MURDER ON MONDAY MORNING

Miss Curley dragged Campion from his bed on Monday morning with a startling story. "One of the typists found him." Her voice was unnaturally businesslike over the phone. "I sent her down to get an address file. The door was locked. I gave her the key from my desk. She screamed from the basement and we all rushed down to see Mr. Paul lying there. Can you come over?"

Mr. Campion put a question and she answered it testily. "Yes, the strong room. Yes, the same room where Mike got the folder last night. Oh, and Mr. Campion"—she lowered her voice—"the doctor says the poor man's been dead for some days."

Again Campion put a query, and this time Miss Curley's tone was awful. "Right in the middle of the room, sprawled out. No one could have opened the door without seeing him."

BANTAM BOOKS offers the finest in classic and modern English murder mysteries. Ask your bookseller for the books you have missed.

Agatha Christie

DEATH ON THE NILE
A HOLIDAY FOR MURDER
THE MOUSETRAP AND
　OTHER PLAYS
THE MYSTERIOUS AFFAIR
　AT STYLES
POIROT INVESTIGATES
POSTERN OF FATE
THE SECRET ADVERSARY
THE SEVEN DIALS MYSTERY
SLEEPING MURDER

Carter Dickson

DEATH IN FIVE BOXES

Catherine Aird

HENRIETTA WHO?
HIS BURIAL TOO
A LATE PHOENIX
A MOST CONTAGIOUS GAME
PARTING BREATH
PASSING STRANGE
THE RELIGIOUS BODY
SLIGHT MOURNING
SOME DIE ELOQUENT
THE STATELY HOME
　MURDER

Patricia Wentworth

MISS SILVER COMES TO
　STAY
SHE CAME BACK

Elizabeth Lemarchand

BURIED IN THE PAST

Margaret Erskine

CASE WITH THREE
　HUSBANDS
THE WOMAN AT
　BELGUARDO

Margery Allingham

BLACK PLUMES
FLOWERS FOR THE JUDGE
TETHER'S END
TRAITOR'S PURSE

Elizabeth Daly

THE BOOK OF THE CRIME
EVIDENCE OF THINGS
　SEEN
THE WRONG WAY DOWN

Jonathan Ross

DEATH'S HEAD

FLOWERS FOR THE JUDGE

Margery Allingham

BANTAM BOOKS
TORONTO • NEW YORK • LONDON • SYDNEY • AUCKLAND

To my publishers this book is respectfully dedicated

*This low-priced Bantam Book
has been completely reset in a type face
designed for easy reading, and was printed
from new plates. It contains the complete
text of the original hard-cover edition.*
NOT ONE WORD HAS BEEN OMITTED.

FLOWERS FOR THE JUDGE

*A Bantam Book / published by arrangement with
Doubleday & Company, Inc.*

PRINTING HISTORY

Doubleday edition published May 1936

Bantam edition / July 1984

ISBN 0-553-24190-7

Published simultaneously in the United States and Canada

*Bantam Books are published by Bantam Books, Inc. Its trademark,
consisting of the words "Bantam Books" and the portrayal of a rooster,
is Registered in U.S. Patent and Trademark Office and in other
countries. Marca Registrada. Bantam Books, Inc., 666 Fifth Avenue,
New York, New York 10103.*

PRINTED IN THE UNITED STATES OF AMERICA

H   0 9 8 7 6 5 4 3 2

NOTE:

In criminal trials it is not customary for witnesses to remain in court during that part of the hearing which precedes their own testimony, but in Rex v. Wedgwood in 1931 in point of fact they did.

FLOWERS
FOR
THE JUDGE

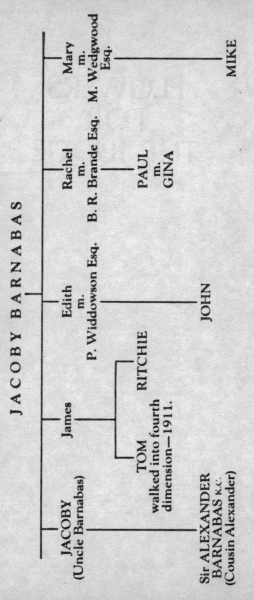

BARNABAS LIMITED
JACOBY BARNABAS

JACOBY
(Uncle Barnabas)

James

Edith
m.
P. Widdowson Esq.

Rachel
m.
B. R. Brande Esq.

Mary
m.
M. Wedgwood
Esq.

TOM
walked into fourth
dimension—1911.

RITCHIE

JOHN

PAUL
m.
GINA

MIKE

Sir ALEXANDER
BARNABAS K.C.
(Cousin Alexander)

1

Damp Dynamite

The story of the little man, sometimes a stockbroker, sometimes a tea merchant, but always something in the City, who walked out of his suburban house one sunny morning and vanished like a puff of grey smoke in a cloudless sky, can be recalled by nearly everyone who lived in Greater London in the first years of the century.

The details vary. Sometimes it was the inquisitive lady at Number Ten who saw him go by, and the invalid propped up in the window of Number Twelve who did not; while the letter which he was about to post was found lying pathetically upon the pavement between the two houses. Sometimes the road was bounded by two high walls, with a milkman at one end and the unfortunate gentleman's wife on her door-step at the other. In this version the wife was kissed at the garden gate and waved at from halfway down the oddly bordered road, yet the milkman saw neither hide nor hair of his patron then or afterwards.

All the stories have their own circumstantial evidence. Only the main fact and an uncomfortable impression are common to all. A man did disappear and there were reasons for supposing that he did so in no ordinary fashion. Also, of course, he never returned.

Most people know of someone who lived in the next street to the hero or victim of the tale, but the ancient firm of Barnabas and Company, publishers since 1810 at the Sign of the Golden Quiver, never referred to the story because the little man had been their junior partner on that morning in May, nineteen hundred and eleven, when he bade a polite "Good morning" to his housekeeper at his front door in the Streatham Crescent, turned out into a broad suburban road and never passed the tobacconist on the corner, but vanished as neatly and unobtrusively as a raindrop in a pool.

At the time there was a certain excitement in the grand Queen Anne house in the cul-de-sac at the Holborn end of Jockey's Fields which bore the sign of the Golden Quiver, but, when it was discovered that the ledgers were still truthful and that Mr. John Widdowson, the other partner, was quite prepared to carry on while his cousin remained disintegrated or in the fourth dimension, the natural conservatism of the firm reasserted itself and the whole disturbing affair was decently forgotten.

However, although a wonder may degenerate into a funny thing after the proverbial nine days and may well become nothing but an uneasy memory after twenty years, the odd disappearance of Tom Barnabas in nineteen eleven created a sort of precedent in the firm, so that in the curious paradoxical way in which the mind works no one thought very much of it when in nineteen thirty-one Paul R. Brande, one of the directors, did not show up for a couple of days.

Gina Brande sat on the couch before the fire in her big sitting room in the top flat on the Sunday evening after Paul went. "Shop tea" was in progress. This function was part of the Barnabas tradition. On Sunday evenings all through the winter it was the custom of the cousins and Miss Curley to meet together to take tea and hold an inquest on the Sunday papers. Sometimes outsiders were present; perhaps a privileged author or visiting American or, on rare occasions, old Caldecott, that patriarch of agents who had known the Old Man.

When Paul had brought Gina back from New York and the firm had recovered from the shock of having a woman and a foreigner on the door-step, she had taken over the responsibility of providing the fire and the meal for the gatherings from John's aged housekeeper and the meetings had moved up from the flat below. It was typical of the two principal directors of the firm that they should have

2

snapped up the lease of the house next door to the office, converted its unsuitability into three flats at considerable expense, and had settled down to live in the Holborn backwater, each convinced that they should or could desire no more.

John Widdowson, managing director, senior cousin, and son of the Old Man's eldest sister, took the centre flat as befitted his position, although in size it would have better suited Paul and Gina, who were quartered above.

The ground floor and basement had been more or less wished upon Mike Wedgwood, the youngest cousin and junior director. Barnabas, Limited did things like that in the holy conviction that through minor discomforts their dignity and prestige were upheld.

The tea party was almost at an end, and as yet no one had referred to Paul. The general feeling seemed to be that the gathering was very peaceful without his crimson-faced didacticism.

Gina had folded herself on the big white sofa with its deeply buttoned back and exaggerated curves. As usual, she looked odd and lovely and unexpected amid that sober gathering.

When Pavlov, the décor man, spoke of her as "the young Bernhardt," he did her a little less than justice. Her small-boned figure, tiny hands and feet, and long modern neck would have disappeared into nothingness in the corsets and furbelows of the 'eighties. Her head was modern, too, with its wide mouth, slanting grey eyes and the small straight nose whose severity was belied by the new coxcomb coiffure which Lallé had created for her and which brought her dark chestnut hair forward into a curl faintly and charmingly reminiscent of the "bang" of the last century.

She was wearing one of her own dresses. The firm, or rather John Widdowson in the person of the firm, had not countenanced his cousin's wife continuing her career in England, and she now only designed for herself, and sometimes for Pavlov, in a strictly dignified and semi-amateur way.

The narrow gown, in a heavy dark green and black silk, accentuated her foreignness and her chic, which was so extraordinarily individual. At the moment she looked a little weary. John's weekly diatribe against the firm of Cheshunt, who flooded the book market with third-, fourth- and fifth-rate novels and advertised the figure of their mighty output with bland self-satisfaction, had seemed even a little longer and heavier than usual.

Curley sat in the corner by the fire. Her plump hands were folded on her knee and her very pale blue eyes were quiet and contemplative behind her spectacles.

Miss Florence Curley was easily the least distinguished-looking person in the room. Her iron-grey hair was not even tidy and her black velvet dress was of that variety of ill-cut, over-decorated and disgracefully expensive garments which are made in millions for the undiscerning. Her shoes were smart but looked uncomfortable, and she wore three rings which had obviously been her mother's. But Curley was the firm. Even John, glancing at her from time to time, hoped devoutly that she would outlast him.

Long ago she had been the Old Man's secretary, in the days when a lady typist was still a daring innovation, and, with the tradition of female service and unswerving loyalty to the dominant male still unshattered behind her, she had wedded herself to the firm of Barnabas, Limited as to a lover.

Thirty years later she loved the business as a son and a master. She knew more about its affairs than a roomful of ledgers, and understood its difficulties and cherished its triumphs with the insight of a first nurse.

In the office she was accepted as a benevolent and omniscient intelligence which was one of the firm's more important assets. Outside the firm she was feared, respected and faintly resented. Yet she looked a rather stupid, plain old woman sitting there by the fire.

It was very warm in the room, and John rose to his feet.

"I shall go back to it, I think, Gina," he said. "Tooth's new one is an odd sort of jumble, but I want to finish it. I'm having him up tomorrow."

John always spoke of "having authors up" when he meant that he had invited them to an interview. It was a traditional phrase of the Old Man's.

4

Miss Curley stirred. "Mr. Tooth is a very self-opinionated young man, Mr. Widdowson," she ventured, and added, with apparent irrelevance: "I saw him lunching with Phillips of Denver's last week. They were at school together, I think."

John, who followed her line of thought, turned round. "It's not as good as his first book," he said defensively.

"Oh, no. It's not," Miss Curley agreed. "Second books never are, are they? Still, I think he's got something in him. I shouldn't like to see him leave us. I don't like Denver's."

"Quite," said John, dry to the point of curtness. "I'll finish it," he added. "It may be just possible."

He moved over to the door, an impressive, interesting-looking person with his tall, slender figure, little dried-up yellow face and close-cropped white hair.

On the threshold he paused and looked back.

"Where is Paul? Do you know, Gina? Haven't seen him since Thursday. Off to Paris again, I suppose."

There was a moment's awkward pause, during which Curley smiled involuntarily. Paul, with his hustle methods, his bombast and his energy, while infuriating his cousin contrived to amuse her. John's remark was his first direct reference to the Tourlette biography affair, and everyone in the room recalled Paul's excited, unconvincing voice rising above the din at the September cocktail party:

"I tell you, my dear fellow, I was so thrilled, so absolutely annihilated, that I just rushed off down to Croydon and got a 'plane—didn't even remember to snatch a bag or tell Gina here—simply fled over there and bought it."

The fact that the Tourlette biography had proved of about the same interest to the British and American publics as the average first book of free verse, and that Barnabas, Limited had dropped a matter of five hundred pounds on the transaction, lent point to the comment.

Gina stirred. All her movements were very slow, and she turned her head with graceful deliberation before speaking.

"I don't know where he is. He hasn't been home since Thursday."

The quiet voice with the unexpected New England

accent betrayed no embarrassment or resentment at either the question or the fact.

"Oh, I see." John also did not seem surprised. "If he comes in tonight you might tell him to drop in and see me. I shall be reading all the evening. I've had a most extraordinary letter from Mrs. Carter. I wish Paul would learn not to enthuse to authors. It goes to their heads and then they get spiteful if a book doesn't sell."

His voice died on a plaintive note and the door closed softly behind him.

Ritchie began to laugh, a dry little cackle of which nobody took the least notice. He was out of the circle, leaning back in a chair in the shadows, a quiet, slightly melancholy or, if one felt sentimental, pathetic figure.

Ritchie Barnabas, brother of the transported Tom, was the only cousin who had received no share of the business under the Old Man's will. He had been younger in nineteen hundred and eight, of course, but not so young as Mike, who had been a baby, nor so young as Paul, who was still at school, nor even so very much younger than John himself. His own explanation of this mystery was never sought, but a clause in the will which charged the beneficiary cousins to "look after" Richard Barnabas threw some light on the Old Man's opinion of this nephew.

It was characteristic of the firm, and perhaps of publishing generally, that they fulfilled this charge by supplying Ritchie with a small room at the top of the building, a reasonable salary and the title of "The Reader." He shared the work with some twenty or thirty clergymen, maiden ladies and indigent schoolmasters scattered all over the country, but his was the official post and he lived in a world of battered manuscripts on which he made long and scholarly reports.

Like some thin and dusty ghost he was often seen on the stairs of the office, in the hall, or tramping home with long flapping strides through the network of gusty streets between the sacred cul-de-sac and his lodgings in Red Lion Square.

No one considered him and yet everyone liked him in the half-tolerant, half-condescending way with which one regards someone else's inoffensive pet.

Every year he was granted three weeks' holiday, and on these occasions he was never missed. Only the increasing height of the piles of manuscript in his dusty room bore witness to the genuineness of his absence.

There was a vague notion among the junior members of the staff that he spent these holidays reading in his lodgings, but no one was interested enough to find out. The cousins simply said and thought "Where's Ritchie? Oh, on holiday, of course . . ." and dismissed him for the more important matter that was always on hand.

There had been from time to time sentimental young women, although these were not encouraged in the firm, who saw in Ritchie a romantic and mysterious figure with some secret inner life too delicate or possibly too poetic for general expression, but always in time they gave up their investigations. Ritchie, they discovered, had the emotional outlook of a child and the mind of a schoolboy. He was also not even particularly unhappy.

Now, when he had finished laughing, he rose and walked over to Gina.

"I shall go too, now, my dear," he said, smiling down at her with the mildest of blue eyes.

There was a minute pause, and he added charmingly: "A delicious tea."

Gina's grey eyes narrowed as she smiled back at him.

"Sweet person, Ritchie," she said, and gave him her hand.

He took it for a moment, and then, after nodding to Curley, grinned broadly at Mike, whom he had always liked, and wandered off to find the door.

The three who were left smiled after he went out, but in a most kindly way. The warm silence remained unbroken for some time. Outside the first waves of the fog were creeping down from the park, but as yet its chill dirtiness had not penetrated into the gracious room.

Miss Curley sat in her corner, placid and apparently lost in thought. Those who knew her were used to Curley "staring through them" and her habit was a time-honoured joke in the office. She found it very useful. Her faded blue eyes were difficult to see behind the gold-rimmed spectacles, and it was, therefore, never easy to be sure whether they were focused upon one or not.

At the moment she was looking at Mike with steady inquisitiveness.

Michael Wedgwood was the son of the Old Man's youngest and favorite sister. His place in the firm had been assured to him since his childhood. He had been barely seven years old at the time of his uncle's death.

As she watched him Miss Curley reflected that his early training might easily have spoilt him altogether. A little boy brought up in cold blood to be a fitting member of any old-established publishing firm, let alone Barnabas, Limited, might have turned out to be a prig or a crank or worse. But there had been mitigating circumstances. The firm had suffered during the war and the Old Man's fortune had been very much divided, so that although the young Michael had been to the right schools he had never had quite enough money, and, in Miss Curley's opinion, there was a sobering quality in poverty greatly to be prized.

Mike had missed the war by a few months and had been actually in training at school when the Armistice was signed. Looking at him, sprawled out in the deep armchair opposite her, Curley wondered if he had not always just missed the big things. Until now she had seen him as an unscathed, untried sort of person. He was twenty-eight or nine, she supposed; kindly polite, good-looking, dependable and quiet; but, although she had understood his popularity, hitherto he had always seemed to her to be a slightly unsatisfactory being. It was as though all the vital part of him had been allowed to atrophy while his charm, his ease and his intelligence had occupied his full stage.

Curley's faded eyes did not blink. He was certainly good-looking. In his full manhood he had more of the Old Man's size and dignity than any of the cousins. The Barnabas features were there, too, the bright, sharp dark eyes, the strong characterful nose and the thin sensitive mouth. Curley's heart warmed towards him.

Now that the suspicions she had entertained for the past few weeks had virtually become a certainty, he had gained tremendously in interest for her, and, curiously, had also gone up considerably in her estimation.

She stole a glance at Gina, resting superb and quiet upon the highbacked couch.

"She doesn't know for certain yet." Curley's thoughts ran placidly on. "He's been careful not to say anything. He wouldn't, of course. People don't nowadays. The passions frighten them. They go on fighting them as though they were indecent. So they are, of course. So are lots of things. But the Old Man—" her lips curled in a faint reminiscing smile, "—he'd have got her. It wouldn't have been nice, his cousin in the firm, but he'd have got her. That was where he was different from these nephews."

Curley's old mouth pouted contemptuously as she considered them: John with his irascibility, his pomposity and his moments of sheer obstinacy; Paul lathering and shouting and making an exhibition of himself; and now the dark horse Mike, who had never really wanted anything before. Would any of them go out bald-headed for their desires, sweeping away obstacles and striding over impossible barriers to attainment, to get clean away with it in the end as the Old Man had done time and time again? Curley did not think so.

Mike was leaning back, his head partly in the shadow, so that only sometimes when the fire flickered was his face visible. Curley felt that he was very careful of his expression on these occasions.

Gina did not glance in his direction, but she was aware of him. Curley knew that by the studied calm, by the odd suggestion of tension which anybody but her, one of the most unemotional of woman, must have found unbearable.

They were "in love," then. A ridiculous but illuminating phrase, Miss Curley reflected, suggesting "an uncomfortable state." It was a very awkward thing to have happened to either of those self-possessed, intelligent young people. Mike had been woken up under his skin, Miss Curley saw with satisfaction. The fever was upon him all right. It showed painfully through his ease and politeness, turning him from a slightly austere personality into something infinitely more appealing and helpless, and at the same time somehow shameful.

Of the girl Curley was not so sure. Her poise was extraordinary. The older woman speculated upon her

9

possible attitude towards her husband. Of course she could
hardly entertain much affection for him. There might
possibly be somewhere in the world a woman thick-skinned
enough to be able to ignore the series of small exposures
which was Paul's life, but not Gina. His fake enthusiasms
and windy lies, which were always being found out, his
unconvincing braggartry—surely no physical passion could
counteract the blast of these upon a sensitive intelligence.

Besides, what consideration did Paul give Gina? His
mind was fully occupied in the hopeless and, in the
circumstances, ridiculous task of putting himself over big.
Where did she think he was now, for instance? Rushing off
on some wild-goose chase, throwing his importance at the
head of some dazzled scribbler, to return on the morrow
drunk with enthusiasm for his own cleverness, only to be
sobered and left sulky by the common sense of his elder
cousin.

No. If Gina had ever loved him, a possibility which
Curley was inclined to doubt, she could not possibly do so
now.

Her reflections and speculations were cut short by an
intrusion into the warm paper-strewn sanctuary. At a glance
from Gina, Mike had leapt to answer the flat buzzing of the
door-bell. There was the murmur of polite greetings in the
hall and he returned with the newcomer.

Curley knew of Mr. Albert Campion by repute alone
and was therefore quite unprepared and a little shocked
when he came wandering in behind Mike. His slender,
drooping figure, pale ingenuous face and sleek yellow hair
were rendered all the more indefinite by the immense and
unusually solid horn-rimmed spectacles he chose to affect.

"Party over?" he enquired regretfully, casting an eye
over the dismantled tea-table and scattered chairs. "What a
pity!"

He shook hands with Curley and Gina, and sat down,
crossing his long thin legs.

"No tea? No party? It must be business then," he
chattered on, smiling affably. "Cheap, clean and trustwor-
thy, fifteen months in last place and a conviction at the end
of it. Detective work of all kinds undertaken at short
notice."

He paused abruptly. Curley's eyes were upon him in frozen disapproval.

Mr. Campion had the grace to look abashed. Gina came to his rescue.

"You haven't met Mr. Campion before, have you, Curley? He gets some people down, but most of us grow used to him in time."

"It's an affliction," said the pale young man, with engaging embarrassment. "A form of nervousness. Think of it as a glass eye and it won't bother you any more."

Curley was only partly disarmed. The world in which she lived was besprinkled with consciously funny young men, most of them ill-mannered nincompoops. The difference between the newcomer and the average specimen dawned upon her slowly. In every case the flow of nonsense was in the nature of a protective covering, she knew, but here it was the reality which was different. Mr. Campion had more than poverty of intelligence to hide.

Meanwhile he was still talking.

"As an American, Gina, you have a thrill coming to you. We are on the eve of a real old London particular, with flares in the streets, bus-conductors on foot leading their drivers over the pavements into plateglass windows, and blind beggars guiding city magnates across the roads for a small fee. It's pretty bad in the Drury Lane vicinity now. I'm wallowing in old-world romance already."

Mike shrugged his shoulders and his dark eyes twinkled lazily.

"I hope you enjoy it," he said. "As a motorist, its romance leaves me cold. You'll hate it, Gina. It has the same effect upon the skin and clothes as a train journey from Paris to the south in midsummer."

"I see. Just another little British trick to entertain the foreigner."

The girl spoke absently, and for the first time Mr. Campion saw that the constraint in the atmosphere was not due to Miss Curley's presence alone.

"Well, ladies and gentlemen," he said cheerfully, "the Professor is here. The *ballon* she is about to mount. Bring out your misfortunes. Lost anything, Gina?"

There was a moment's awkward silence, and whereas

11

Miss Curley's astute mind took in the whole situation, Mr. Campion, who was not in possession of the facts, perceived that he had made a gaffe. Mike glanced at Gina imploringly. Miss Curley leant forward.

"If you three want to talk business, my dear, I'll get my things."

Gina hesitated, and a faintly deeper colour spread over her face. It was the first trace of embarrassment to destroy her poise, and was all the more expressive because of its restraint.

"It's not exactly that, Curley," she said. "I don't know— you might be able to help us in a way—and yet——"

She broke off deliberately. Miss Curley leant back in her chair.

"I'll stay," she said firmly. "It's about Paul, isn't it? He'll turn up, my dear. He always does. All the cousins like to disappear now and again. It's quite a tradition in the family."

She had broken the ice completely, and there was a hint of relief in Mike's laugh.

"A sort of affectation," he murmured. "Good old Curley! You see through us all, don't you?"

Miss Curley eyed him. "I *see*," she said dryly.

"Wait a minute for Mastermind to catch up," said Mr. Campion protestingly. "What's happened to Paul?"

Gina turned slowly toward him, two bright spots of colour in her face.

"I suppose it's just foolishness," she said, "but I asked Mike to get you to come over for a sort of unofficial talk. Paul hasn't been around since last Thursday, and after all, he does live here—and—and——"

"Quite," said Campion, hurrying to the rescue. "I see your point perfectly. Whereas it's one thing to call in the police, it's quite another to pretend you haven't noticed your husband's absence for three days."

"Exactly." She looked at him gratefully and went on talking, the hint of pride in her soft lazy voice making it extraordinarily appealing. "I suppose some wives would have gone haywire by this time, but with me—I mean with us—it's different. We—well, we're post-war people, Albert. Paul leads his own life, and so do I, in a way."

She paused wretchedly, only to hurry on again, forcing herself at her fences.

12

"What I'm trying to say is, there's nothing really unusual in Paul going off for a day or two like this without thinking to tell me, but I've never known him to stay away quite so long without my hearing even indirectly of him, and this morning I felt I ought to—well—just mention it to somebody. You do understand it, don't you?"

"Ye-es," said Mr. Campion a little dubiously.

The heavy white lids closed over the girl's eyes for a moment.

"It's not unheard of," she said, half defiantly. "Lots of people do the same sort of thing in our crowd. He may be anywhere. He may turn up tonight or tomorrow or next week, and I shall feel a fool for making such a fuss."

"Let me get this straight." Mr. Campion's precise voice was as friendly as any in the world. "I take it the dear fellow may easily have gone to a cocktail do, drifted on to an all-night binge with some of the gang, and finished up with a hangover at a week-end house-party."

"Yes," said the girl eagerly, anxious, it seemed, to convince herself. "Or he may have rushed over to Paris about this exhibition scheme he's so keen on. But even so, I don't see why he should have taken so long about it."

Mr. Campion pricked up his ears. "Is that the rare manuscript exhibition at Bumpus's in February?" he enquired.

Mike rose to give Gina a light. "Yes. Paul's putting his weight into it. It's going to be a stupendous affair. Practically the whole of the Leigh Collection will be on view."

"But not *The Gallivant*, I suppose?" murmured the visitor, venturing Miss Curley's disapproving stare.

"No, I'm afraid not." Mike seemed genuinely regretful. "Paul put up the suggestion, I believe, but John vetoed it promptly. The firm of Barnabas is hanging on to its past."

The Gallivant, that precious manuscript of Congreve's unpublished play, set down by his own hand and never printed even in his unsqueamish age, had come into the possession of the firm of Barnabas very early in its dignified career. There had been something vaguely unsavoury in the story of its acquisition, some unpleasant business of the gift of a few pounds to a starving antiquary, but that was ancient history and half forgotten.

The present grievance, shared by scholars and collectors alike, was the fact that, through a certain Puritan streak in Jacoby Barnabas, the late Old Man himself, the manuscript was never permitted to be copied or even read. John respected his uncles's wishes, and it remained therefore one of the firm's assets only.

"Too bad," said Mr. Campion aloud, and forgot *The Gallivant* as he returned to the main subject. "No line on Paul anywhere at all, then?" he said slowly. "You don't know where he went on Thursday night, for instance?"

Gina shook her head. "No. As a matter of fact, I expected him home that evening. We—er—we had some things to discuss, and I arranged a quiet meal here for seven-thirty. When he didn't show up by nine o'clock I got peevish and went out."

"Yes, yes, of course." Campion was studying her face. "When you say you went out—you didn't go to look for him?"

"Oh, no, of course not." Her cheeks were flaming. "I phoned down to Mike and we went off to the Academy to see the revival of 'Caligari.'"

Something made Mr. Campion glance at his friend. He caught the man with the visor up and a warning light flashed through his brain.

Mr. Campion was old-fashioned enough to take the marriage contract seriously, but he was also sufficiently sophisticated to know that the nicest people fall in love indiscriminately and that while under the influence of that pre-eminently selfish lunacy they may make the most outrageous demands upon their friends with no other excuse than their painful need.

It suddenly occurred to him that what Gina probably needed most was a reliable and discreet enquiry agent capable of handling divorce, and was on the point of telling her so in the friendliest of fashions when he was saved from the blunder by a remark from Miss Curley.

"Where do you *think* he is, Gina?" she said baldly. "Running round the lovely Mrs. Bell?"

Once again Gina flushed, but she laughed as she spoke:

"No, Curley, I know he's not. As a matter of fact, I phoned this morning and asked her if he was down there.

Oh, no, if it was only something like that it would be simply my own affair, wouldn't it? I mean it would be quite unpardonable of me to discuss it like this. No, I can't think where he is. That's why I'm telling someone. I mean, I'm all right. I can amuse myself. I can come down on Mike to take me around."

She smiled shyly at the other man.

"Of course," he said abruptly. "You know that. At any time."

"Oh, my hat!" reflected Mr. Campion, just as Miss Curley had done. "A genuine passion. She hasn't even been told."

His interest in the affair promptly revived.

"I say," he began diffidently. "I don't want to be inquisitive, but I must ask this. Any row between you and Paul?"

"No." Her slanting grey eyes met his squarely. "None at all, at the moment. That's another thing that made me wonder. I saw him for a moment in the office on Thursday afternoon. He'd been lunching with Caldecott and he said then that he'd come here for dinner and we'd talk. No one seems to have seen him after four. He wasn't in his room when Miss Netley took some letters for him to sign just before five. I know that because she phoned me on Friday morning to ask if she should do them herself, as they ought to go off. John phoned to ask where he was, too. He was offended with Paul for being 'so damned offhand,' as he called it."

She paused, a little breathless, and sat up on the couch, the glowing end of a cigarette between her fingers as she glanced round for an ashtray.

Mike rose and came towards her, his cupped hand held out.

"I'll take it—and chuck it in the fire," he said hastily.

She drew back in surprise. "Not like that. It'll burn you," she protested.

He did not speak, but nodded to her, his whole body expressing urgency and unconscious supplication. It was a ridiculous incident, so trivial yet curiously disquieting.

Bewildered and half amused, the girl dropped the burning fragment into the hand and Campion glanced away involuntarily so that he might not see the man's satisfaction at the pain as he carried the stub over to the fire.

The return of John Widdowson a moment later restored the trend of general thought. Gina's faithful charwoman, who had returned to do the tea things, had met him on the staircase and admitted him with her key. He nodded to Campion and glanced across at Curley.

"That book of clippings on *The Shadow Line* Fellowes sent us, Miss Curley; do you know where it is? It was a rather ornate little red thing, if I remember. What did we do with it? Send it back?"

Miss Curley considered. Somewhere neatly pigeon-holed in her mind was the information. It was this gift for relatively unimportant detail which had made her so valuable in her youth, and now in her age her skill was a fetish.

"It's on a shelf with a lot of other miscellany on the right of the doorway in the strong room," she said at last, not without a certain pride.

Mike, who caught Mr. Campion's expression of polite astonishment, hastened to explain.

"The strong room is a bit of an anachronism these days," he said. "It's a sort of fortified basement in the cellar at Twenty-three and dates from the days when authors insisted on being paid cash down in gold. We haven't much use for it now, so it's used as a junk cupboard for odds and ends we don't want to lose—addresses and that sort of thing. It's a very fine affair. Tin-lined walls in the best Victorian style."

"All very interesting," said John dryly. "Would you like to run round there and get that folder?"

Mike hesitated. The older man's tone had been unnecessarily peremptory and he was in the mood to resent it.

"I'll get it for you, Mr. Widdowson. I know just where it is." Curley was already on her feet.

"Rubbish, Curley. I'll get it. The key's in your desk as usual, isn't it? All right. I shan't be a moment."

Mike strode out of the room and John sat down in the chair he had vacated.

"Fog's getting very thick," he remarked, leaning forward to jab unceremoniously at the fire.

At sixty-three, John, the eldest of the cousins, was as forceful a personality as he ever had been. Campion, leaning back in the shadows, had opportunity to consider him. A spoilt child of his profession, he decided. A little tyrant nurtured in his uncle's carefully prepared nursery. Still, he had met his battles and had fought and won them. Not a weak face, by any means.

Conversation became desultory. Curley never expanded in John's presence, and Gina was lost in her own unhappy thoughts. Mr. Campion did his best to keep the ball rolling, but without great success, since his peculiar line in small talk was hardly appreciated by the elder man. Long silences were bound to occur, and in the last of these they heard Mike's quick steps in the passage outside.

Just for a moment a wave of apprehension touched them all. It was swiftly gone, but the sight of the young man with the red and gilt folder in his hand was somehow reassuring.

Campion might have fancied that he was unduly jumpy had it not been for John, who, after peering at his cousin inquisitively, enquired abruptly:

"What's the matter? Seen a ghost?"

They all glanced at the newcomer. His dark face was a little paler than usual and he was certainly breathless. However, he seemed genuinely surprised.

"I'm all right. A bit out of training, that's all. Fog's getting very thick outside."

John grunted, and, taking his folder, trotted out again. Campion took up the main conversation where it had left off and spoke reassuring words.

After a while Miss Curley left, and presently Mr. Campion followed, leaving Gina and Mike by the fire. Campion had reflected upon the peculiarities of other people's lives and had dismissed Gina and her truant husband from his mind by the time he turned in just after midnight, so that it came with all the more of a shock to him when Miss Curley dragged him from his bed at ten o'clock the following morning with a startling story.

"Miss Marchant, one of the typists, found him, Mr. Campion." Her voice was unnaturally businesslike over the phone, and he had a vision of her, hard, cool and practical in the midst of chaos. "I sent her down to get an address file as soon as I got here, about half an hour ago. The door was locked. I gave her the key from my desk. She screamed from the basement and we all rushed down to see Mr. Paul lying there. Can you come over?"

Mr. Campion put a question and she answered it testily, as though irritated by his obtuseness.

"Yes, the strong room. Mike got the folder from it last night. Yes, the same room. Oh, and Mr. Campion—" she lowered her voice—"the doctor's here. He seems to think the poor man's been dead for some *days*."

Again Campion put a query, and this time Miss Curley's reply did not sound irritable. Her tone was awful, rather.

"Right in the middle of the room, sprawled out. No one could have opened that door without seeing him."

2

Funeral Arrangements Later

There are moments which stand out in clear detail in the recollection of an hour of horror. They are seldom dramatic, and those who are haunted by them are sometimes puzzled to discover why just they and none other should have been singled out by the brain for this especial clarity.

Neither Mike Wedgwood nor Miss Curley ever forgot the instant when the doctor looked up from his knees and said half apologetically:

"I'm afraid we shall have to move him after all. I can't possibly see here."

It may have been that the bounds of their capacity for shock had been reached and that his words coincided with the moment immediately before the first degree of merciful callousness descended upon them and they were able to begin again from a new level. But at any rate, the scene was photographed indelibly upon their minds.

The extraordinarily untidy room stood out in every detail. They saw with new eyes its lining of dusty junk-packed shelves, only broken at the far end where an old-fashioned green and black safe replaced the cooking range which had once been there. They saw the heavy table which took up nearly the whole of the centre of the room, heaped high with books and files and vast untidy brown-paper parcels.

They were even aware of the space beneath it; that, too, fully occupied by flimsy wooden boxes whose paper contents would have overflowed had it not been for the books piled carelessly on top.

The fog, which enveloped the city and now crept into every corner, hung about the air like smoke, giving the single swinging bulb a dusty halo. The body lay upon its back, the head in the shadow of the table ledge and the sagging legs and torso sprawled out towards the doorway where they stood.

The doctor rose stiffly to his feet and faced them. He was a short man, grizzled and of a good age, but still spruce, and his little eyes were shrewd beneath his fierce brows. In contrast with his sombrely smart clothes his bare forearms, muscular and very hairy, looked slightly indecent.

"Where can we take him?" he enquired.

Miss Curley, who took it for granted that the question was addressed to her, considered rapidly. Space at Twenty-three was restricted. In the basement, besides the present room, there were only the packers' hall at the end of the passage, the stock room, or the little washroom next door, none of them suitable resting-places for a corpse. Upstairs the amenities were even less inviting, since the business of the day had begun and the staff was already hysterical.

She glanced at the table.

"If we move those things on to the floor and spread a sheet on the table you'll be right under the light, Doctor," she said. "I'll get a better bulb."

The little medical man looked at her curiously. He knew Paul had been a director, and although he did not expect office employees to have quite the same attitude towards a dead man as a family might have adopted, he was surprised to find an absence of the general tendency of laymen to get the body to the most comfortable place possible at the earliest moment. Aloud he said he thought Miss Curley's a most sensible suggestion.

Mike stepped into the room, avoiding the piteous thing upon the floor, and began to shift the dusty papers to the ground on the opposite side.

The place was dry from the furnace on the other side of the passage, with occasional icy draughts from the door into the yard. Mike worked like a man in a nightmare, his tall thin figure and deep-lined sensitive face looking curiously boyish and despairing.

The doctor bent down once again, and as he worked he grunted to himself at intervals and made little breathing sounds.

Miss Curley returned with a new electric light bulb and a pair of sheets borrowed from Mike's own flat next door. Her face was grim and she moved with a suppressed energy which made the doctor look at her sharply, but Curley was all right as long as she kept going.

It was she who superintended the changing of the bulb, a feat which Mike performed with unwonted clumsiness, and she who spread one sheet over the table and stood ready with the other, waiting for the doctor to move.

The two men glanced at each other. Mike was younger and considerably stronger, but he was very pale and there was sweat upon his forehead.

Doctor Roe spoke briskly. His calm was very comforting. Thirty-five years of general practice had built up an impersonal yet friendly shell which quite concealed the rather inquisitive, ordinary little man inside.

"I'll take the shoulders, Mr. Wedgwood," he said. "If you would grip the feet, now. That's right—just above the ankles. Are you ready? Now then . . ."

Mike looked down at the square-toed brown shoes. They were familiar. They were Paul's. This dreadful helpless thing lying on the dusty floor was Paul himself. Only the physical effort of lifting steadied him. Deliberately he forced his eyes out of focus so that he should not see his cousin's face. Miss Curley's expression was quite enough.

"That's right," said the doctor. "Ah!"

And afterwards, when he looked up and saw them:

"Perhaps you'd care to wait for me outside? This—ah—isn't a very pleasant business."

In the stone corridor outside the door Mike gripped the iron banisters of the staircase which ran up beside him and hung there for a moment, his crisp shorn head pressed against the stone.

"God, Curley, this is awful," he said at last. "Where the hell is John?"

"He's coming." Miss Curley's voice was sharp. "I sent round word to him as soon as I'd phoned the doctor. The woman said he'd been up half the night reading and wasn't dressed yet, but that he'd come over right away. It's a terrible thing. I haven't sent anyone to tell Gina yet."

"Gina? Of course—I say, Curley, I'll do that. Later—not now. She might come down and see him . . ."

He broke off.

Miss Curley's sympathy for him returned and the softer emotion crowning the fear nearly undid her. She took off her spectacles and dabbed at her eyes petulantly.

Mike was silent, his brows drawn down so that his eyes seemed deep sunken and darker even than usual.

At the top of the staircase on the floor above somebody paused and a greyer shadow thickened against the wall over their heads.

"Miss Curley! Oh, Miss Curley."

A girl's voice, tremulous with its owner's effort to appear unconcerned, floated down to them.

"Mr. Tooth is here."

"Put him in the waiting room, Miss James. Put every visitor in the waiting room."

Mike spoke before Miss Curley could open her mouth and footsteps above pattered away.

The doctor came out in what seemed an extraordinarily short space of time. They pounced on him, besieging him with questions, and as he washed his hands in the little toilet next to the strong room he talked to them over his shoulder.

"He's been dead about three days, I should say. Very difficult to be more accurate once the period of rigor mortis has passed. But I put three days as the minimum. How odd he should not have been found before."

For the first time Miss Curley noticed that his eyes were sharp and curious under his fiery brows, and unconsciously she spoke defensively.

"This room is very seldom used, Doctor. It's virtually a safe, you know. It's really extremely lucky that we found him this morning."

"But he must have been missed," the doctor persisted. "Surely his wife . . . ?"

"Mr. Brande was a man of very uncertain habits." Miss Curley had not meant to interrupt with such chilling asperity, and Mike attempted to come to the rescue with clumsy friendliness.

"We had begun to wonder where he was. We were only talking of it last night. No one thought of looking in there, naturally."

He stopped abruptly and as clearly as though he had proclaimed it aloud it became obvious that a startling recollection had occurred to him. He grew suddenly crimson and stared at Curley, who did not meet his eyes. The doctor regarded them both with interest.

"I see," he said hastily. "I see. And now, Mr. Wedgwood, is there any heating apparatus down here at all?"

Mike looked bewildered. "How do you mean? Do you want a fire? There's the main coke furnace under the staircase here if——"

"That's what I'm asking you," interrupted the doctor shortly. "Let's have a look at it."

Together they inspected the central-heating system and the stove built into the tiny cellar-like cupboard under the staircase.

The doctor asked a great many questions and measured the distance between the cellar and the strong-room door with ridiculously exaggerated strides.

To Curley, who was only bearing up under the shock with great difficulty, the performance seemed absurd.

"But how did it happen, Doctor?" she demanded impatiently. "How did he die? That flush on his face—it's very unusual, isn't it? How did it happen?"

"That, madam," said the little man, eyeing her with a pomposity which was oddly disquieting, "I am attempting to decide."

On the whole, it was very fortunate that John should have arrived at that particular moment. He came running down the stairs, his head held slightly on one side and his excellently cut clothes looking out of place in the draughty dinginess of the basement.

He brushed past Mike and Miss Curley and shook hands perfunctorily with the doctor.

"Where is he?" he demanded.

Although no one who actually saw him during those first five minutes could possibly have doubted that John was genuinely shaken by his cousin's death, a catalogue of his words and actions would have been misleading. He moved towards the door of the strong room with little, jerky, birdlike steps, paused for a moment on the threshold and peered in at the sheeted figure on the table.

He made no attempt to enter but stepped back sharply after a second's contemplation, beating his long ivory hands softly together, cymbal fashion.

"Terrible," he said shortly. "Terrible. We must get him out of here. We must get him home."

Mike recognized that tone of quiet authority. When John spoke like that his commands were automatically carried out. The younger man turned to him.

"Gina doesn't know yet," he said. "Let me warn her, at least. Give me five minutes."

"All right. But he can't stay here, poor fellow."

Both cousins had completely forgotten the doctor, and his diffident demur came as a surprise to them.

"Mr. Widdowson," he ventured, "I hardly know whether I can advise——"

"My dear sir——" John turned upon him with raised brows, "——he can't stay here in the office, in the strong room. Can you give me any valid reason why he should not be moved?"

The doctor hesitated. He had no story ready, no actual ground on which to stand. It was a situation in which the stronger personality was bound to triumph. Mike mounted the staircase.

"Give me five minutes to tell her," he said over his shoulder.

As for Miss Curley, she hurried up to her office and phoned Mr. Campion.

Gina was pottering in the big living room, clad in a severe man-tailored pyjama suit, when the woman admitted her visitor. She looked up from the hearth rug, where she was sorting her morning's correspondence, when he entered, and his vision of her, kneeling there in the warm navy blue suit, was the only lovely thing in all that day. He remembered afterwards that her red mules made little blobs of color on the white rug and her face turned to his was radiant with sudden pleasure.

"Mike, my pet! How nice to see you. Too early for some coffee? I'm just going to have some."

Conscious that the charwoman was hovering behind him, he hesitated. All the old insufferable phrases crowded into his mind: "Gina, my dear, you must prepare yourself for a shock." Or, "I have bad news, I'm afraid." Or, "Gina, something terrible has happened."

Now that the moment had come they stuck in his throat and he was only conscious of her sitting there smiling at him, sane and lovely and adorable by a fire.

"He would like some, Mrs. Austin, please." Gina smiled at the woman and waved her hand to the sofa. "Sit down, animal, and don't stand there goggling at me. What's the matter? Can't we go to the Athertons this afternoon after all? Good heavens, it doesn't matter. Don't look like that."

Mike sat down heavily and raised his eyes to hers.

"Paul's dead," he said.

She had been in the act of placing a couple of envelopes in the flames when he spoke, and now her arrested movement, the shoulder half turned, the head bent, was more expressive than any sound she could have uttered. He dropped down on the rug beside her and put a hand on the small woollen back.

"Gina, I didn't mean to say it like that. Oh, my God, I am a fool!"

She turned to him at once. Her face was very pale, her eyes wide and dark.

"Tell me," she said quietly. "How did it happen? A car smash?"

"No." He paused. She was so close to him.

Presently he heard himself talking in a guarded unnatural way which he was unable to correct.

"He's been at Twenty-three the whole time. They've only just found him. They're going to bring him up here. You—you had to be told, you see."

"But of course I had to be told." Her deep soft voice had sharp edges. "Mike, what's happened? Was it suicide?"

"I—we—we don't know."

"But why should he? Why? Oh, Mike, why should he? We hadn't even quarrelled. He had no reason, surely. Surely, Mike?"

"Hold on, old dear." The man was gripping her shoulder tightly and she leant back into the crook of his arm.

Mrs. Austin set the coffee tray down on the table behind the sofa with a clatter and stood looking over it at them with the shrewd glance of a mendicant pigeon. Things *were* happening! She had been thinking they must get a move on for some time now, but if a man ignored his wife, well, he was asking for trouble; that was her opinion.

Gina became aware of her. She moved quietly to her feet.

"My husband is dead, Mrs. Austin," she said. "They don't know how it happened."

The full arc of Mrs. Austin's knitted bosom swelled. Her long face with its festoon of chins grew blank and she emitted a long thin sound midway between a scream and a whistle.

"No!" said Mrs. Austin. "Here," she added hastily, clattering with the coffee-jugs, "you drink this, dear. You'll need it."

Gina sat in the big white chair, and sipped the coffee obediently, while the other woman stood before her and watched her face. Mike glanced at the woman wonderingly. Hitherto Mrs. Austin had been a mechanism to open doors in his life. Now she had miraculously become a personality.

It was as though a shadow had taken substance.

"Will they be bringing him up here, dear?" she demanded, and behind her ill-contrived sorrow Mike detected an awful secret glee.

25

Gina looked at Mike. He was still poised awkwardly, half kneeling on the rug at her feet.

"They are coming now, aren't they?" she said.

He got up stiffly. "Yes—yes, they are. But look here. Gina, there's no need for you to do anything, unless you want to, of course. I mean——"

He broke off helplessly, the situation beyond him.

"Oh," said Mrs. Austin, her little green-grey eyes fixed on him with dreadful understanding, "I think I take your meaning, sir. Oh, well, there's no need for the poor lady to see her husband for a bit. I'll do all the necessary."

She crossed over to the girl and laid a kindly crimson hand on her shoulder.

"Don't you worry, dear. Don't you worry at all."

Mike felt himself gaping at her with fascinated horror. There was a ghastliness about this practical side of death which overtopped the sum of frightfulness which had confronted him in that short morning. Mrs. Austin was kind; sympathy and friendliness oozed from her every pore; and yet she was enjoying the tragedy with all the shameful delight of the under-entertained.

He glanced at Gina. She was thinking, her face white, her eyes dark and blank.

He found himself feeling that she ought to cry and yet being relieved that she did not. He knew it would never occur to her to adopt any conventional attitude. The sudden loss of Paul could hardly be a great emotional tragedy, but it was naturally a tremendous shock.

He was looking at her, trying to divine her thoughts, when Mrs. Austin touched his sleeve.

"I'd like a few words with you outside, sir, please," she said, and before the elaborate solemnity which scarcely veiled the exuberant curiosity which consumed her he was helpless. He followed her meekly.

The fog was not yet at its worst, but the streets were as dark as at midnight and the waves of bitter, soot-laden air softened and blurred the edges of familiar objects until London was like an old brown lithograph chalked by a man with no eye for detail.

In the basement at Twenty-three John had taken

charge of the proceedings, the doctor hovering ineffectually
at his side. One of the smaller packing tables had been
taken off its trestles and upon it the sheeted body of Paul
Brande now lay. Under John's supervision the whole affair
was being managed very decently.

Old Dobson, the chief packer, a bull-necked individual
with arms like the forelegs of a cart horse and a red rim
round his head where a cap had sat, took the head of the
improvised stretcher, while the foot was supported by a Mr.
Peter Rigget from the Accounts Department. Mr. Rigget
had somehow appeared upon the staircase at the critical
moment and, much to his delight, had been invited to
assist. He was a squat, insignificant-looking young man,
long in the body and short in the leg, with a solidarity which
would become fleshy in a few years. It was his misfortune
that he looked like the popular conception of the less
attractive black-coated worker, even to the pink sensitive
nose and the very shiny gold pince-nez. In a rather futile
effort to combat this disadvantage he wore his very black
hair *en brosse*, and, to his eternal credit, spent much of his
spare time in the Regent Street Polytechnic Gymnasium
hardening his muscles.

With a certain amount of assistance from the doctor,
therefore, he was quite able to manage the task for which
he had angled.

Mr. Rigget had been waiting to get into the heart of the
excitement downstairs ever since his sensitive perceptions
had got wind of it less than three minutes after the
discovery of the body, for it was a tragic fact that, in spite of
his struggles against his destiny, Mr. Rigget remained what
he had been born and reared to be, an inquisitive, timid,
dishonorable person with a passion for self-aggrandizement
which was almost a mania.

"Not through the street." John made the statement
sound like an edict. "We shall have to go the back way,
through the garden and into the basement at Twenty-one.
We can't have a crowd in the front of the office. Are you
ready?"

Not for the first time during the past ten minutes the
doctor shot a curious glance at the elegant, elderly head of
the firm. John Widdowson's complete preoccupation with

27

his own particular aspect of the tragedy, and his utter disregard for any sort of pretence at conventional grief, was something unique in his experience.

He found it all the more puzzling because he did not know the man well and did not realize that it was the outcome of lifelong habit and was nothing to do with the unusual circumstances.

The procession moved off out into the yard through the narrow door between the strong room and the furnace cellar. Once in the fog the picture became macabre. The massive Dobson was blurred and transfigured into a shadow of heroic size, while Peter Rigget, bending forward under the weight, became foreshortened and spread out into something dwarfish and deformed.

The white burden between them widened and narrowed at every new angle which its path dictated, and the folds of the sheet hung limply in the cold still air.

They went down the stone way between the garage and the loading shed and turned sharply to the right, negotiating a little-used gate in the wall with difficulty.

Their progress through the other house was even more awkward, and both John and the doctor were forced to lend every assistance as they struggled and panted up the seven flights of stairs.

Mrs. Austin admitted them with red-eyed reverence as long as the door was open and whispering efficiency as soon as it was shut. She and the doctor understood each other instantly, and for the first time that morning the professional man received the mixture of awe and clumsy but well-meant assistance to which his long professional life had accustomed him.

"Mrs. Brande's quite laid out, poor thing," Mrs. Austin announced in a stage whisper, adding with ambiguous sentimentality, "Mr. Wedgwood's with her, comforting her as only he can. I've told him not to let her come out for a minute or two."

John looked at the woman as though he wondered what rather than who she was, and followed Dobson and Peter Rigget into the spare room, where nearly all the best linen had been set out by Mrs. Austin because a doctor was coming.

Dobson left at once, glad to go, but Peter Rigget lingered until bidden sharply by his employer to return to work.

Meanwhile, Mrs. Austin turned back the sheet.

John went out of the room. He felt he could not possibly be of any assistance, and he found the situation disagreeable.

Mike had only escaped from Mrs. Austin when the knock at the door heralded bigger game. He and Gina had barely spoken when John came in. He stood eyeing their questioning faces absently for a moment, his mind clearly upon other things, but as he sat down he addressed the girl.

"We brought him up, Gina, because he couldn't possible stay down there."

"But of course not. Of *course* not," she said, her deep voice rising a little. "What's the matter with you all? Of course they must bring him to his home. I'll go to him."

Mike stood in her path and she looked up at him.

"You're not protecting me, you're frightening me," she said, and swung round to John. "Where did it happen, John? Where has he been all this time?"

"In the strong room." He still spoke impersonally, his mind preoccupied.

"In the strong room?" The girl repeated the words as though she doubted her senses. "But I thought that place was kept locked; locked from the outside and the key in Curley's desk."

John blinked at her. "It's all very terrible, I admit, my dear, but there are so many things to think of besides details."

Gina sat down suddenly. The change in her face was extraordinary. She looked haggard, blue-shadowed and years older.

"Mike," she said unsteadily, "you were down there last night."

"In the strong room? Were you really, Mr. Wedgwood? You must excuse me, but this is very curious indeed, isn't it?"

Little Doctor Roe stepped forward from the doorway, where he had been hesitating for the past few moments.

29

"Doctor, this is Mrs. Brande." John's voice was gently reproving.

The little man was pulled up short. He looked uncomfortable.

"Er—quite, quite; I see. Er—may I say how extremely sorry I am, madam? I am afraid you must have had a very great shock." Doctor Roe's best professional manner was to the fore as he pressed Gina's hand, but he returned to Mike immediately.

"You went down to the strong room last night?" he repeated.

"Yes, Doctor, I did." Mike's tone sounded over-friendly in his eagerness to explain. "Yes, I did. I went down for a folder for my cousin. I took the key out of the desk where it is always kept, unlocked the door, found the book, relocked the place and put the key back and hurried up here. I was only in there for a second but I—I didn't see anything."

There was a long pause. The doctor's eyes had become like John's, veiled and introspective.

"Well," he said after what seemed an interminable silence, "there will be certain formalities, you understand." He coughed.

"Formalities?" John looked up. "I don't quite understand. What was the cause of death, Doctor?"

The professional man hesitated. "I shouldn't like to commit myself just now," he murmured at last. "My opinion will be tested by post-mortem before the inquest."

"Inquest?" John stiffened. "Really? Surely that's not necessary in a case like this?"

The authoritative tone somehow saved the question from sounding absurd.

The little doctor stood like a Trojan on the one piece of ground he knew to be firm.

"Mr. Widdowson," he said, "I did not attend your cousin before his death. I am not at all sure how he died and I am afraid I must refuse to grant a certificate."

"And what exactly does that mean?" John's tone was, if anything, slightly contemptuous.

The doctor looked profoundly uncomfortable.

"The case will automatically come under the cognizance of the Coroner as an uncertified death," he said slowly. "I—er I am afraid I can do nothing more."

He still hovered, his eyes beneath their heavy brows interested and bright.

Gina pulled herself together with an effort.

"Doctor," she said, "I think I will go to my husband. Will you come with me, please?"

She moved quickly out of the room, the little man at her heels.

Mike strode restlessly up and down. The cousins were not communicative as a family and a crisis did not loosen their tongues. John remained silent for some considerable time. Finally he said:

"Inquest, eh? How extremely like Paul—flamboyant to the end."

Mike stared at him, but he went on in a perfectly normal tone:

"Ring down to Miss Curley, will you? Tell her to come up here herself and bring a notebook."

Mike hesitated, opened his mouth to speak, but thought better of it and went out obediently. He had just finished phoning in the little booth at the far end of the hall when the doctor and Gina came out of the spare room. He hung back to wait for her.

The little man was all kindliness.

"Leave it all to me, Mrs. Brande," he said, holding her hand. "I quite understand. The shock has been very great. Don't worry. Leave it all to me."

It passed through Mike's mind that Gina was like that. There was something essentially feminine about her, something that inspired a spirit of protection in the most unlikely breasts. However, there was nothing shrinking about her as she came hurrying down the corridor towards him.

"Oh, Mike, what *has* happened?" she demanded. "What are you and John doing? What are you hiding?"

"Hiding? My dear girl——" Mike was aghast. "You must forgive old John," he went on hastily. "He's much more knocked up than he shows, and after all, the firm does mean such a lot to him that he can't help thinking of it even at a time like this."

The girl placed her hand on his arm and looked up into his eyes.

"Mike," she said, "I do believe you actually mean all

31

this rubbish. My dear, don't you see, the doctor won't give a certificate. He's not satisfied. How could he be in the circumstances? How could you be? How could I be? I've asked him to report to the Coroner. He was obviously going to anyway. Oh, Mike, are you listening to me? Do you understand?"

"I only know that this ghastly thing has happened to you, of all people," he said. "Look here, Gina, don't get alarmed. We'll fix it somehow so that you don't have go to the damned inquest."

The girl passed her hand over her forehead.

"Oh—oh, dear God!" she whispered, and crumpled at his feet.

Mike carried her into her bedroom.

It was over three quarters of an hour later when Mr. Rigget came creeping up the stairs. John held up his hand warningly as Mrs. Austin showed the excited young man into the room. It was one of John's peculiarities that he regarded himself as the undisputed owner of any room in the two buildings, and the fact that he was now using his bereaved cousin-in-law's studio as an office did not strike him as being in any way unfitting or extraordinary.

". . . suddenly at his place of business, Miss Curley," he was saying. "Funeral arrangements later. That's for the *Times, Morning Post* and *Telegraph*. The other paragraph Mr. Pelham can send out to the places he best thinks fit. Mr. Rigget, what do you want?"

The final phrase was uttered in such a complete change of tone that Miss Curley stared violently. But Peter Rigget was not quelled. For one of the few times in his life he was the bearer of important news.

"Mr. Widdowson," he burst out, "there are two men at the office asking for you. I slipped out through the garden and came up the back way to warn you."

"To warn me?" John eyed the young man with a nice admixture of distaste and astonishment. "What are you talking about? What two men?"

"Well, sir," said Mr. Rigget flatly, cheated of his drama, "one of them's a Coroner's Officer and the other is a plain-clothes man. They only send the plain-clothes man, sir, when it's—serious."

3

Design for an Accident

Mr. Campion sat in the waiting room at the Sign of the Golden Quiver and reflected philosophically that it is often the fate of experts to be called in and left in a corner. The young woman who had admitted him had been very firm: he was to wait.

As he sat in the shadow of the mahogany mantelpiece and sniffed the leather and tobacco-scented air he regarded the room with interest. There are publishers whose waiting rooms are like those on draughty provincial railway stations: others that resemble corners of better-class bookshops, with the wares tastefully displayed; and still others that stun by their sombre magnificence and give the odd impression that somebody very old and very rich is dying upstairs: but the waiting room at Twenty-three expressed the personality of Barnabas, Limited and was solid and comfortable and rather nice, like the dining room of a well-fed mid-Victorian household.

Mr. Campion caught himself glancing at the polished side tables and supposing the silver had gone to be cleaned. Apart from a few early editions in a locked glass and wire-fronted cupboard there was not a book in the place.

A portrait of Jacoby Barnabas, the uncle of the present directors, hung over the mantelpiece in a grand baroque frame. Head and shoulders were life size, and it was evident from a certain overpainting in the work that the artist had striven with some difficulty for a likeness.

It showed a strong, heavily boned man of sixty odd with the beard and curling white hair of a Victorian philanthropist, but the light eyes set deeply in the fine square head were imperious and very cold and the small mouth was pursed and narrow amid the beautiful fleecy whiteness of the beard. A grim old boy, thought Mr. Campion, and turned his attention to the other visitor, who stood stiffly on the other side of a centre table which ought to have had a silver epergne upon it.

He was a fat young man with a red face, who looked less as though he had a secret sorrow than a grievance which was not going to be a secret very long. He regarded Mr. Campion with what appeared to be suppressed hatred, but as soon as the other ventured to remark inanely that it was a nice foggy day he burst out into the spasmodic but more than eager conversation of one who has been in solitary confinement.

Mr. Campion, who thought privately that all young persons who voluntarily shut themselves up half their lives alone, scribbling down lies in the pathetic hope of entertaining or instructing their fellows, must necessarily be the victims of some sort of phobia, was duly sympathetic. Moreover, his curiosity concerning the business downstairs was fast becoming unbearable and he was glad to have something to crowd it out of his mind.

The fat young man flung himself down in a chair.

"I'm waiting to see Mr. Widdowson," he said abruptly. "I usually see Brande, but today I've got to go to the Headmaster. They're all infernally casual, aren't they? I've been here half an hour."

In view of all the circumstances Mr. Campion did not know quite what to say, but his silence did not worry the other man, if indeed he noticed it at all.

"I expect Brande will be down in a moment," he went on explosively. "Do you know him? A nice chap. Very enthusiastic. Gets all het up about things. He's made a lot of difference to this place since he left the army. He was in the States for a bit, you know, and then came back and started putting a bit of pep into this mausoleum."

He paused again but only for breath. Since neither of them even so much as knew the other's name Mr. Campion found him quite extraordinarily indiscreet, but he recognized the symptoms and understood that people who are forced to spend long periods alone can rarely chat noncommittally. The fat young man's tongue was running away with him again.

"Brande married an American, you know," he said accusingly. "Extraordinarily pretty girl, I believe. It seems a pity they don't . . ." He broke off hastily and rose to his feet again, glaring at Campion this time as if he had discovered him trying to surprise him into a confidence.

Mr. Campion looked comfortingly blank and as the other retired to a corner, crimson with rage and confusion, he rose himself and, wandering across to the heavily curtained windows, peered through them into the fog.

"I wonder where Brande is," said the plaintive voice behind him after a pause.

Mr. Campion stiffened and controlled the insane impulse to say, "There goes his body, anyway. Looks a fishy little procession, doesn't it?" and turned back into the room just as the door opened and a girl came in.

She was neither particularly good to look at nor possessed of an arresting personality, but she caught Mr. Campion's interest at once. She was small and very dark and affected the coiffure of a medieval page and a small straight blue serge dress with a white collar and cuffs. The effect aimed at was a twelve-year-old schoolgirl but the result was ruined by the maturity of her face, hands and neck. She smiled at the fat young man.

"Oh, Mr. Tooth," she said, "I'm so sorry you've been kept waiting. I'm afraid Mr. Widdowson won't be here today. He's been called away. Would you mind very much if we wrote you?"

Mr. Tooth grew red and then pale with indignation and Mr. Campion was inclined to sympathize with him.

"I'll go in and see Mr. Brande, then," said Mr. Tooth with dignity. "He's not engaged, is he?"

"Oh, no, he's not engaged, but I'm afraid you can't see him." There was a quality in the girl's voice which was hard to define. She was enjoying the situation, certainly, but she was not bursting to come out with the news. Rather, she was being unduly secretive about it. Mr. Campion was interested. Why should the staff of Barnabas, Limited have decided to try to keep Paul's death a secret? The death of a man is a hopeless thing to hide from his friends; after all, it is no little peccadillo or temporary embarrassment from

35

which he may be expected to recover and afterwards prefer not to have discussed.

"Miss Netley, is there anything wrong?" Mr. Tooth had caught the savour of unrest in the air and Campion watched the girl. She did not look in the least confused.

"Well, he won't be here today," she said, not so much evasively as tantalizingly. "I'm so sorry."

A great desire to get to the heart of the trouble downstairs passed over Mr. Campion and unobtrusively he moved to the door. Mr. Tooth he dismissed from his mind. Their interests, he felt, did not meet. But there was something very curious about Miss Netley, something about her personality which was peculiar. He made a mental note of her name.

The wide entrance hall at Twenty-three was of a very simple plan and Mr. Campion had no trouble in locating the basement stairs. He sauntered through the gloomy shadows and stepped slowly down the first flight. He did not move furtively and at the first sound of his shoes upon the stone there was a warning cough from below and three men in packers' aprons slid out of a doorway below him and made for their own domain. The first two walked with their faces averted and the third glanced sharply but ineffectually at the young man's grey figure in the fog.

"Door not even locked, and plenty of visitors. The police will be pleased," murmured Mr. Campion as he wandered on towards the scene of the trouble which had been so neatly pointed out to him.

In the entrance to the strong room he paused. The retreating packers had not thought to switch off the light and the whole scene lay before him, inviting him to examine it. It was not difficult to see where the body had lain, especially as he had Miss Curley's telephoned description of its discovery firmly fixed in his mind.

The bare table puzzled him at first but it did not take a very acute mind to reconstruct roughly what had happened after the body had been found.

As Mr. Campion glanced at the heterogeneous collection of books and papers which Mike had heaped upon the floor his sympathy for any police detective who might come after him grew more intense. Since so much damage had already been done he had no hesitation in entering the room. One more set of footprints in the dust, he decided, could do little harm.

The construction of the place interested him immensely. It was clear that it had at one time been part of the kitchens of the house and its subsequent alterations had done something to enhance the dungeon-like qualities of the domestic offices of the eighteenth century.

The walls appeared to be lined first with some sort of metal and then with asbestos, while the window which had been immediately on the right of the doorway had been bricked up and covered by the shelves which ran all round the walls.

Mr. Campion sniffed the air. It was still stuffy, in spite of the open door, yet, as it seemed impossible that a room of its size could have been left entirely without ventilation, he took the opportunity of examining the outside wall.

Yet fog had penetrated even here and he could not understand it at first until his search was rewarded by the discovery of a tiny iron grating let into the wall directly beneath one of the lower shelves, where a brick had been displaced. The two centre bars of the grating had been broken, leaving a ragged hole some two inches in diameter.

At this hole Mr. Campion looked very thoughtfully. By squatting down on his heels he found that he could peer through the broken ventilator into some half-lit chamber beyond, which he erroneously decided was the loading shed.

He spent some time considering the shelf below the ventilator and restrained with difficulty his impulse to touch the papers thereon.

When at last he straightened his back and continued round the room his face was much graver than usual and narrow vertical lines had appeared between his eyebrows.

At the far end of the room, between the safe and the table, the chaos was indescribable, but, looking at it, Campion was inclined to think that it was the outcome of years of untidiness rather than the result of one frenzied five minutes indulged in by any hasty or excitable person.

It passed through his mind that the term "businesslike" rarely applied to business people. There are degrees of muddle to be found in the offices of old established firms which transcend anything ever achieved in a schoolboy's locker.

The strong room at Twenty-three seemed to have become simply one of those useful places where nothing is ever cleaned up, so that anything deposited therein may reasonably expect to remain in safety until it is again needed.

All the same, it occurred to him as he looked round that the amount of odds and ends which three generations of Barnabas directors had considered worth keeping was distressing when viewed in the bulk.

The safe, he decided, could well be the centrepiece in any museum which an enterprising burglars' guild might establish for the edification of junior members. It was massive enough in all conscience and looked as if it had been built to withstand shell-fire, but it opened with a key, a large key if the size of the highly decorated hole could be taken as a guide.

He was still looking at it when hasty footsteps pattered down the passage and the door leading out into the yard banged. Feeling a little guilty but not really deterred, Mr. Campion continued his tour.

Lying on a dusty parcel of manuscript on the shelf nearest the table he came upon an anachronism. It was a bowler hat, nearly new and only very slightly dusty. Turning it over gingerly he saw the initials "P.R.B." inside, and on the door below was a neatly rolled umbrella.

Mr. Campion's frown deepened. The problem as he saw it had certainly a great technical interest, apart from its personal side. A man, dressed for the street, found dead in his own strong room, the door locked on the outside, four days after he disappeared, presented a situation provoking thought.

Campion took another look at the ventilator and wished he might see the body.

A few minutes later he was examining the door of the room and had just decided that at no time had the lock been forced or picked when the pattering feet returned, this time from the courtyard. There was a rush of bitter air as the door swung open and next moment somebody paused and looked in at him.

Mr. Rigget and Mr. Campion exchanged glances.

For some seconds Mr. Rigget hesitated, torn between a desire to see what was going on upstairs and an inclination to investigate Mr. Campion's unexpected presence. He took stock of the stranger carefully, his eyes round and excited behind his glittering pince-nez.

He decided almost immediately that Mr. Campion was not a detective. Mr. Rigget's knowledge of detectives was small and his opinion bigoted. A thrilling alternative occurred to him and he came forward ingratiatingly.

"Could *I* help, I wonder?" he suggested, lending the offer a tinge of the underhand. "I shouldn't want my name mentioned at first, of course, but if there's anything you want to know . . . ?"

He broke off promisingly, adding a moment later as Campion's expression did not change:

"You're a journalist, of course?"

"There's no 'of course' about it," said Mr. Campion. "What's on the other side of this wall?"

"A—a garage," said Rigget, startled into speech.

Mr. Campion's eyebrows seemed in danger of disappearing.

"How many cars?"

"Only one. Mr. Wedgwood keeps his Fiat there. Why?"

Mr. Campion ignored the question. Instead he snapped out another.

"Who are you?"

Neither his tone nor manner fitted in with Mr. Rigget's idea of the jolly, hard-boiled journalist he had seen so often on the films. He grew crimson.

"I have a position here," he said stiffly.

"Fine," said Mr. Campion heartily. "Toddle along and keep it up."

"You are a journalist, aren't you?" said Mr. Rigget, now considerably alarmed.

"Certainly not." Campion looked astonished by the suggestion.

"But you're not a detective. It wasn't you who came in with the Coroner's Officer just now."

"Ah! He's here at last, is he?" said the pale young man with interest. "Splendid! Good morning."

"Shall I tell him you're waiting?" Mr. Rigget's slender pink nose quivered as he caught a glimpse of this exciting chance to visit, if only for a moment, the heart of the enquiry.

"No," said Mr. Campion. "It wouldn't be true." And, brushing past his would-be informant, he moved quietly out of the room and mounted the stairs.

Mr. Rigget stood irresolute. Some instinct told him that it would not be wise to follow immediately. Moreover, the sense of mingled shame and apprehension, inevitable aftermath of a too hastily seized conclusion, was upon him. The scene of the trouble, on the other hand, was not a healthy spot in which to linger with the police in the house. In default of any other retreat Mr. Rigget shut himself in the washroom.

Mr. Campion hurried up the stairs. His face was unusually blank and there was a strained expression in his pale eyes. He had made a discovery, or at least he had unearthed a possibility which, if it should prove to be substantiated by other facts, was going to lead to serious trouble.

At the top of the stairs he hesitated. His next step presented difficulties. He was not at all sure of his own place in the proceedings. Miss Curley had invited him to the house presumably on her own initiative; therefore he was not working with the police but in the interests of his friends. In view of everything Mr. Campion was inclined to wonder what their interests would prove to be.

However, his curiosity overrode his caution and he considered the best means of getting the information he needed.

He was still hesitating in the fog-laden hall, wondering if he should take the bull by the horns and go up to Gina's flat, when he caught sight of a shadowy figure drifting down the stairs from the floor above. Ritchie, of course; Mr. Campion had forgotten him. He stepped forward, his hand outstretched.

"Mr. Barnabas," he began, "I don't know if you remember me——"

The tall looser built man paused abruptly and a pair of astonishingly mild blue eyes peered into Campion's own.

"Yes," he said. "I do. You're a friend of Mike's, aren't you? Albert Campion. You're the man we want. You've heard, of course?"

Campion nodded. The sense of shock and regret which he had missed in the office was here very apparent. Ritchie looked haggard and the bony hand he thrust into Campion's own shook.

"They've only just told me," he said. "One of the secretaries came up to my room. I was reading. I didn't dream . . . Mike went down there last night, you know."

He paused and passed his hand through his tufty grey hair.

"Twenty years ago . . ." he added unexpectedly. "But it was May then . . . none of this awful fog about."

Mr. Campion blinked. He remembered now the other's habit of flitting from subject to subject, linked only by some erratic thought process at which one could only guess. However, he had no time to study Ritchie Barnabas's eccentricities at the moment. There was something very important that he had to find out at once.

"Look here," he said impulsively, "I'm at a great disadvantage. I really haven't any business here at all, but I do want a few words with someone who has seen the body. Do you think—I mean, could you possibly . . . ?"

Ritchie hesitated. "I'll see what I can do," he said at last, adding abruptly, his eyes fixed anxiously upon Campion's like a dog who is attempting to talk: "The body . . . that was the terrible part of it then. . . . Nothing . . . not a sign. Poor young Paul!" And afterwards, in an entirely different tone: "A mild day it was, inclined to be misty. But no fog like this."

He turned away and had gone halfway up the stairs again when he paused and finally returned.

"Go upstairs to my room," he said. "It's right at the top of the house. Forgive me for not thinking of it before."

He went off again, only to turn at the landing to look back.

"I'll meet you there," he said. "Come up now."

Mr. Campion found his way to Ritchie's office with

41

some difficulty. It lay at the very top of the house and was approached by a small staircase set behind the panelling of a larger room. Campion discovered it only by accident, having caught a glimpse of the swinging door as he put his head into the last room on what had at first appeared to be the top floor.

The office itself was a fitting place for its owner. It was very small and was built round an old-fashioned brick chimney, to which it seemed to cling for support. Apart from two dilapidated chairs huddled close to the minute fireplace, the whole place was a mass of manuscripts. They jostled and sat upon each other in tall unsteady piles rising up to meet the sloping ceiling.

A little window through which the fog now looked like a saffron blanket held up to the light filled one alcove, and, save for this and the glow from the fire, the place was in darkness.

Campion found the switch and a dusty reading lamp on the mantelpiece shot into prominence.

He sat down to wait. After the chill downstairs the room felt warm and musty, the air spiced with the smell of paper. It was a very personal place, he decided; like an old coat slipped off for a moment regretfully.

He had barely time to let its unexpected charm take hold of him when Ritchie returned. He came scrambling up the staircase like some overgrown spider, his long thin arms and legs barking themselves recklessly on the wooden walls.

"She's coming," he said. "Won't be a moment. Had to powder her face. Too bad . . . a child, Campion . . . only eighteen. Very pretty . . . typist or something. Good family . . . been crying . . . making statement."

He sat down.

Mr. Campion, who had deduced that he was not talking about Miss Curley, had an inspiration.

"You've got hold of the girl who found him?"

Ritchie nodded. "Terrible experience! Glad to get away from them all. Nice girl."

He brought a packet of cigarettes out of his pocket and lit one thoughtfully. He had replaced the package when, with a word of apology, he produced it again and forced a rather battered cigarette upon Campion.

42

"You knew Paul well?" he said. "Poor fellow! Poor fellow! You didn't? Oh, I see. . . . Well, it's a shock for everybody. It must be. . . . Dead three days, they say. Can't have been. Mike was there last night. Doctors don't know, do they?"

Mr. Campion was slowly getting used to this somewhat extraordinary method of conversation. He had experienced this jerky chatter before, but in Ritchie's case the man had a disconcerting way of fixing one with his gentle blue eyes with an earnestness which was somehow pathetic. It was evident that he wanted to be understood, but found speech very difficult.

In spite of his preoccupation with the pressing matter on hand, Campion noticed that the elder man used long sweeping gestures, completely meaningless in themselves, and he began to understand why the intolerant Jacoby Barnabas of the portrait in the waiting room had found this particular nephew so unsatisfactory.

Although he was still obviously very shaken, Ritchie seemed more at ease now that he was back in his own little room. He glanced about it, caught Mr. Campion's eye and smiled shyly.

"Been here twenty years, reading," he said.

Campion was taken off his guard.

"No remission for good conduct?" he said involuntarily.

Ritchie looked away, and for the first time the younger man was aware of something not quite frank about him.

"Get away sometimes," he said. "Week or two now and again. Why not . . . ? Must live."

His tone was so nearly angry that Campion almost apologized. He had the uncomfortable impression that the man was hiding something.

He put the idea from him as absurd, but the impression remained.

Ritchie was puffing furiously at his cigarette, his long thin fingers with their enormous knuckles gripping the little flattened tube clumsily.

"Strong personality," he said, his blue eyes once again fixed on Campion's face. "Moved very quickly . . . did foolish things. But to be found dead . . . terrible! Have you ever been in love?"

"Eh?" said Mr. Campion, completely taken aback.

"Don't understand it," said Ritchie with a wave of a long bony arm. "Never did. Paul didn't love Gina. Extraordinary. Mike's a good boy."

Campion was sorting out the possible relations between these disjointed ramblings when there was a movement on the stairs below and Ritchie got up.

"Miss Marchant," he said.

He disappeared for a moment, to return almost at once with a very pretty girl. She had been crying, and was still near tears. As he caught sight of her Mr. Campion was inclined to agree with Ritchie's sympathetic outburst. It certainly did seem a shame that this little yellow-haired girl with the big frightened eyes and demure, intelligent face should have been subjected to what must have been a very unpleasant experience.

Ritchie was already performing the introductions. He was less jerky and more at his ease when speaking to the girl, and there was a gentleness about him which was very attractive.

"Sit down," he said, taking her by the hand and leading her into the room. "This is Mr. Campion, a very clever man, not a policeman."

He peered down into her face and evidently thought he saw tears there, for he pressed a large white pocket-handkerchief into her hand without any explanation.

"Now," he said, squatting down between them on the dusty boards, "tell him."

Campion leant forward. "I'm awfully sorry to trouble you, Miss Marchant," he said. "It must be most unpleasant for you to go all through this again. But you would be doing me and Mr. Barnabas a very great service if you'd answer one or two questions. I won't keep you long."

The girl made a rather pathetic attempt at a smile.

"I don't mind," she said. "I'm glad to get away from them all. What do you want to know?"

Mr. Campion approached his point gingerly. It was not going to be easy.

"When you went down to the strong room this morning," he began, "did Miss Curley give you the key or did you take it out of her desk?"

"I—I took it. It was hanging on a little hook screwed into the underside of the flap at the back. It always hangs there."

"I see. And you just took it and went straight downstairs?"

"Yes. But I've told all this to the Coroner's Officer." Her voice was rising, and Mr. Campion stretched out a soothing hand.

"I know," he said. "And it's really very kind of you to tell it to me again. When you unlocked the door and went in, what did you do?"

The girl took a deep breath.

"I switched on the light," she said. "Then I'm afraid I screamed."

"Oh, I see. . . ." Mr. Campion was very grave. "You saw him at once?"

"Oh, yes. He was just inside the door. My foot nearly touched his foot. When I turned on the light I was looking straight down at him."

Ritchie nodded at her, and with a wave of a flail-like arm encouraged her to use the handkerchief he had just lent her. There was something so extremely comic in the gesture that just for an instant laughter crept out behind the tears in the round eyes.

Mr. Campion proceeded cautiously.

"Look here," he said very gently, "this is going to help a lot. Try not to think of the man you found as someone you've seen in the office, someone you've worked for; think of him just as a thing, a rather ugly sight you've been called upon to look at. What struck you most about him when you first saw him?"

Miss Marchant pulled herself together. Mr. Campion had been speaking to her as though she were a child, and she was a modern young woman of eighteen.

"His colour," she said.

Mr. Campion permitted himself a long intake of breath.

"He was pink," said the girl. "I didn't think he was dead, you see. I thought he'd fallen down in a fit—apoplexy or something. I went up to him and bent down, and then I saw he was dead. He was bright, bright pink, and his lips were swollen."

"And was he lying quite naturally?" said Mr. Campion, anxious to lead her away once the vital fact had been ascertained.

Miss Marchant hesitated. "I think so. He was on his back and stretched out, his hands at his sides. It wasn't—nice."

"Terrible!" said Ritchie earnestly. "Terrible! Poor girl! Poor Paul! All frightful . . ."

He hurled his cigarette stub into the fire and searched frantically for another, hoisting his gaunt body from side to side as he fought with his pockets.

Miss Marchant glanced at Mr. Campion.

"That's all," she said. "I ran out and told Miss Curley and the others after that."

"Naturally." Campion's tone was soothing and friendly. "Where was the hat?"

"The hat?" She looked at him dubiously for a moment, her brows wrinkled. "Oh, his bowler hat . . . of course. Why, it was there on the ground, just near him."

"Near his head or near his hand?" Mr. Campion persisted.

"Near his shoulder, I think . . . his left shoulder." She was screwing up her eyes in an effort of recollection.

"How was it lying?"

Miss Marchant considered. "Flat on its brim," she said at last. "I remember now. It was. I caught sight of the round black mound out of the corner of my eye and I wondered what it was at first. His umbrella was there too, lying beyond it, where it must have fallen when he fell."

She shuddered involuntarily as the picture returned to her, and looked younger than ever.

"On the left?" laboured Mr. Campion. "On *your* left?"

"No, *his* left. I told you. The side furthest from the table."

"I see," said Mr. Campion, and his face became blank. "I see."

Ritchie shepherded Miss Marchant to the floor below. When he came back his mild blue eyes rested upon Campion eagerly.

"Clearer?" he enquired, and added abruptly: "Sounds like gas, doesn't it?"

Mr. Campion regarded the other man thoughtfully. It had been slowly dawning upon him for some time now that Ritchie's disjointed phrases and meaningless gestures were disabilities behind which a mind resided. However, this last shrewdness was unexpected.

"Yes," he said slowly. "It does. Carbon monoxide, in fact. Of course one can't possibly tell for certain without taking a blood test but Miss Marchant's description does indicate it. Besides, it fits in damnably with one or two things I noticed downstairs."

Ritchie heaved a sigh of relief. "Garage next door to the strong room," he remarked. "Fumes must have percolated somehow. Accident. Poor Paul. . . ."

Mr. Campion said nothing.

Ritchie clambered into the chair Miss Marchant had vacated and sat poring over the fire, his immense bony hands held out to the tiny blaze.

"Carbon monoxide," he said. "How much of it will kill?"

Mr. Campion, who had been reflecting upon the problem for some time, gave a considered opinion.

"I'm not sure of the exact proportion," he said, "but it's something very small . . . just over four per cent in the atmosphere in some cases, I believe. The trouble with the stuff is that it's so insidious. You don't realize you're going under until you've gone, if you see what I mean. The exhaust of a car is pretty nearly the pure stuff."

Ritchie nodded sagaciously. "Dangerous," he said. "No ventilation down there with the door shut."

". . . And locked." The words were on the tip of Mr. Campion's tongue, but he did not utter them.

Ritchie continued. "Shouldn't have been there," he said. "Paul always poking about out of hours. Silly fellow . . . sorry he's dead."

The last remark was not put in as an afterthought. Every line of Ritchie's gaunt body indicated his regret, and his tone was as expressive as the most elaborate speech.

"I didn't know him well," said Campion. "I met him at most four or five times."

Ritchie shook his head. "Difficult chap," he remarked. "Great egoist. Too dominant. But good fellow. Impulsive. Not in love with Gina. Dreadful accident."

Mr. Campion's mind wandered to the little grating under the shelf in the strong room, and presently, when he and the other man went down the stairs together, it was still in his thoughts.

Ritchie was frankly overcome by the horror of the accident. The locked door and the time of death were both points that he had evidently shelved as minor details, while the significance of the position of the hat and umbrella had escaped him entirely.

As they crossed the hall, two policemen in plain clothes came up from the basement. Campion recognized one of them as Detective-Sergeant Pillow of the special branch. The man glanced up as he passed, and nodded, satisfaction in his little black eyes.

As Campion caught sight of the curious burden he carried, his heart missed a beat. Carefully wrapped round the middle with a dark handkerchief, its ends looped into drooping bows and its protected centre clasped in the Sergeant's stubby hand, was a length of rubber tubing such as is sometimes used for the improvisation of a shower-bath. Sergeant Pillow carried it as though it were his dearest possession.

4

Relations

To Gordon Roe, Esq., Surgeon.

London.
To wit.
Sir,

By virtue of this my Order as one of His Majesty's Coroners for the County of London you are hereby required to be and appear before me and the jury on Tuesday the ninth of February at eleven o'clock in the forenoon at the Court in the Parish of St. Joan's, Holborn, and then and there to give evidence on His Majesty's behalf touching the death of Paul Redfern Brande and to make or assist in making a post-mortem examination of the viscera of the Head, Chest and Abdomen of the body of the said Paul Redfern Brande without an analysis and report thereon at the said inquest. And herein fail not at your peril.

Dated the second day of February, 1931.

P. J. Salley,
Coroner.

Doctor Roe patted his pocket absently as he entered the hall of Gina's flat on the Friday following the discovery of Paul Brande's body and the Coroner's summons crackled responsively. The little doctor was following the anxious Mrs. Austin down the passage to the studio with a certain amount of curiosity.

"I really think you ought to have a look at her, Doctor." The charwoman spoke in a hushed voice and without looking round as she ploughed over the thick carpet in her soft shoes. "Not a mite of sleep she hasn't had. You can see it in her face. I said to her I said, 'You have the doctor, dear. After all, he can't make you worse nor what you are at present.' And she said to me, 'I think I will, Mrs. Austin.' 'Lie down,' I said, but she wouldn't, and there she is sitting in front of the fire like a lily."

Her speech lasted until they reached the door, but just before she entered she laid a plump, damp hand upon his own and looked up at him, a gleam of conspiratorial excitement in her eyes.

"Have they found out anything yet?"

Doctor Roe coughed. "I really don't know, Mrs. Austin," he said pleasantly. "I'm not a policeman, you know. Now where is our patient?"

Mrs. Austin raised her eyebrows, and, with many

ostentatious precautions against noise, tiptoed heavily into the room.

"Here's the doctor, dear," she said in a sepulchral whisper which might well have given her employer a heart attack had their entry been really quiet.

Gina was sitting in one of the big white armchairs in a tailored black wrapper which contrasted with the pallor of her face and the brilliance of her eyes and hair. She made a pathetic attempt at a smile.

"I'm glad to see you, Doctor," she said. "Won't you sit down? That'll do, Mrs. Austin."

That good lady left the room, making it plain that she did so against her better judgment. Doctor Roe remained upon his feet. His professional personality inclined to heartiness and was seen at its best astride a hearth rug.

"Well, now, Mrs. Brande," he said, "what's the trouble? Not sleeping, eh? Well, of course, that's not to be wondered at, but you can help yourself much better than anyone else can, you know. You need courage, young lady, great courage. Any other symptoms? Eating well?"

Gina leant forward, her small white hands clasped together, her elbows resting on her knees.

"Doctor," she said, "what's happened about my husband?"

The little medical man stiffened, and something that was half alarm, half resentment, flickered in his eyes.

"I came here to discuss your health, Mrs. Brande," he said warningly.

"Oh, Doctor . . ."—the soft New England accent slurred the words—". . . I don't mean to offend you. I don't understand professional etiquette and that sort of thing, but can't you see that the thing that's making me ill is not knowing what's going to happen—what is happening. What are the police doing? Why was the inquest on Tuesday adjourned for seven days? What do they expect to learn from the post-mortem?"

"My dear lady . . ." Doctor Roe's voice conveyed that his sense of decorum was outraged . . . "I'm a medical practitioner. I'm not a detective. You sent for me to ask advice about your health, and I'm prepared to give it to you. I can see you want sleep and I can prescribe something that will see to that. But I don't know anything about your other trouble, and if I did I couldn't discuss it. It would be most improper."

"But even if you're a doctor, you're human." The girl's voice was quivering. "Don't you see you're the only person who knows what the police are thinking? Just imagine my position. . . . my husband disappeared ten days ago. Four days later he was found dead. Without any warning, without any explanation, the police arrived. My husband's body was taken away. I was summoned to appear at an inquest the next day. It lasted five minutes at the outside. My cousin-in-law gave evidence of identification, and the Coroner adjourned for seven days. I've been subpoenaed for the second part of the inquest, and of course I shall go. Yet when I went out yesterday I was followed."

She paused, and the nervous tension behind her eyes was vivid and painful.

"If only they said *something!*" she said. "If only they told me! It's being kept in the dark that's getting on my nerves. Why are they watching me? Why should they think that I might run away? What's happening?"

Doctor Roe was not entirely impervious to the appeal of a very pretty woman, but there is perhaps no professional man who must protect himself more carefully than the physician.

"I'm very sorry for you," he said quite genuinely, "but I can't tell you anything about the police. They have their own methods and go about their affairs in their own mysterious way."

He frowned and looked slightly uncomfortable. Doubtless the recollection of his unpleasant morning's work with the police surgeon in the mortuary had returned to him. But he pocketed his sympathy. Some things were safe, others were not. He attempted to be consoling and at the same time noncommittal.

"I shouldn't worry," he said. "You have yourself to think of now, you know, and we mustn't have your health letting you down. Let me have your wrist, please."

He felt her pulse and compared it with his watch.

"A little excited," he announced, "but not seriously. I'll send you round something to make you sleep. You'll feel

51

very much better in the morning. This period of suspense is very trying, I know, but you must try and pull yourself together. You've had a very great shock—a very great shock indeed—and your grief has naturally worn you down?"

The inquisitive soul which lurked behind the physician in Doctor Gordon Roe prompted the faint question contained in the last remark, and the girl responded to it without thinking.

"It's not grief," she said. "Not real grief. I'm sorry for Paul, but I was not in love with him."

Doctor Roe started. Even his most mischievous and unworthy hopes had not included a statement quite so damaging. He was both shocked and frightened by it.

"Come, come, you don't mean that, Mrs. Brande," he said peremptorily. "You're overwrought."

The girl looked at him in surprise for a moment and then her nerves seemed suddenly to fail her altogether.

"How horrible you all are!" she said explosively. "If I'd said that before my husband died you wouldn't have thought anything of it—no one would—and yet it's just as true now as it was then. Now I've only got to say that I didn't love my husband and you look at me as though you thought I'd murdered him."

Doctor Roe was panic-stricken.

"I—I must protest. Really!" he murmured into his collar, and made for the door, from which he summoned Mrs. Austin. "Get your mistress to bed," he ordered so sharply that she wondered whether he had divined that she had listened outside the door, and, having done what he considered was his duty, made his escape.

Meanwhile in a small flat over the police station in Bottle Street, Piccadilly, Mr. Campion was sitting at his desk attempting to write letters and at the same time to take a comparatively intelligent share in a conversation which he was holding with someone in the room next door.

"It's goin' to be a nasty case," a thick, inexpressibly melancholy voice announced bitterly. "Anyone can see that with 'alf an eye. You keep out of it. You don't want to get notorious. The way your name's been gettin' about lately you're a positive publicity 'ound."

"I resent that," said Mr. Campion, writing "hound"

irrelevantly in the midst of a note to his bank manager and crossing it out again. "These people are my friends, you know."

"All the more reason you want to keep away," said the voice, adopting this time a flavour of worldly wisdom. "Friends'll ask you to do things what strangers would never dare. It's a sex crime, I suppose you know that?"

"What?" said Mr. Campion. He had removed his spectacles, which somewhat obscured his vision when writing, but now he replaced them and laid down his pen.

"Sex crime," said the voice from within. "You've bin pretty lucky so far keepin' out of that sort of degradation, but you won't look so pretty trailin' about with the mud of the cheap Press all over you. I couldn't associate meself with you after that, for one thing. You'll lose all your old friends."

"Lugg," said Mr. Campion sternly. "Come in here."

There was a rumble in the other room as though a minor earthquake had disturbed it, and, preceded by the sound of deep breathing, Magersfontein Lugg surged into the room.

His girth was increasing with the years and with it his melancholy. He had also achieved a certain sartorial elegance without losing his unconventionality in that direction. At the moment he was clad in what appeared to be the hind legs of a black elephant, a spotless but collarless boiled shirt and a black velvet jacket.

His employer surveyed him coldly. "The *vie de bohême*, I see," he observed. "How are the tiny hands?"

Mr. Lugg shook his head ponderously. "Turn it aside with a light word if you like," he said mournfully, "but here we are, all respectable, nice, good class and the first nasty eruption that breaks out you're in it up to the neck."

"Where did you get that coat?"

"'Ad it made for me," said Mr. Lugg, with intent to snub. "It's a gentleman's 'ouse coat and very smart. All the wear just now. I bought it because I see in the paper that a certain important relative of yours is not too well, and if anything 'appened to 'im and you were suddenly called to take your place in the world I should like to be prepared."

"Yes, well, of course, you're revolting," said Mr.

Campion, getting up. "Ten years ago you climbed up the side of a three-story house with the agility of a monkey, let yourself through a skylight, opened a safe and got away as clean as a whistle and now look at you. You couldn't steal a bag of sweets from a two-year-old in a pram."

"I shouldn't want to, I hope," said Mr. Lugg, with dignity. "Besides," he added, lowering his puffy white lids over his little black eyes and achieving a superbly virtuous expression, "them things all belong to the past. It's the future we've got to think of, and that's why I do 'ope you'll steer clear of anything with a nasty flavour. It looked very bad in the evening newspapers and not at all the sort of thing you want to get our names mixed up with."

"You've gone soft, Lugg," said Campion, with regret. "I haven't given you enough work lately. I don't think there's much in this case for you, either."

"I'm glad to 'ear it." Mr. Lugg was positive. "When they was all talking about it at the club, discussin' the details, I said to myself, 'I do 'ope I keep out of this. It isn't as though we're on the side of the police.'"

Mr. Campion perched himself on the edge of the desk and wrapped the folds of his thin and rather dilapidated silk dressing-gown around his bony form.

"When you say 'the club,' do you mean that pub in Wardour Street?" he enquired.

A wooden expression crept into Mr. Lugg's face.

"No. I don't go there any more. I took exception to some of the members. Very low type of person, they were. If you want to know, I go to a very quiet, respectable little place in a mews up Mayfair way. There are several nice people there in me own line of business."

"Gentlemen's gentlemen, I suppose?" said Mr. Campion sarcastically.

"Exactly," agreed Mr. Lugg belligerently. "And why not? A nice superior class of people I meet and I hear all the gossip."

"I'm disgusted with you." Campion sounded genuine. "You make me sick. I've a good mind to sack you."

"You try," said Mr. Lugg, with a return of his old fire. "I'd like to know where you'd be—as helpless as a babe unborn. I've trained you not to be able to do without me.

You drop the case and we won't say anything more about it. Nothin' could be fairer than that.

"After all," he went on persuasively as he noticed no sign of capitulation in Mr. Campion's expression, "once sex rears its ugly 'ead it's time to steer clear. You know that as well as I do."

Mr. Campion's mystified expression deepened.

"You're not trying to be funny?" he suggested.

"Do I ever try to be funny?" said Mr. Lugg, with justifiable reproach. "It's not a funny subjec'."

Campion stirred. "Where did you get this—this sex idea?" he said. "I thought the papers were very reticent. They must be, of course, the law of libel being what it is."

"Readin' between the lines," said Mr. Lugg darkly. "Libel or no libel, if you reads the newspapers properly it's always clear what's 'appened. It's not what they say: it's the way they say it."

Campion frowned. "There's a lot of truth in that, unfortunately," he observed. "After your little mug between the lines, what do you deduce?"

"The wife did it, of course. They published 'er photograph. Did you see it? Nice-lookin' little bit—just the type."

Mr. Campion shuddered. "Lugg, you've done it this time," he said. "Get out."

Before the vigour of the command Mr. Lugg was abashed.

"No offence, Cock," he said hastily. "I don't know anything about the inside story. I'm only tellin' you how it appears to the man in the street. That's what you want to know, isn't it?"

Campion was silent for a moment, a slightly less vacuous expression than usual upon his pale, inoffensive face.

"I know these people, Lugg," he said at last. "They're all right, I tell you. Charming, straightforward, decent people. Mrs. Brande is one of the most delightful women I've ever met, and yet you see, apart from the tragedy of losing her husband, her portrait appears in the newspapers and the opinion in the Mayfair pubs is that she did him in."

Mr. Lugg was rebuked, but it was not his temperament to admit the fact.

"The tragedy of losin' 'er 'usband?" he said contemptuously. "That's good, that is! Hadn't the fellow been missin' since the Thursday and found dead in the office next door on the Monday? That's not my idea of a nice lovin' wife. Lets 'er old man be missin' three or four days and doesn't say a word."

"She sent for me," said Mr. Campion.

"Ho, she did, did she?" Lugg was interested. "That makes all the difference. Still, it didn't come out in the Press, did it? So how was I to know, or anybody else? Who do you think done it?"

Mr. Campion passed his hand over his fair hair and his eyes clouded.

"I don't know, Lugg," he said. "I don't know at all. I'm on the inside, you see, and yet you and your pals at the club have fixed the guilt already."

"Ah," said Mr. Lugg, "and I shouldn't be at all surprised if we wasn't right. Outsiders see most of the game, you know. You mark my words," he went on, gathering confidence, "before we know where we are up'll crop some nice young fellow she's 'ad her eye on. There'll be the motive and—there you are!"

Mr. Campion's reply was silenced by the trilling of the front-door bell. Lugg pressed his tongue against the back of his front teeth and emitted a clucking sound expressing both annoyance and resignation.

"What a time for anyone to come visitin'," he said.

Moving across the room, he opened the bottom drawer of a bureau and took therefrom, to Mr. Campion's horror, a remarkable contraption consisting of a stiff collar with a black bow tie attached. With perfect solemnity and a certain amount of pride, Mr. Lugg fastened this monstrosity round his neck by means of a button at the back, and moved ponderously out of the room, leaving his employer momentarily speechless.

Mike came into the room unannounced. The last two or three days had made a great difference in his appearance. His shorn black curls seemed to have receded a little and the skin over his forehead looked taut and lined. The old sleepy expression was still lurking in his eyes, but there was anxiety there also.

"I had to come round," he said abruptly. "I want to see you." He paused and glanced hesitantly at the sepulchral figure behind him, and Campion took the hint.

"That's all right, Lugg, please," he said.

The old ex-burglar raised his eyebrows. "I shall be in the kitchenette, sir, if you should require me," he said in so affected a voice that Campion gaped.

Mike was in no condition to notice extraneous details, however. As soon as he was alone he threw himself down in one of the deep chairs by the fire and sighed.

"This is damned awful, Campion," he said. "Losing old Paul's bad enough, but you can't imagine what it's been like this week. We haven't been able to call ourselves our own. Gina seems to be going to pieces altogether. Is there any way of finding out what the police have in their minds? I know you'll do your best for us. Have you found out anything?"

Mr. Campion, who was employed with a cocktail-shaker at the cabinet on the other side of the room, spoke over his shoulder.

"I went down to Scotland Yard," he said, "but Stanislaus Oates is on leave, and Tanner and Pillow, the men in charge of your business, were quite polite, but they weren't giving anything away. However, I shouldn't worry. Old Salley, the Coroner, is a good scout; a fierce old boy, rather abrupt, but hasn't held the office all this time without learning a thing or two. Have the police been round much since the postponement?"

"Round much . . . !" Mike groaned. "They're living in the office. We've all made statements till we're black in the face. Gina had a beastly experience, too. I persuaded her to go out a bit—sitting indoors brooding was doing her no good. She had a luncheon date with the Adelaide Chappel woman—the soprano. They went down to Boulestin's, and afterwards Madame Chappel had to go to Cook's, of all places. She always books through them, apparently, and she was off to Belgrade to sing in a concert there. Gina had nothing better to do, and went with her. She got the impression she was being followed, and actually saw a detective enquiring about her from a clerk. Since then there's been a man outside the flat. It's damnable, Campion, absolutely damnable! Why shouldn't she turn up at the inquest? Why shouldn't any of us? What have the police got up their sleeves?"

Mr. Campion handed his guest a cocktail before he spoke.

"What about all these statements you've been making?" he said. "I suppose they've been questioning you on your original essay dictated to the Coroner's Officer?"

"Have they not!" Mike spoke explosively. "I've gone over all that a dozen times, and so has Gina, to say nothing of poor old Curley and the poor little beast who found the body. They come to see us every day. This morning they were on a new track."

He drank the cocktail without tasting it and his eyes were fixed anxiously on Campion.

"They ask questions the whole time," he said, "but they never tell you anything. Today it was all the Thursday night stuff. Can you remember what you did last Thursday night—not yesterday, but the week before?"

Campion pricked up his ears. "Thursday night?" he said. "Did they ask everybody?"

"Oh, rather! I asked Pillow—a funny little chap, Campion, a sort of good-class head gardener, the last person on earth to be a detective—if they'd fixed the time of death, but he wouldn't say anything. Simply smiled surreptitiously."

Mr. Campion sat down on the edge of the opposite chair.

"Did he ask you about any special time on Thursday?"

"Yes. Between eight and nine o'clock. You've never heard such a tedious business. The whole office went through it. Poor Curley was nearly off her head. John couldn't remember where he was and she had to hunt up engagement books and phone through to inquisitive friends and business acquaintances. Finally it transpired that he was at the dinner given by the Quill Club to Lutzow, the psychologist. The secretary remembered him arriving at ten to eight and he didn't get back till eleven or twelve. Curley herself appears to have been in a Tube train on the Morden line. I was out until ten to nine. Gina was alone in the flat waiting for Paul. All simple ordinary activities, but difficult to remember when you're asked suddenly. Frankly, what's worrying me is that as far as I can see there's an ordinary explanation for the poor chap's death. The carbon monoxide must have soaked into the room and gassed him. The explanation of the locked door I suggested to Pillow was something like this: I think he went down there, let himself in, and left the key in the lock. The door swung to, and someone else, one of the employees, saw the key in the lock, turned it and took it upstairs and put it back in its place. Now they're probably too frightened to admit it."

Mr. Campion considered. "What did Sergeant Pillow say to that?"

Mike shrugged his shoulders. "Oh, you know what these policemen are! They're so darned clever. He said he'd look into it, and went on questioning me."

"How's your cousin taking it?" Mr. Campion put the question mildly.

"Who? John?" Mike permitted himself a faint smile. "He's quite fantastic. Simply doesn't realize that anything's up. Treats the police as though they were literary agents he'd never heard of, and spends his spare time thinking out little obscure paragraphs to send to the newspapers explaining why the funeral has been delayed. John's only thinking about Barnabas, Limited. He's believed so long that its reputation is sacred that he doesn't recognize a scandal when it comes along. He's had all the staff in crêpe bands, if you please, and has made arrangements for a very quiet and respectable funeral at Golders Green on the day after the inquest."

Campion replenished the empty glass.

"Mrs. Brande doesn't mind all these details taken off her hands, of course," he ventured.

"Gina? Oh, no." Mike spoke bitterly. "I think Gina always realized that Paul belonged to the firm more than to her. He—well, he neglected her in an impossible fashion, you know."

He lowered his eyes as he spoke and busied himself lighting a cigarette.

Mr. Campion did not speak, and after a pause the other man went on.

"Paul wasn't a subtle soul at all," he said, "and he had

the disconcerting habit of working himself into a fever to get hold of beautiful things and then forgetting all about them. It was the same with everything. He didn't appreciate the things he had."

Mr. Campion heaved a piece of coal into the centre of the blaze.

"As much as you might have done?" he suggested softly.

Rather to his surprise, Mike's dark eyes met his own squarely.

"That's the trouble," the younger man said quietly.

"How far has it gone?" enquired Mr. Campion.

"Not at all, thank God." Mike spoke fervently. "She's not particularly interested in me. I've just been about and we've naturally gone around together, but that's all. You don't understand Gina, Campion. No one does. I hope to heaven we can keep her out of this."

Mr. Campion was silent. For a moment he was aware of forces and counter-forces beneath the surface of the quiet lives surrounding Barnabas, Limited. There were revelations to come, he knew, some of them hideous, some of them piteous and others fantastic in their unexpectedness. He also knew that the man in front of him did not dream that once the searchlight of police and Press was turned on them there could be nothing hidden, nothing protected, and that beneath the glare little intimate things would stand out in unnatural prominence.

Aloud he said: "You ought to have married years ago, Mike."

The other man stirred. "I'm damned glad I didn't. Things are complicated enough as they are. Forget it and shut up about it. I don't know why I come to you, blethering about my secret affairs when there's open trouble to discuss. Hullo, who's this?"

His last remark was occasioned by the sound of a woman's voice in the hall. They had not heard her ring, and when Lugg showed the black-clad figure into the room a moment later they were taken by surprise.

"Gina! What are you doing here?" Mike rose to his feet and went towards her. All trace of his nerviness of a moment before had vanished. He had himself well in hand, Mr. Campion noticed approvingly.

Gina stared at him without a word of greeting and turned abruptly to Campion.

"You didn't mind me coming, did you?" she said hastily. "I'm going mad sitting up alone in the flat, wondering what the police are thinking. I even sent for the doctor, but he wouldn't tell me anything. Albert, what are they going to *do* on Tuesday?"

"Talk and talk and talk for hours, and write it all down by hand in the copybook," said Mike easily. "Look, here, suppose you come and sit down in this expensive-looking chair and let Campion give you a White Lady."

She turned to him and her wide grey eyes searched his face anxiously. He met her scrutiny smiling.

"Things are going to be all right," he said. "There's nothing to worry about. You look very fine. Did you design all that white collaretting? What d'you call it—a jabot or a bertha?"

"Mike, I can't bear it," she said, turning away from him. "Albert, tell me, what's happened?"

She sat down in the chair as she spoke and her pale face was raised to Campion's appealingly.

"He doesn't know any more than we do, Gina, but he says the Coroner is a wise old boy who isn't likely to make mistakes."

Mike spoke soothingly and pulled another chair forward and sat down in it between them. The girl seized at the straw of comfort.

"Still, people do make mistakes, don't they?" she said slowly. "To the police things look different, worse then they are. I could see that when I was interviewed by Inspector Tanner last night. I told him something, and I could see as he wrote it down that he thought—well, that he thought about it in a different way from the one in which it happened."

"Tell us about it." Campion handed her a glass as he made the suggestion.

She hesitated, and some of the colour returned to her face.

"It doesn't seem so important now," she said. "I'm behaving very badly, I'm afraid."

"Let's have it."

"Well—" Gina cleared her throat, "—I didn't know you were going to be here, Mike. It's something you don't know about, and you'll probably be surprised or shocked, but there was my side to it, and it wasn't all my fault."

She hesitated again, and the two men watched her as she sat there, so small and fragile in her sophisticated clothes.

"The Inspector was asking me about Thursday night. I told him Paul and I were going to discuss something over a meal and that I waited in for Paul until nine o'clock, when I phoned Mike and asked him to take me out."

She paused and her eyes met Campion's gravely.

"The Inspector asked me what Paul and I were going to talk about, and I told him. When he heard, he seemed to think it important. It was only an impression I got, of course, and yet . . ."

"What were you going to discuss with your husband?"

Campion saw the danger signal before he heard her confirming words.

"A divorce. I'd been trying to get Paul to give me one for some time," she said.

"A divorce?" Mike's whisper seemed to fill the room. She turned slowly round to him.

"Don't," she said. "Don't! No reproaches—not now. I'm just telling you what I told the Inspector."

A tremor passed over the younger man's face and it occurred to Campion that she did not realize her injustice.

"The Inspector was very interested," Gina went on. "He asked me if we'd spoken of it before, and I told him we had, lots of times, and that Paul wouldn't hear of it. But on the Wednesday I went to see a solicitor and that brought matters to a head. I knew where I stood. I knew I was tied to Paul if he—he—wouldn't desert me or beat me, so I begged him to have an evening at home so we could discuss it."

"You told the Inspector all this?" Mike's voice was very quiet.

"He got it out of me," she said helplessly. "Does it matter, Albert, does it matter? Will it make any difference?"

Mr. Campion rose to his feet. His face was very grave.

"I don't think so," he said at last, hoping his voice carried conviction. "You weren't quite alone in the flat when you were waiting for Paul, were you? I mean your woman was there to serve dinner?"

"Oh, yes, of course." Gina spoke carelessly. "Mrs. Austin was there until eight o'clock."

"Eight o'clock?" Mr. Campion's brows were rising.

She nodded. "I couldn't keep the woman all night," she said. "When Paul was a whole hour late for our conference and the dinner was spoiled, I told her I didn't care when he came in and I sent her off."

"Oh dear!" said Mr. Campion, and, after a little pause, again, "Oh, dear!"

5

Inquisition

It is perhaps not extraordinary that the mixture of anxiety, irritation and excitement typical of the backstage of amateur theatricals is nearly always reproduced at the moment when a family sets off for a public performance, be it wedding, funeral, or as in this case, inquest.

John had arrived, already dressed for the ordeal, at Gina's flat no later than half past eight in the morning of Tuesday, the 17th. By a quarter of nine he had phoned Mike three times and had upbraided the startled Mrs. Austin because Curley had not yet appeared.

Gina very wisely kept to her own room and left him to rampage up and down the studio.

When Curley came, pink and breathless with the exertion of climbing the stairs, he pounced upon her with a grunt of relief.

"We've got to be there in less than an hour," he said. "We don't want to be late. Let me see, there's Scruby to come yet. Hang the fellow! I told him to be punctual. You told him, Miss Curley, over the telephone. We were all to meet here at nine o'clock. I thought I'd made that quite plain."

Miss Curley, who was making frantic and futile efforts to tuck her wispy grey curls under the tight headband of her fashionable but unbecoming tricorne, was apologetic.

"He has a long way to come, Mr. Widdowson. He lives out at Hampstead, you know. Don't you remember, I told you he said we weren't to wait for him, but he'd meet us at the court."

John sank down in a chair, placing his speckless bowler on a table within arm's reach.

"Well, I suppose as a lawyer he knows well enough it doesn't do to be late for court proceedings," he said. "But I should have liked him to have been here. Miss Curley, go and ring down to Mike. Tell him we're all waiting. No one seems to realize the publicity involved in an affair of this sort, and not at all the right sort of publicity for a firm of our standing. I was fond of Paul, as you know, Miss Curley, but this final piece of sensationalism makes it very difficult for one to respect his memory as one would have liked."

"Oh, well, he won't do it again," said Miss Curley absently, and then, realizing the impropriety and inanity of the remark grew crimson with confusion.

To her relief John did not appear to have heard. He was entirely absorbed with his own angle on the tragedy.

"It's holding up everything. There's three quarters of the Spring list to come out and the Autumn one not half made up," he observed. "Still, we must put all that behind us now. We've all got to be calm and courageous. We must see this thing through with dignity and then we must bury our grief and get on with the work."

He seemed to be much more at ease after he had delivered this little homily and Miss Curley suspected that he had been saving it for a larger audience which had not materialized. She glanced at him curiously. He was getting older than she had thought, she decided, and wondered why it was that the cares of a firm aged a man so much more unattractively than the cares of a family. There was a great deal that was positively inhuman about John.

"Mr. Wellington rang up yesterday," she said, drawing

on her short black suéde gloves bought for the occasion, "and he asked me in confidence whether I thought you'd mind if he made an attempt to get into the public part of the court today. He wanted to make it very clear that he was not going after copy, but simply as an old friend of yours and Mr. Paul's."

The mention of the distinguished author's name seemed to cheer John immensely.

"Oh, not at all, not at all. I hope you told him not at all," he said. "Like to feel we had friends there. It did go through my mind that we might ask one or two people, but it didn't seem our prerogative, so to speak."

Miss Curley looked at him sharply, but there was no shadow of a smile upon his deeply lined, yellow little face.

"I wore a band," he said. "I think we all ought to wear bands, don't you? Mourning's out of fashion I know, nowadays, but it looked well, I thought. I told Mike about it."

Miss Curley was growing calmer. There was something extraordinarily soothing about John's attitude towards the terrifying business. At night, when she went home and she had a little leisure to think of the facts, she found herself growing frightened of the disaster which had overtaken them, but back in John's presence the habit of a lifetime reasserted itself and she found herself adopting his attitude against her better judgment.

When the Dresden clock on Gina's mantelpiece chimed the quarter John could bear it no longer.

"We must go," he said. "It may take us several minutes to find a cab at this hour of the morning. We don't want to be late. Getting about in London is very difficult."

Miss Curley hesitated. "It couldn't possibly take us more than ten minutes on foot, Mr. Widdowson," she said. "The court's only just round the corner. And, anyway, there's a cab rank at the end of Bedford Row."

"All the same, I wish you'd ask Mrs. Brande to come in here at once." John was fidgeting. "As for Mike, I don't know what the boy's up to. With so many Press people about we can't afford to make a bad impression."

When Miss Curley was out of the room he rose to his feet and walked over to the long mirror on the far side of the room and stood there for a moment, surveying himself critically. No one who saw him could have dreamed for a moment that he regarded himself as anything but the Head of the Firm. His poise and stance proclaimed it. He was faultlessly dressed in a dark suit and overcoat, upon which the crêpe band was only just visible. His short grey hair was clipped to a point at which it would seem that its growth was discouraged and his perfect hat completed the picture.

He looked, as he hoped, a distinguished public man, shaken, but not bowed, by private grief.

He turned away from the mirror as Gina and Miss Curley entered. It did not occur to him for a moment to apologize for having commandeered her room for the family meeting place. Instead he regarded her critically and on the whole with approval.

Her black clothes suited her. They were smart yet very severe. The only touch of softness was the crisp white ruff at her throat, and to this he took exception.

"I don't know that I should wear that, Gina," he said. "It's very nice, my dear, very becoming, but I don't know whether it's quite the thing for an occasion of this sort. Let me see how you look with it off."

The girl stared at him. Her face was drawn and colourless and her eyes had receded until there were dark hollows where they should have been. She looked ill and on the verge of collapse.

She plucked at the ruff obediently, but the touch of its crispness against her fingers seemed to steady her. She stared at him coldly.

"Don't be absurd, John. I'm not going to appear on the stage. Leave me alone—for God's sake, leave me alone!"

The man was obstinate, but like others of his generation he had a horror of nerves in women.

"Just as you like, my dear," he said coldly. "Just as you like. But I do think you'd look better without it."

"What the hell does it matter what she wears?"

Mike spoke from the doorway, where he had just appeared.

John fixed his younger cousin with a disapproving stare.

"There's no need to lose your temper," he said stiffly. "I'm only trying to think what would be wisest and most

dignified for us all to do. We share a common misfortune
and we are going to share a common ordeal."

Mike swallowed his temper. "That's all right, John," he
said. "But you might remember that Paul was Gina's
husband."

"Paul was my cousin and my partner," said John, with
dignity.

There was a pause and Miss Curley seized it.

"I think we should all go down now, Mr. Widdowson,"
she ventured. "It'll take us two or three minutes to get
down to Bedford Row."

Mrs. Austin put her head round the door, and they
stared at it not without justification, since it was adorned by
all the rakish splendour of Mrs. Austin's "Best that had once
belonged to a titled lady."

"I think I'll slip along now, M'm, if you don't mind,"
she said. "I don't want to be late."

Gina turned to her eagerly. "Mrs. Austin, I'll come
with you. We'll go together."

She moved unsteadily across the room and the charwoman put an arm round her.

"That's right, duck," she said. "You come along with
me. You've lost your 'usband and there's nobody else but
me in *this* room that knows what that means."

And with this Parthian shot she swept the girl out into
the passage.

"Gina's gone mad. . . . Stop her, Mike. Who is that
woman? Where are they going?"

John was halfway out of the door before Mike detained
him.

"They're going to the inquest," he said wearily. "We're
all going to the inquest. Hundreds of people are going to be
there—it's not just our show. And for God's sake come
along."

Miss Curley touched his arm. "I think Mrs. Brande
should come with us," she said.

The boy looked at her curiously. "Oh, let her go," he
said. "She's escaped from this family, Curley. Let her go
with her friends."

In the end they all straggled down Bedford Row
together, Gina and Mrs. Austin stumbling along in front

and John, in high dudgeon, stalking between them and Mike and Curley, who brought up the rear. They arrived at the court with fifteen minutes to spare.

There were still remnants of the last week's fog hanging about the city and the court seemed to have trapped more than its fair share. To Gina at least the whole place seemed to be filled with a thick brown mist, through which the faces of people she knew and did not know loomed out towards her and peered at her questioningly, only to disappear again in the general maelstrom.

She avoided Mike and clung to Mrs. Austin, whose grim determination to assert herself and whose contempt for the police and all their works made her a very comforting pillar on which to lean.

Mike and Curley remained side by side. The old woman's shrewd eyes took in every detail. She saw the Press benches were crowded and had the presence of mind to nod to the immaculately dressed Mr. Wellington, who was doing his best to look sympathetic at a distance of twenty feet.

John had buttonholed old Scruby, the firm's solicitor, and was talking to him rather than listening to what he had to say, as was his custom.

Scruby was a little skeleton of a man with sparse white hair that had yellow lights in it. At the moment he was peering at his client with protuberant pale blue eyes. As his practice largely consisted of libel and copyright he felt somewhat out of his element in the present situation and was doing his best not to say so. Mike, catching sight of the two of them, experienced a sense of sudden irritation well-nigh unbearable.

Scruby evidently had an inkling of the seriousness of the situation, but it was quite beyond him to impress his fears upon John, whose principal concern seemed to be the probable newspaper reports.

A pale young man with horn-rimmed spectacles, accompanied by an enormous person in a long black overcoat, sidled into the back of the court. Mr. Lugg and Mr. Campion were not on speaking terms that morning. No open rupture had occurred, but each, it seemed, thought it better not to intrude himself upon the other's private thoughts.

The inquest began in an unorthodox way. Mr. Salley addressed the jury. His voice, like his appearance, which was small and fierce, was unexpected. It was deep and very quiet, with a quality of naturalness which took Gina by surprise. He was like the best type of country doctor, she decided; blunt and straightforward and obviously completely without fancies of any sort.

His first words to the jury provoked furious activity at the Press table. He leant over his desk and his sharp eyes ranged over the seven embarrassed-looking citizens.

"Before you hear the evidence in this case," he said, "perhaps it would be as well if I defined your duty to you. I do this because possibly some of you may be under a misapprehension concerning this important matter, due to recent misleading criticisms of Coroners and Coroners' juries which have appeared in the Press.

"In the laws of England your duties are specifically laid down. There can be no question about them. They are clear and rigid.

"First of all let me repeat the oath which you took before me on this day one week ago. I must ask you to listen carefully and judge for yourselves what is the meaning of these very plain words."

He paused and they blinked at him owlishly. Taking a card from his desk he peered at it through his spectacles.

"This is your oath," he said, "listen to it—understand it. 'I swear by Almighty God that I will diligently enquire and a true presentment make of all such matters and things as are here given me in charge on behalf of our Sovereign Lord the King touching the death of Paul Redfern Brande, now lying dead, and will, without fear or favour, affection, or ill-will, a true verdict give according to the evidence and the best of my skill and knowledge.'

"There," he said, throwing down the card. "You have each of you repeated these words and I now ask you to consider to what you stand pledged. When the evidence has been set before you the law will demand of you that you answer several questions, and I think it will be as well if I told you now what those questions will be.

"Firstly, you will be required to state who the deceased was. Then how and where he died and afterwards how he came by his death."

He paused and regarded them steadily.

"This will constitute the first part of your verdict. But afterwards, and it is this point to which I want to call your attention because there has been much mischievous and misleading rubbish talked and written about it, you may possibly be called upon to answer another question. There is set down in Halsbury's *Laws of England,* a book whose authority cannot be questioned, the following incontrovertible decree. It is there stated that if the jury find that the deceased came by his death by murder or manslaughter those persons whom they find to have been guilty of such an offence, or of being accessories before the fact of murder, must be pointed out. It is the jury's responsibility, and they are in duty bound, if they know the persons guilty, to say their names."

Everybody in court save the seven people to whom these sober words were addressed seemed to be more than startled by them. The jury merely looked uncomfortable and cold. In the back of the court Mr. Lugg nudged Mr. Campion.

The Coroner had not quite finished.

"I wish to make it clear that this duty of yours does not apply in any particular or special way to the case you are about to hear today. It is your general duty. It is the duty of all Coroners' juries and I have called attention to it because I have found so much misapprehension on the subject, not only among the public, but even among members of the legal profession.

"Now we will hear the first witness."

6

By These Witnesses

Gina shrank back in her seat and waited for a merciful unreality to settle over the proceedings. In the past embarrassing or even harassing situations had always had for her this mitigating quality. Today, however, it was absent.

Instead the reverse seemed to have taken place. Faces seemed clearer, their less pleasing qualities emphasized, while each spoken word appeared to be charged with underlying menace.

The Coroner and the jury took on a Hogarthian quality, and those witnesses whom she knew resembled brilliantly cruel caricatures of themselves.

She tried to disassociate herself from it all, and to look upon the enquiry as though it were a play, but it was not possible even when she forced her eyes out of focus and persuaded her ears to hear only meaningless unrelated sounds.

Presently she found herself listening intently to Miss Marchant giving evidence about the discovery of the body. The Coroner was taking her gently through her written statement, but his tone became peremptory at the point where the actual appearance of the corpse was mentioned, warning her that any display of nerves which she might have contemplated would not be received sympathetically.

The fair-haired girl stepped down, relieved and a little nettled, the colour in her demure face heightened and her blue eyes embarrassed. The jury looked studiously disinterested.

The two doctors followed, one after the other. Consequential little Doctor Roe bustled forward, giving everyone in the court the impression that he wished to appear in a great hurry. Gina stirred uneasily. Was this awful clarity to be the peculiarity of the whole enquiry? In other circumstances Doctor Roe's hurry might have passed as genuine, but here in court it seemed monstrously overdone, his self-importance and his vanity painfully obvious.

The repetition of his statement already made to the police went slowly on, the Coroner interpolating an occasional question and writing down the replies with unhurried calm.

Gina tried to fix her mind on the evidence, but the mannerisms of the man, his love of the Latin cherished by his profession, his unction and gratification at his own importance obtruded themselves and all but eclipsed his information.

The Coroner kept him only a very short time, and the police doctor, a wholly unexpected person called Ferdie, appeared upon the stand.

Doctor Ferdie was a Scot from Dundee, and thirty years of work in London had not robbed him of his accent. He was a vast, untidy old person draped in elephant-grey clothes which managed to convey that there was something extraordinary about their cut without being actually peculiar in any definable particular. His face was seamed and rucked like the bark of an oak and from out its mass of indentations two very bright and knowing blue eyes peered at the world.

He cocked an eye at the Coroner with the confiding air of a trusted expert confronting an old client and the whole court became alive.

Preliminaries, the names and addresses of witnesses who had attested to Doctor Ferdie that the body of Paul Redfern Brande was the body of Paul Redfern Brande and not any spare corpse which might have been lying around at the time; the little matter of the warrant for examination and the address of the mortuary were all disposed of with perfunctory speed, and the doctor passed on to the external appearances of the body indicative of the time of death.

"The body was that of a well-nourished pairson," he remarked, his bright inquisitive eyes fixed upon the Coroner. "Not sae lean an' not sae stout. Just ordinary, ye see. There was no death stiffening, or, as ma colleague

Doctor Roe here would put it, rigor mortis. I examined the body carefully, and in my opeenion death had taken place within three to five days."

He paused and added confidentially:

"There were certain signs, ye see."

The Coroner nodded comprehendingly and turned to his personal notes.

"The man was last seen alive on Thursday afternoon, January the twenty-eighth; that is to say, somewhere between ninety-four and ninety-five hours before you saw him," he began at last. "In your opinion would the condition of the body be consistent with the suggestion that his death took place within an hour or so of his disappearance?"

Doctor Ferdie considered, and Gina found her heart beating suffocatingly fast.

"Ah, it might," he said at last. "It might indeed. But I couldn't commit myself, ye see. There were definite signs of the beginning of decomposition and in ordinary condeetions these do not appear until after the third day. But I wouldn't go further than that."

"Quite." The Coroner seemed satisfied, and after he had written for some moments he looked up again. "In regard to these ordinary conditions, you have said that the deceased was a well-nourished person of normal weight."

"Ah, he was," Doctor Ferdie agreed. "A healthy normal pairson."

"I see. Did you examine the room where the body was found?"

"I did."

"Was there anything about it which might have hastened or retarded the natural decomposition of the body?"

"No. It was a cool dry room, very badly ventilated, but otherwise nothing extraordinary."

"I see." The Coroner glanced at the jury, who made a visible effort to appear more intelligent. "Would the coolness hurry the termination of the period of death stiffening?"

The doctor cocked an eye again and spoke to the jury rather than to the Coroner.

"No, ye see, it would rather tend to prolong it."

"Death might easily have taken place between eighty-eight and eight-four hours before you saw him, then?"

"Ah, it might." The Scotsman hesitated. "I'd say it was very probable."

"Thank you, Doctor." The Coroner wrote again. "Now, as to the cause of death . . ."

Doctor Ferdie cleared his throat and launched into a careful and extremely delicate description of the colour of the face and chest, followed by a technical account of the autopsy which he and Doctor Roe had performed.

Gina's head began to swim. The brutality of the facts related in the soothing Scotch voice produced in her a sense of outrage.

She turned her head and caught a glimpse of Mrs. Austin. The woman was watching her with kindly but almost hungry eyes.

"Feel faint, duck?" she whispered hopefully.

Gina shook her head and passed her tongue over her dry lips. Mrs. Austin seemed disappointed.

Doctor Ferdie was still talking.

"It's lairgely a question of the colour of the bluid, ye see. I applied Haldane's test, and in my opeenion there was between forty and fifty per cent of carbon monoxide in the bluid. I took a test-tube containing a one per cent solution of the bluid to be examined. Then in a second tube I put a solution of normal bluid of like strength. Then I took a third tube an' . . ."

On and on it went, the details explained with endless patience to the seven self-conscious individuals whose acute embarrassment had given place to a sort of settled discomfort.

By the time Doctor Ferdie left the stand there could have been no reasonable doubt in anybody's mind that Paul Redfern Brande had died from carbon monoxide poisoning, and no very great question but that he had done so within eight hours of his last appearance in the office.

The doctor lolloped back to his seat and the Coroner's Officer, a plump uniformed person with a sternly avuncular manner, produced the next witness.

At the back of the court Mr. Campion sat up as Miss Netley walked hesitantly forward. Her schoolgirl affectation

74

was enhanced today and she looked little more than fourteen in her severe blue jacket and sailor hat.

She gave her evidence in a very low voice, but her timidity did not quite ring true, and even Mr. Lugg's sympathetic expression faded into one of doubt as her plaintive answers reached him.

The Coroner was very gentle with her, and she smiled at him confidingly as he helped her through her very simple tale. It transpired that she had been Paul's secretary and that so far as anybody knew she had been the last person to see him alive.

"You say Mr. Brande went out of the office at about half past three of the afternoon of Thursday, the twenty-eighth of last month, and that was the last time you saw him alive? Is that so?"

"Yes, sir."

"And you say here"—the Coroner went on, tapping the statement upon his desk—"that when Mr. Brande went out he seemed to be excited. Suppose you tell the jury what you meant by that?"

Miss Netley blushed painfully.

"I don't know, sir," she stammered at last. "He just seemed to be excited."

Some of the Coroner's tenderness vanished.

"Was he pleased or worried? Alarmed? Anxious about something?"

"No, sir. He was just—excited."

Mr. Campion pricked up his ears. There it was again, that same indefinable thing he had noticed about the girl before. She wanted to be tantalizing and did not mind appearing a fool in order to achieve that end.

"How did you know he was excited?" the Coroner suggested.

Miss Netley considered.

"He moved as though he was," she said at last.

Mr. Lugg nudged his employer and made an expressive depreciatory gesture with his thumb, an indication which in the days of his vulgarity would have been accomplished by the succinct expression "Out her!"

The Coroner breathed deeply through his nose.

"You just knew by the way he moved that he was excited?"

"Yes, sir."

The Coroner returned to facts.

"How did you know it was half past three when Mr. Brande went out?"

"Because," said Miss Netley, "the afternoon post comes at five-and-twenty minutes past three."

"And the post had just come when Mr. Brande went out?"

"Yes, sir." Her expectancy was as evident as if she had expressed it in words.

The Coroner looked up.

"Did anything come by the post for Mr. Brande?"

"Yes, sir. One letter."

"Did you see it?"

"I saw it was addressed to him and I handed it to him," she said. "It was marked 'Personal.'"

The court began to sit up and even the police looked interested.

"After Mr. Brande had read the letter, did he decide to go out?"

"Yes, sir."

"Did he tell you where he was going?"

"No."

"Did he say when he was coming back?"

"No."

"Did he say anything at all?"

"No, sir."

The Coroner sighed.

"You are here to give us all the help you can, Miss Netley," he said sternly. "To return to this excitement you noticed in Mr. Brande; had it anything to do with the letter?"

The girl considered.

"It may have had," she said. "I noticed it after he had read the letter. He got up hurriedly, put on his hat and coat and went out."

"What did he do with the letter?"

"He put it in the fire, sir."

"And that's all you know about this business?"

"Yes, sir."

The Coroner glanced at the written page in front of
him.

"All you can tell us, then, is that a letter came for your
employer at five-and-twenty minutes past three on the
twenty-eighth, that it was marked 'Personal,' and that after
he had read it he thrust it in the fire, put on his hat and coat
and went out and was never seen again alive as far as you
know?"

"Yes, sir."

"You've taken a great deal of time to tell us that, Miss
Netley. You're not hiding anything, are you?"

"Hiding anything, sir?" The big dark eyes grew round
and shocked. The small mouth trembled. The years
dropped away from the girl until she looked a child. "Of
course not, sir."

"All right. You may sit down."

Miss Netley returned to her seat with all eyes upon her
and Mr. Campion wondered. She was not quite the
ordinary notoriety-seeker, and once again he made a mental
note of her name.

The next witness was Detective-Inspector Tanner. He
was tall, thick-set, and the possessor of a figure predestined
to wear a uniform. His face was expressionless, but
forbidding in structure, while his light blue eyes looked
shrewd and obstinately honest. He gave his evidence in a
flat careful voice, obviously different from the one in which
he usually spoke. He made his statement with the awful
conviction of the slightly inhuman, while the Coroner
nodded to him from time to time and wrote it all down.

In the beginning it was the same story told from yet
another angle. Gina glanced restlessly round the court and
was startled to catch Mike's eyes resting upon her. He
looked away abruptly, but she had seen and turned back to
the witness, her body suddenly cold.

Mrs. Austin leant against her.

"Bear up, dear," she murmured.

The Inspector was making a great point of the fact that
the body had been moved by the doctor after its discovery.
Doctor Roe was recalled and stated amid much self-
conscious protestation that the step had been necessary, or
so he had been assured by Miss Curley and Mr. Michael
Wedgwood.

77

Having successfully shifted the blame from his own shoulders to theirs, he bustled back to his seat and the Inspector was recalled.

As soon as he reappeared a tremor of interest passed through the whole court. The Press men scribbled vigorously and Mr. Lugg leaned forward to catch a glimpse of the Barnabas party seated in front of him.

"After I and my colleague, Sergeant Pillow, had taken statements from the witnesses present on the premises at Number Twenty-three, Horsecollar Yard, I made a detailed search of the said premises."

The flat voice droned out the words like a child reciting.

"In the room where the deceased was discovered I noticed a small ventilator beneath one of the shelves which surround the room. The ventilator is situated three feet from the ground and five and a half feet from the ceiling. This ventilator is not easily observed by anyone entering the room because it is hidden by the projection of the shelf beneath which it is situated. I and my colleague removed the ventilator from its position and took it to headquarters as evidence."

There was a sensation as the ragged piece of iron was produced and solemnly handed round to the jury.

"I observed," Inspector Tanner continued, "that two of the centre bars of the ventilator had been recently broken. The sharp metal edges were bright and there were signs indicative of force having been used upon them. I also noticed a quantity of soot of a certain nature sprayed over the papers and débris on the lower shelf beneath the ventilator. My colleague and I then examined the lock of the door of the room and found that it had not been tampered with in any way. We then traced the outside wall of the building and discovered that the ventilator gave into a garage used by the directors of the firm. In the garage was a twenty-horse-power Fiat car, number PQ 348206, which we subsequently discovered belonged to Mr. Michael Wedgwood, junior partner in the firm of Barnabas, Limited and first cousin to the deceased.

"Continuing our search, we entered the building next door, known as Twenty-one, Horsecollar Yard, where the

78

residences of Mr. Michael Wedgwood, Mr. John Barnabas and the deceased are situated. Among some miscellany in the passageway outside the heating plant of these premises we found a length of rubber pipe, eight feet three inches in length and one and a half inches in diameter. As far as we could ascertain it had once formed part of a shower-bath apparatus, but did not appear to have been used for this purpose for some considerable time. One end of the pipe had been hacked off recently and the other end, which was fitted with a nozzle designed to fit over a water tap, had been considerably stretched and mutilated.

"The pipe was black with soot on the inside and the nozzle end showed signs of burning."

He paused again and the length of tubing was passed round.

The inference was obvious and the Inspector proceeded to show how the cut end of the tube had passed through the ventilator and was able to point out the indention some six inches from the end where it had been held by the ends of the broken bars.

Gina closed her eyes. It seemed to her for a moment that everyone was staring not at the exhibit but at herself. She dared not look at Mike. At her side Mrs. Austin was breathing heavily, her eyes snapping with excitement.

The Coroner took the Inspector over his statement very carefully.

"In your opinion, Inspector, this pipe was passed through the ventilator recently?" he suggested.

The Inspector stated that in his opinion there was no possible doubt whatever about the matter; he went on to say that the other end of the pipe had been tested in connection with the end of the exhaust pipe on the Fiat and finished up by producing that part of the car.

The jury stared at these three component parts and on their faces there appeared a gleam of something that could only be called satisfaction.

The Inspector stepped down and for a moment the court was full of whispers. Old Mr. Scruby was talking to John with an animation and authority quite foreign to his nature. Two or three reporters slipped out of their places and Mr. Lugg turned to Campion triumphantly.

"What did I tell you?" he murmured. "Here it comes."

Mr. Salley restored order and the next witness was thrust forward. He was a small square person with a large head, respectable clothes and innocent baby-blue eyes. It transpired that his name was Henry Cecil Pastern and that he had an expert knowledge of central-heating plants.

He made his statement with machine-gun rapidity.

"On the evening of the twenty-ninth of last month, at the invitation of Detective-Inspector Tanner, I made a detailed investigation of the boiler situated in the basement of the premises known as Twenty-three, Horsecollar Yard. It is a type of stove well known to me and when I examined it I found no defect of any kind whatsoever. Nor did I find evidences of any repairs having been made to it at any time. The stove is a comparatively new stove, not more than eighteen months installed. I do not see how any water gas or carbon monoxide gas could have escaped from it into the basement at any time."

Careful and scrupulously fair questioning by the Coroner made it clear to the jury and the court that Mr. Pastern knew perfectly well what he was saying and that even if his words had a slightly official flavour they did in fact represent his true and honest opinion.

It was during the interval after this evidence that Gina caught sight of Ritchie leaning forward in his seat, a bewildered expression upon his face. The sight of him almost made her laugh. He was so hopelessly out of place. So were they all, John, Curley and certainly poor Mr. Scruby. She found herself wishing desperately that it would end. It was a nightmare which had gone on too long.

The midday adjournment came unexpectedly. Miss Curley came bustling over, consternation on her plain plump face and her tricorne thrust unbecomingly to the back of her head.

"I've got to go with Mr. John and Mr. Scruby. They want to talk," she said breathlessly. "Will you be all right, my dear?"

"No one shall touch an 'air of 'er 'ead while I'm beside 'er," said Mrs. Austin valiantly but unnecessarily.

Gina was amazed at herself. One part of her mind was half irritated, half amused by the banality of the woman.

But there was another which was timidly grateful for her support.

As she came out of the court clinging to Mrs. Austin's arm she caught a glimpse of Ritchie mooching along, his hands in his pockets, his chin thrust out, and his lean, rangy figure looking unexpectedly distinguished. He did not see her but wandered over to Mr. Campion, who was standing in the lobby with a funereal individual whose face was only vaguely familiar to her.

The two women came out into bright sunlight completely unaware of the extraordinary picture they presented. Gina, with her hair sleeked beneath her Schiaparelli hat and her severe black suit clinging to her exquisitely fashionable figure, made a contrast with Mrs. Austin's exuberant Sunday Best which was positively arresting.

For a moment they stood hesitating, startled by the staring group on the pavement and the battery of cameras thrust mercilessly into their faces.

Glancing round her wildly, Gina suddenly saw Mike.

He was standing on the fringe of the crowd, his face turned towards her. As their eyes met he made an involuntary step forward, but immediately afterwards, as though a sudden recollection had occurred to him, he turned away and made off down the road at an exaggerated pace.

Somebody in the crowd laughed hysterically and Mrs. Austin gripped her firmly by the arm.

"If you ask my opinion," she said firmly, "what you want is a small port."

7

The Lying Straws

The woman came forward to the stand self-consciously, constraining her natural gait into little mincing steps and holding her large hands, exaggerated by impossibly ornate gloves, in an affected position neither comfortable nor becoming.

John Widdowson turned to Mr. Scruby.

"Who's this?" he demanded with the startled expression of an author at rehearsal finding an unexpected character in his play. "I've never seen her before."

"Ssh," said Mr. Scruby apprehensively as the Coroner's glance shot towards them.

John gobbled in silence and the witness took her place.

She was a large woman, asthmatic and unhealthy-looking, with a white face, a pursed mouth, and gold pince-nez looped to her ear with a small chain. She wore a cheap black fur coat much too small for her and had filled up its deficiency in front with a heavily frilled blouse. She gave her evidence in tones of staggering refinement.

For a moment she was so absorbed by her unusual prominence and a delicacy either real or assumed that she did not hear the Coroner when he asked her name, but was at length prevailed upon to inform the court that she was Mrs. Rosemary Ethel Tripper, that she lived in the basement flat at Number Twenty-five, Horsecollar Yard, and that her occupation was assistant caretaker with her husband of the two blocks of offices, Numbers Twenty-five and Twenty-seven. She also took the oath.

Once again the sense of outrage crept over Gina. She realized that the police were under no compulsion to broadcast their affairs, but when those affairs were so very intimately her own it seemed unnecessarily cruel to have kept her so much in the dark.

At the Coroner's request Mrs. Tripper cast her mind back both to her statement and the evening of the twenty-eighth.

"I had been to the pictures with a lady friend," said Mrs. Tripper with the air of one recounting an interesting social experience. "I parted with her at the end of the street—at about five minutes to seven o'clock, I should say it was—and then I entered my flat and went straight into the kitchenette, where I made myself a cup of tea.

"Going into the bedroom to change my shoes, a habit I have had from a girl, I suddenly said to myself, 'Why, there's that car started up!'"

She paused triumphantly and the Coroner coughed.

"Perhaps you'll explain to us, Mrs. Tripper," he said, "what exactly you meant by that?"

Mrs. Tripper was taken off her balance.

"I was referring to the car in the garage at Number Twenty-three," she said sharply, her refined accent temporarily deserting her. "Although we can't hear the car in the daytime, of course, because of the traffic, any time after six o'clock the Crescent is so quiet you could hear a pin drop and of course you can hear the car then, because the walls are so thin—I often say it's a disgrace."

"The Crescent?" said the Coroner enquiringly.

The faint colour flowed into Mrs. Tripper's pale face.

"Well then, the Yard," she said defiantly. "Horsecollar Yard. It's really a crescent."

"I see," said the Coroner and bowed his head over his papers. "What time was it exactly, Mrs. Tripper, when you thought you heard the car start up?"

"I heard it start up at ten minutes past seven," said Mrs. Tripper. "I left my friend at five minutes to. Five minutes to walk up the street, five minutes to make myself a cup of tea, and five minutes to go into the bedroom."

"Five minutes to go into the bedroom?" enquired the Coroner in some astonishment.

Once again Mrs. Tripper was put off her stride.

"Well, let's say five past seven I heard the car," she temporized.

"Are you sure you heard the car start up soon after you came in?" said the Coroner with some asperity.

"Yes, I did. I heard it as plain as anything when I was in the bedroom after I'd had my cup of tea."

"I see. And how long did you stay in the house?"

"Till about half past seven," said Mrs. Tripper promptly. "And the car was running all the time. It was running when I went out. I noticed it because I said to myself, 'It's bad enough to hear that engine being turned on and off, without having it running in your ear the whole time,' and I meant to speak to the janitor at Twenty-three about it."

"You say about half past seven, Mrs. Tripper—" the Coroner was very gentle. "Could you be more exact?"

"Well, I *think* it was half past seven. Anyway I left the house and went down to wherever I was going, and when I got there it was ten minutes to eight—because I saw the clock."

"Where was this?"

Once again Mrs. Tripper flushed.

"It was a shop in Red Lion Street—a fried-fish shop, if you must know. It was very foggy and I hadn't been able to get about to do my ordinary shopping, and I knew my husband would like something hot for his supper and so I thought I might as well try some of their more expensive pieces. Some of these places are very high class, and the Red Lion shop is very nice indeed."

"Quite, quite," said the Coroner, rather taken aback by the vehemence of her confession. "You went straight to the fried-fish shop when you left your house and you arrived there at ten minutes to eight?"

"Yes, I did."

It was evident that Mrs. Tripper was torn between the desire to acquire kudos by admitting to a knowledge of interesting facts and irritation at having to disclose the more humble activities of her private life.

"And when I returned," she went on triumphantly, "the car was still running. I heard it turned off at ten minutes to nine or thereabouts."

The Coroner leant forward across the desk.

"I feel these times are important, Mrs. Tripper," he said. "I wonder would it be possible for you to cast your mind back and think of any concrete fact by which you can fix them? For instance, are you quite sure that it was not half past eight, or even a quarter past nine, when you heard the car turned off?"

Mrs. Tripper's narrow black eyes behind her gold pince-nez snapped.

"I've told you there was a clock," she said. "Haven't I? I stood talking in the shop a little while and suddenly I looked up and saw it was a quarter to nine. 'Oh, dear!' I said. 'My husband comes in for his supper at nine,'—he goes down to the club on Thursdays—'and I must get home,' I said. I remember saying it. I hurried off and I got home at ten minutes to, as far as I can judge."

The Coroner returned to his notes.

"I see that it took you twenty minutes to get from your home to the fried-fish shop, Mrs. Tripper, and only five minutes to get back . . ."

Mrs. Tripper's mouth set obstinately.

"That's all I can tell you," she said. "I hurried back and as far as I can judge it was ten minutes to, because my husband came in just as I'd got everything on the table, and he's always punctual. I came in at the door, I listened, and I heard the car still running. Then just as I was saying something to myself about it, off it went."

As she stepped down off the stand a sigh passed round the court and the jury whispered together.

Gina felt that she was crouching in her seat. She dared not think ahead. In her heart she felt there was nothing to be gained by thinking. There was a slow inexorable quality about this enquiry. Nothing could deter it. It was simple, brutal and unescapable.

She was still dithering when she heard her own name called, but for the first time, as she walked to the stand, she felt the longed-for sensation of remoteness. A wall of apathy seemed to have descended between her and the nightmare around her. Faces became vague and indistinct, voices heard from afar off.

She gave her name, her address and the fact that she was Paul's wife with a calm detachment which passed for extreme self-possession. Her voice was soft and carefully modulated and she held herself rigidly.

She repeated the oath calmly, unconsciously imitating the lack of expression of the Coroner's Officer.

The Coroner became a nonentity, a questioning machine, gentle and not at all unpleasant. He took her quietly through her statement. She remembered making it, remembered signing it, but only in an impersonal far-off way as though it had not been of very great interest.

"I last saw my husband at two o'clock on the afternoon that he disappeared. It was only for a few minutes. I went into his office and caught him, as he had returned early from lunch. We had a short conversation. Then I went back to my flat. I never saw him again alive."

She was completely unaware of the impression she was creating.

The average British crowd is quick to admire beauty, especially in distress, but there is a curious streak in the temperament which makes it distrust the quality of smartness, especially when it is allied, however remotely, to something questionable or suspicious.

The fact that she was a foreigner told in her favour naturally—foreigners may be forgiven for having chic—but her calm weighed heavily against her. Widows should weep and emotional display is not only expected but demanded of them.

The questioning continued.

"You say in your statement, Mrs. Brande, that you expected your husband to come home to dinner at half past seven and that you waited for him until nine, at which time you rang up your husband's cousin, Mr. Michael Wedgwood, who took you to see a film. Were you not worried when your husband did not appear for dinner?"

She repeated the word. "Worried? No. I don't think so. I was annoyed."

It occurred to her that she might explain that Paul was always late for appointments with her, that his neglect of her, his indifference to her feelings, had rendered her completely impervious to the sensation of alarm where he was concerned, but she did not want to explain. It seemed so unnecessary to go into details to all these stupid gaping people, who could never be expected to understand. She held her tongue.

The Coroner went on.

"You say that when you went to see your husband in his

office that afternoon you had something very particular to ask him. What was it?"

"I wanted to impress upon him that he must dine with me that evening, because I wanted to talk to him."

It appeared to occur to the Coroner that she was making no effort to help herself and he bent forward.

"Mrs. Brande," he said, "how long have you been married?"

"Four years."

"Would you say your marriage has been a happy one?"

"No," she said, more vehemently than she intended. "No, I don't think it was."

There was excitement in the court and John would have risen had not Mr. Scruby held him down. The Coroner pursed up his lips.

"Perhaps you'd like to amplify that, Mrs. Brande," he said. "This is a court of enquiry, you know, and we want to arrive at the truth. Did you quarrel with your husband?"

"No," she said. "We were indifferent to one another."

As soon as she had spoken she was sorry. The publicity of the whole business struck her again, but not forcibly enough to make her angry. She was past anger.

The Coroner sighed and his manner became a little less friendly.

"Mrs. Brande," he said, "you made this statement voluntarily to the Inspector and the Coroner's Officer, I understand?"

"Of course," she said stiffly. "I had nothing to hide."

"She's a cool one." The court's comment was almost audible.

"Of course not," the Coroner agreed. "You say in your statement that you were particularly anxious to confer with your husband on the evening of the twenty-eighth because you wanted to persuade him to help you to get a divorce?"

"Yes," she said.

"You do not wish to add anything to that statement now?"

"No, I don't think so."

The Coroner looked at her under his eyebrows. He had seen many frightened women and to him her reaction was not incomprehensible, but his duty was to enquire and she was not helpful.

"Why were you so anxious to talk to him about it at that particular time, Mrs. Brande?"

"It is all in the statement," she said wearily. "I told Inspector Tanner that I had visited a solicitor and found out exactly how I was placed. I realized that I could not get a divorce from my husband unless he assisted me."

There was an audible murmur in the court and little Mr. Scruby bounded to his feet. The Coroner acceded to his request that he might be allowed to question the witness and Gina became aware of the little man staring at her anxiously across the crowded room.

"Had you had any violent quarrels with your husband upon this subject, Mrs. Brande?"

"No, of course not," she said in some surprise. "It was only that we saw really very little of each other and I wanted Paul to consider my point of view."

Mr. Scruby sat down, not at all sure that he had been of any real assistance. The Coroner returned to the statement.

"You say you had ordered dinner in your flat for half past seven. Were you alone?"

"No. I had my charwoman, Mrs. Austin, with me."

"I see. And you waited for your husband until nine o'clock?"

"Yes, until almost nine."

"Was your charwoman with you then?"

"No. I let her go about eight o'clock. I saw no point in keeping her after that."

"You were pretty sure your husband would not come then?"

"I thought it extremely unlikely."

"Yet you waited for him yourself?"

"Yes. I hoped, you see."

The jury stirred. This was more like it.

"And at nine o'clock, or nearly nine o'clock—eight fifty-five, to be exact—you rang up Mr. Michael Wedgwood in the flat below and suggested that you go out together? The rest of the evening you spent in a picture palace?"

"Yes. That is true."

There was a long pause while the Coroner wrote.

"Now," he said at last, "were you in the habit of ringing up Mr. Wedgwood and suggesting that he should take you out?"

She hesitated. Something odd about the question warned her to be careful, but there was no time for adroit manoeuvring, even had she been capable of it.

"Yes," she said. "I was. We have been about a good deal together."

Mr. Campion felt the hair on his scalp rising and Mr. Lugg granted him a single reproachful glance.

"You were very great friends?"

"Yes. We are."

"Are you lovers, Mrs. Brande?"

She stared at him, hardly believing that she had heard the words. She was so completely taken aback that for a moment she was silent and during that instant of stupefaction her anger and indignation were transmuted into helplessness. The old apathy reclaimed her.

"No," she said evenly.

"You are not shocked by the suggestion?"

She opened her mouth to protest violently but thought better of it.

"It is too utterly ridiculous," she said and the proud quiet words were momentarily convincing.

A few unimportant questions followed and she was allowed to step down. She walked to her seat with the eyes of the whole court upon her, but it was not until she saw Mrs. Austin's sympathetic but horribly knowing face raised to hers that she realized quite what had happened.

Panic seized her. What had she said? What were they all driving at? The blood drained out of her face and Mrs. Austin caught her arm.

"Put your head between your knees," she whispered. "Shall I get you out?"

Gina had sufficient strength to shake her head and to turn her eyes resolutely towards the desk. She knew that John was staring at her angrily and in imagination she could see the startled little face of Mr. Scruby by his side.

Mike was the next witness.

The jury were wide awake now and their interest was not assumed. They had completely forgotten their own prominence and were absorbed by the story being unfolded so lucidly before them.

Gina did not take her eyes from Mike's face during the whole of his evidence. She felt she was seeing him for the first time. He was extraordinarily handsome, with the tall, lank Barnabas figure and the crisp curls shorn tightly to his head.

To those who knew him he betrayed his nervousness. He spoke with a drawl not natural with him and the ease of his stance was assumed.

His written statement was necessarily brief. He admitted helping the doctor to move the body on to the table and afterwards up to the flat, and gave a brief account of his cousin's position and activities in the firm.

The Coroner questioned him about the strong room. Evidence that had been given by other witnesses concerning its use was confirmed by him and he repeated that the car in the garage belonged to him.

"The yard gates are kept locked," he said, "but not the garage itself. I never considered there was any need for that."

The Coroner returned to the question of the strong room.

"I see in your statement, Mr. Wedgwood," he said, "that you admit to having visited the strong room on the night of the thirty-first, three days after your cousin's disappearance and on the evening before the discovery of his body."

The excitement at this point was intense and the Coroner had to enforce silence.

Mike's lank form seemed to be leaning back upon the air and his drawl became more pronounced.

"That is so," he said.

"Will you describe exactly what you did upon that occasion? It is all written down, I know, but I should like to hear it from you again."

Mike complied. He described how he had left the flat on Sunday night, had gone into the darkened office, taken the key from its usual place, opened the strong room and taken the folder which John had needed from its shelf, and had come away, locking the door behind him.

The Coroner seemed puzzled and he took the young man through the story again and again. Finally Mike's evidence was interrupted while Miss Curley and Miss Marchant were called to describe the exact place in which the body was found.

When the Coroner returned to Mike again his tone was peremptory.

"Can you offer any explanation why you did not see the body of your cousin on Sunday night?" he said.

"I'm sorry, I can't. It wasn't there. Or, if it was, I didn't see it."

Mike's exasperation was not unmixed with defiance. The Coroner dismissed the matter for the time being and went back to the Thursday night.

"Mr. Wedgwood," he said, "will you tell us what you did from three o'clock in the afternoon of Thursday the twenty-eighth until you answered the telephone at nine o'clock and went out to a picture palace with Mrs. Brande?"

Mike stiffened slightly and when he spoke his tone was defensive.

"I worked in my office all the afternoon," he said slowly. "My secretary was there the whole time. I left about half past five, intending to go to a cocktail party, and because it was slightly foggy and I was early I decided to walk. The house I intended to visit was in Manchester Square, but before I reached it I changed my mind and decided that I would go on walking."

He paused. The Coroner was looking at him and the seven pairs of eyes from the jury benches watched him narrowly.

"Yes?" said the Coroner.

"Well, I went on walking," said Mike lamely. "I had various things on my mind and I wanted to think them out. I went on walking until about half past eight. Then I got on a bus and came home."

The Coroner's pen traced idle designs on the blotting paper in front of him.

"Half past five till half past eight," he said. "That's three hours. It's a long time to walk on a foggy winter night, Mr. Wedgwood. Can you tell us where you went, exactly?"

"Yes. I went down to the far end of Westbourne Grove.

I walked down Holborn, Oxford Street, Edgware Road, Praed Street, and Bishop's Road. Then I turned back and I went up one of those long terraces to the Park, I cut through from Lancaster Gate to Hyde Park Corner and came up Piccadilly. I went up Shaftesbury Avenue, Charing Cross Road and I took a bus at St. Giles's Circus. It's a long way and I was not walking fast."

"Did you stop anywhere? Speak to anyone?"

"No. I don't think so."

"Well, can you tell us, Mr. Wedgwood, why you went to Westbourne Grove? Had you any purpose in going there?"

A faint smile passed over the man's expressive face.

"Yes, I had, vaguely. I meant to visit a shop there. There's a little secondhand jeweller's and curio shop about halfway down the right-hand side. I don't know the name of it. When I got there it was shut. It was Thursday anyway— I'd forgotten that."

The Coroner was inclined to be impatient.

"You must see that this is a very unsatisfactory story," he said testily. "You say you walked nearly four miles to visit a shop and found it shut. Had you any particular purpose in going to that shop?"

"No, not really. I mean, nothing urgent." Mike seemed unduly embarrassed. "I thought I might find something of interest there, I have done so before."

"Some piece of jewellery?"

"Well, yes."

"I see." The Coroner paused significantly. "Well, then, when you found the shop was shut you walked back for no other reason than that you wished to walk?"

"That is so."

"And it was cold and slightly foggy—not a pleasant night for walking?"

"No, it wasn't. But I didn't really mind about that. I had things on my mind and wanted to work them out."

"Those things, I see, Mr. Wedgwood, were private affairs which have no bearing on this case?"

"They were business matters," said Mike briefly and unconvincingly.

"When you returned home to Horsecollar Yard what did you do?"

"I went down through my own flat, out of the back door, through the gate in the wall to the garage behind the office, and started my car."

The court gasped.

"Why did you do that?"

"The fog had cleared a little and I thought it would probably be quite bright in the country. I thought I would go out somewhere by myself for a run round."

"You were tired of walking?" observed the Coroner dryly.

"Yes, I was."

"According to your evidence, Mr. Wedgwood, you had nothing to eat all this time . . ."

"No. I wasn't hungry. I just wanted to be by myself."

"And so you started up the car?"

"Yes. I always do that. I let her run for a little while, five or ten minutes at the outside, before I take her out into the traffic in the cold weather. I find she runs much more easily."

"And then?"

"Then I remembered that the key of the yard gates was in my coat in the flat. I went up to get it. While I was there Mrs. Brande rang up and explained that Paul had not returned and I suggested that we should go out somewhere. As it was too late for a theatre we went to a film. Before I went up to fetch Mrs. Brande I returned to the garage and switched off my car engine. I estimate it had been running seven minutes."

"I see." The Coroner cleared his throat. "Now there are just one or two questions I want to ask you concerning this statement. When Mrs. Brande told you that her husband had not returned and that he was two hours late for an appointment, weren't you alarmed? Didn't you wonder what had happened to him?"

"No. Paul was like that. He was a most erratic person. Neither Gina—I mean Mrs. Brande—nor we at the office ever knew when he was going to turn up."

The Coroner wrote.

"But on the Sunday, Mr. Wedgwood, when you were having tea—with others—at Mrs. Brande's flat, didn't you wonder then what had happened to your cousin?"

"I did. I thought he had stayed away rather a long time, but I wasn't worried. As I say, my cousin was unreliable."

"Well, then, one other point. You say you were getting your car out, intending to crawl through the fog until you got to the open country, because you wanted to be by yourself. And yet as soon as Mrs. Brande phoned you you suggested you should take her out to see a film? How do you explain that?"

Mike shrugged. "I don't explain it," he said. "I'm just telling you what happened."

"Mr. Wedgwood, is there a love affair between you and Mrs. Brande?"

"Certainly not."

"You have never at any time treated her in any way other than as your cousin's wife?"

"Never."

"You realize you are on oath?"

"I do."

"Very well. Will you stand down, please."

Much to everybody's astonishment, including her own, the next witness was Mrs. Austin.

She swept forward, a fine belligerent figure, skirts and streamers flying, and after climbing into position turned and surveyed the court, Coroner and police with self-possessed hostility.

She gave her name as Mrs. Dorothy Austin; her age (which was unasked) as forty-two; and an address in Somers Town.

"I've been visiting my lady, Mrs. Brande, for nearly four years now," she explained, "and if anybody knows her I do."

The Coroner looked up and smiled.

"We will stick to your statement as much as possible, Mrs. Austin," he murmured. "You say here that you were in the habit of arriving at Mrs. Brande's flat at eight o'clock every morning, that you stayed until twelve and returned again to cook and wash up after the evening meal if necessary."

Mrs. Austin concurred.

"I don't see anything wrong in that," she said.

"No, no, of course not. Now, during your visits to the flat you have had an opportunity of studying your employer and her husband. Would you say their married life was a happy one?"

"No, I wouldn't," said Mrs. Austin vehemently. "If my husband had treated me as Mr. Brande treated my lady I'd have left him long ago. It was only her sweet nature that made her put up with him as long as she did."

From the back of the court Gina looked at the woman imploringly, but there was no way of stopping that well-meaning tongue or forcing a little enlightenment into that short-sighted mind. Mrs. Austin imagined herself a counsel for the defence and already saw her name large in the newspaper as the champion of the downtrodden wife.

Pleasant, sturdy Sergeant Pillow looked down his nose. When he had taken her statement it had seemed to him almost a pity that she should have been so very much "in the mood," but after all the truth was the truth and the more easily it came out the better for everyone.

The Coroner had hardly any need to speak at all. Mrs. Austin not only remembered her statement but was quite willing to amplify it.

"They never came to blows—I will say that for them," she said, "but I often think it's a pity they didn't. The way he neglected her! Half the time he wasn't there at all and the other half he didn't notice she was there. No one could blame her if she went out a bit with Mr. Mike. A lady's got to have someone to take her about. She can't sit up like a sparrow on a housetop, not going anywhere. It's more than human nature can stand."

The Coroner interrupted the flow.

"Mrs. Austin," he said, "you say that you rarely stayed at the flat later than nine o'clock in the evening and never arrived there before eight o'clock in the morning. You are therefore not in a position to say whether, in the absence of Mr. Brande, Mr. Wedgwood ever stayed in the flat at night?"

"Well, of all the minds!" she began indignantly, but was silenced by the Coroner.

"You must answer me 'Yes' or 'No.' Did you ever know for a certainty that in the absence of Mr. Brande Mr. Wedgwood had stayed in the Brandes' flat overnight?"

"No," said Mrs. Austin, choked by the constraint put upon her. "But if he had I wouldn't have blamed him—or her, and that's the truth."

"That'll do," said the Coroner. "Now you were in the room, I understand, when Mr. Wedgwood came to tell Mrs. Brande that her husband was dead. I want you to describe that scene a little more fully than it is set down here. You admitted Mr. Wedgwood to the flat at about ten o'clock on Monday morning, the first of February. Do you remember that?"

"As clearly as the night my husband died," said Mrs. Austin a little unnecessarily.

"Very well. Now before Mr. Wedgwood arrived you saw your mistress?"

"Of course I did. I'd been running in and out of her room all the morning."

"At that time Mr. Brande had been missing for three days and four nights. Did Mrs. Brande seem worried?"

Mrs. Austin considered.

"Not exactly worried. I think she was relieved to be without him. One of us passed the remark that it was strange he hadn't come in."

"It did not occur to you that any harm might have befallen him?"

A ray of recollection flickered over Mrs. Austin's broad face.

"Now I come to think of it, I did say when I brought in her morning tea, 'I see the master's not back. I wonder if he's been runned over.'"

"Ah. And what did Mrs. Brande say to that?"

"Oh, she turned over on her side and said, 'No such luck,' or something like that."

Anyone of a more sensitive nature than the worthy Mrs. Austin must have noticed the tremendous sensation she was providing. The Coroner picked her up.

"When you say things like this, you must realize what they mean," he said severely. "Did Mrs. Brande use the actual words 'No such luck' in reply to your suggestion that her husband had been run over and killed?"

Mrs. Austin looked abashed.

"I think her actual words were, 'No, there's no escape that way.' I took it to mean 'No such luck.'"

"You're sure of these words, Mrs. Austin? Are you—yes or no?"

"Yes, I am. 'No, there's no escape that way'—that's what she said."

"And after that no mention of Mr. Brande was made?"

"No."

"You say you remember Mr. Wedgwood coming to the flat at ten o'clock that morning very distinctly. Will you describe it, please?"

"There was a ring at the bell," said Mrs. Austin dramatically. "I was just going to make some coffee, but I popped off my apron and opened the door. There stood Mr. Mike, white as a sheet, his hands twitching, his eyes starting out of his head. I knew at once something was up."

"Not unnaturally." The Coroner opened his mouth to say the words, but thought better of them. Instead he wrote down "Seemed greatly agitated" and put a further question.

"I see that you took Mr. Wedgwood into the room where your mistress was kneeling by the fire in pyjamas. Do you remember what she said?"

"Yes. She said, 'Mike, my pet, I'm glad to see you,' and asked him if he'd have some coffee. Her face lit up—she looked quite different."

"Then you went out of the room?"

"Yes, to make the coffee."

"And when you came back, what did you see then?"

"They were clinging together," said Mrs. Austin, with sentimental relish. "Clinging together on the hearth rug like a couple of children. Of course, when they heard me they sprung apart—as was only natural, me being an older person—and my lady said, 'My husband's dead, Mrs. Austin.' 'No!' I said. 'Yes,' she said. I give her some coffee quick. Then we all had some coffee and Mr. Wedgwood told us that they was bringing the body up. I made him come out and give me all the details so I should know what to get ready. As soon as he could he slipped back to her."

"Then you can't tell us any more about the conversation which took place between them after the death had been discovered," said the Coroner firmly. "Can you tell us what effect the news had upon your mistress? Did she seem surprised?"

"Surprised? She was horrified! I never saw such a change in anyone in all my life. One moment she was a bright laughing girl, not a care in the world except Mr. Brande's neglect and mental cruelty to her, and the next she was a drawn haggard woman, as you might say."

"Yes, but was she surprised?"

"She was thunderstruck, if you ask me," said Mrs. Austin.

Mr. Scruby, who jumped up some little time before and had only just succeeded in catching the Coroner's eye, begged to be allowed to put a question.

"When you say your mistress was in pyjamas, Mrs. Austin," he said, "do you mean her night clothes?"

The woman stared at him. "No, I don't," she said. "It's a new fashion. Little serge romper suits. Ladies wear them in the morning about the house. Very nice and respectable, they are, something after the style of a naval uniform."

"Thank you." Mr. Scruby sat down amid a titter of laughter and Mrs. Austin's appearance in the limelight came to an end.

She went back to her seat bursting with pride.

"I showed 'em," she said, sitting down beside Gina. "They didn't get much change out of me—nosy parkers!"

Gina said nothing.

The last witness was so well known to the whole of the Barnabas group that they stared at him in astonishment in this new setting. He was a little wizened person, very spruce and smart, but so nervous that he was almost incoherent. He gave his name as William Robert Dyke and explained that he was the janitor in charge of Twenty-one and Twenty-three, Horsecollar Yard, and had been in the employment of Messrs. Barnabas, Limited for twenty years.

He identified the piece of rubber tubing reluctantly as part of an old shower-bath attachment which he had saved some years before when it had been thrown out of Mike's flat during a spring-cleaning. Thinking that it might come in useful at some time or other, he had hung it over a large nail on the wall of the cupboard next to the furnace at Number Twenty-one, where a great deal of other odds and ends were stored. The cupboard had no door and its contents were easily visible to anyone and everyone who passed in and out of the building by the basement garden exit.

On the morning of Friday, the twenty-ninth, the day after the deceased had disappeared, he had noticed it lying upon the floor beside the other rubbish and had picked it up. He thought it looked a little dirty, but had not examined it carefully, simply replacing it upon its nail and forgetting it until the Coroner's Officer questioned him about it on the following Monday morning.

And there, with astonishing abruptness, the larger part of the enquiry came to an end.

Gina sat quite still. She did not want to look about her. Miss Curley tried to catch her eye, to give her a timidly reassuring nod, but the younger woman did not stir nor did she ever raise her eyes from her white-gloved hands folded tightly in her lap.

John and Mr. Scruby were conversing animatedly in whispers while Mr. Campion leant back in his seat, his arms folded and an even more vacuous expression than usual upon his face.

Outside the later editions of the evening papers were being unfolded at windy street corners by excited youths. Home news was scarce and the "Strong-Room Mystery Inquest" was a godsend.

Much had been made of the morning's disclosures and a photograph of Gina and Mrs. Austin leaving the court appeared on the front page of each paper.

Inside the courtroom the sense of drama was growing. It had been by no means a tedious inquisition and now there was breathlessness in the air as the Coroner began to sum up. From beginning to end he was scrupulously fair. His deep, matter-of-fact voice lent no hint of theatricality to his oration, but rather brought a salutary commonplaceness into the business, reminding his hearers that they were enquiring into the death of a man of no less or more importance than themselves.

He dissected the evidence of the various witnesses, but was careful to make no comment.

"Let me quote to you from a very old and respected book," he said at last, leaning across his desk and addressing the jury intimately. "I refer to Burke's *Justice*. There these words are set down for our instruction. I will read them to you.

> "*It is peculiarly the province of the jury to investigate and determine the facts of the case. They are neither to expect nor should they be bound by any specific or direct opinion of the Coroner upon the whole of the case, except so far as regards the verdict, which in point of law they ought to find as dependent and contingent upon their conclusions in point of fact. The verdict should be compounded of the facts as detailed to the jury by the witnesses and of the law as stated to them by the court.*'"

He looked up from his book.

"I have told you the law. You know what you must do and what questions you must answer. You may now consider your verdict."

The jury retired and were gone only fifteen minutes. When they returned the foreman was perspiring and the faces of the others were studiously blank. On ascertaining that they were agreed Mr. Salley put the first question, his pen poised.

"Who do you find the deceased was?"

The foreman, his voice squeaky and breathless with discomfort, spoke hurriedly.

"We find, sir, that he was Paul Redfern Brande, of Twenty-one, Horsecollar Yard, of this parish."

"How do you find that the deceased met his death?"

"Sir, we find that he met his death by poisoning from carbon monoxide gas."

"Where do you find that he died?"

"In the strong room in the basement at his place of business at Twenty-three, Horsecollar Yard, of this parish, on the twenty-eighth day of January in this year."

The Coroner wrote rapidly.

"Do you find how he came by his death?"

"Yes, sir. We find that he was murdered wilfully and with malice aforethought."

There was a long pause and the court was unnaturally silent. The reporters waited like greyhounds in the traps and Inspector Tanner sat up, his ears pricked.

The quiet voice of the Coroner continued.

"That is the first part of the verdict. We now come to the final question, about which you already know. You have declared that the deceased was murdered. If you know who is guilty of this terrible offence it is your duty to say his name. From the evidence which you have heard, do you find anyone so guilty? Remember, you must speak from the certainty in your hearts and not from any suspicion, but if you have that certainty it is your bounden duty to speak. Do you find anyone guilty of the murder of Paul Redfern Brande?"

"Yes, sir, we do." The foreman's voice squeaked ridiculously as his nervousness robbed him of his breath.

"Then will you say his or her name?"

The foreman gulped.

"We find that Michael Wedgwood did wilfully murder his cousin Paul Redfern Brande."

Gina's head fell forward and she sank against the woman at her side.

John struggled to his feet, his dignity forgotten in his astounded horror.

The Coroner went on evenly.

"Do you find anyone guilty of being accessory before the fact of murder?"

"No, sir." The foreman mopped his dripping forehead. "We find no one guilty of being accessory before or after the fact."

8
Presumed Innocent

Since the arrest which he had just made was not technically legal until the Coroner had finished with the jury's formalities and had signed the warrant, Inspector Tanner was content to wait patiently in a corner of the anteroom while John and Mr. Scruby monopolized his prisoner.

Mike stood looking at the two elderly men with unseeing eyes. He was pale and the lines of his face had deepened, leaving the skin taut and his skull oddly apparent, but his body had not lost its ease or his manner its natural lazy calm.

The sudden catastrophe seemed to have burnt up over him like the flare of a new gas mantle, leaving him visibly the same but stricken with a new vulnerability.

As though conscious of this he held himself mentally apart from the others, whose thoughts and words were still protected.

John was frankly hysterical. Little pinkish pouches had appeared in the loose flesh beneath his jaw and his eyes were flickering.

"We must keep our heads," he was saying, his long bony fingers gripping Mr. Scruby's arm with painful pressure. "We must keep our heads. It's a monstrous mistake—we know that. The Coroner has exceeded his powers and in due course he will be reprimanded and removed, but meanwhile the publicity involved is terrible. No compensation can make up for it."

"Mr. Widdowson, Mr. Widdowson." Mr. Scruby's timid voice was imploring. "This is not the time. We must talk later when we can see what is best to be done. Now we have only a few moments and I want to assure Mr. Wedgwood that we shall leave no stone unturned to defend him at his trial. You will receive a visit from someone at my office to discuss the defence," he hurried on, speaking directly to Mike. "Rest assured that we shall do everything in our power."

Mike was vaguely aware of an anxious, sympathetic face raised to his and he nodded to it gratefully.

John gaped at them both. The pouches in his neck quivered and his lips moved helplessly.

"But it was an accident. Obviously an accident. I *know* it was an accident."

"Doubtless," said Mr. Scruby dryly, and added with unexpected briskness: "It now remains for us to prove it. I do not know at this juncture, of course, what line the defence will take. That is for Counsel to decide."

John sat down suddenly on the bench which ran round the dirty pale green walls. He looked very old.

Mr. Scruby eyed him thoughtfully for a moment and returned to Mike.

"I need hardly advise you not to discuss your—ah— your situation with anyone at all until I or someone from my office can see you," he murmured. "Keep as cheerful as you can and——"

He broke off abruptly and swung round. The Inspector was interviewing someone at the door. After a considerable amount of whispering he stepped back to admit Mr. Campion, and behind him Gina and Miss Curley.

The Inspector was sympathetic.

"They'll clear off in a little while," he said confidentially to Campion. "You told your man to take the car round to the back of Chequers Street, did you? That's right. You'll be able to get the ladies away quite comfortably in a minute or two. It's the newspaper photographers, not the crowd, today. The crowd won't come until the trial."

His voice flattened and died as he became aware that they were all listening to him. He returned to his corner and presently, as Sergeant Pillow came to relieve him, went down to the courtroom for the warrant.

Mr. Scruby had stepped aside as the newcomers entered and now, his mild eyes unexpectedly shrewd, he watched the meeting between Gina and Mike. No woman, however lovely, is really improved in appearance by any of the tragic emotions, but to some a certain interestingness is lent by crisis. Now that the worst had come Gina had achieved a cold poise and an almost porcelain hardness in her face which gave her features a new decision. She looked at Mike and their eyes met steadily.

Mr. Campion and Miss Curley were firing remarks at John, practically speaking, at random, and Mr. Scruby was the only frank observer of the meeting.

For a moment Gina's lips moved, hovered over words, rejecting them unspoken. Finally she said the one thing which her brain had refused to consider ever since the discovery of the body. The words were jerked out of her, her voice unnatural.

"It's happened then," she said.

For an instant the man's self-possession wavered and the nakedness of his heart was exposed. The expression rushed back into his eyes and incredulity mingled with the other emotion there. He recovered immediately, however, and for the first time since the verdict a smile appeared upon his wide mouth.

"The vanity of the woman!" he said, and turned away.

The damage was done. The colour poured into the girl's face, her poise was destroyed and she stood awkwardly, suddenly looking very young and gawky.

There was a moment of acute discomfort and then the door opened once more, and Sergeant Pillow rose to admit a telegraph boy with an envelope for John.

The old man tore it open with hands that trembled uncontrollably and, because it was his habit to do so at the office, read the message aloud.

> *"Astounded have not been informed. Incalculable harm may result incomprehensible neglect. Do nothing till arrive. Barnabas."*

John looked up, genuine astonishment in his eyes.

"God bless my soul! Cousin Alexander," he said. "I never thought——No, no answer, boy. Miss Curley, give him sixpence."

Mr. Scruby came forward dubiously.

"Alexander Barnabas, the counsel?" he enquired, and

there was no telling whether there was reverence or sheer apprehension in his tone.

John blinked at him. "Yes, my cousin. My uncle's only son. Took silk a good few years ago now. Great man in criminal cases, I believe. Great reputation——"

"Oh, yes," said Mr. Scruby gently, "I know him," and there was a little silence.

It was broken by the return of Inspector Tanner.

"You can get the ladies away comfortably now, sir," he said meaningly, and Mr. Campion, who saw that there was nothing to be gained by waiting, turned to Gina enquiringly.

She went with him willingly, almost eagerly, and Miss Curley followed after leaving a whispered message with the Sergeant for John, who had begun to talk to Mr. Scruby again, and a friendly handclasp with Mike.

In the doorway Gina hesitated without looking back, and the man under arrest, glancing up, caught a last glimpse of her small black figure, her head bent and the soft arc of her chestnut hair showing under her black hat.

At one of the back doors of the court Mr. Lugg sat proud and disapproving in the shining glory which was Mr. Campion's new Lagonda. He sprang out with an agility astonishing in one of his bulk and bundled the two women somewhat unceremoniously into the back.

"Now let's sheer off before we're seen," he said in a husky undertone to his employer.

Mr. Campion, who had the same idea but for less selfish reasons, slid in behind the wheel and the great car moved away.

When they were held up in a traffic jam in Holborn he glanced over his shoulder.

"I'm going to take you back to my flat for half an hour or so, Gina, if you don't mind," he said. "These Press photographers are tenacious beggars, and you don't want to run into a battery of them waiting on your door-step."

The girl did not answer, but Miss Curley's voice, brisk and practical, came from the darkness of the hood.

"I'm so glad you thought of it, Mr. Campion," she said. "It had been on my mind. Of course, I hadn't liked to suggest it." And in a lower voice they heard her add: "Keep your head well down, my dear. You'll feel better."

"I'm all right," said Gina, and her voice sounded unutterably weary.

The person who did not approve of the suggestion was Mr. Lugg. Mr. Campion caught a glimpse of his face reflected in the windscreen and smiled in spite of himself.

It was a dark, wet night and they were caught in the home-going rush, so that it took them some considerable time to reach Bottle Street.

There the lights were subdued and shed little puddles of radiance on the streaming pavements. Campion took Gina's arm and steered her towards the brightly lit entrance beside the police station. Miss Curley followed him and Lugg put the car away.

As Campion and the two women came up the staircase to the small hall on the second landing which contained Campion's front door, a woman rose from the chair which was the only furniture in the minute passageway and stepped forward.

Her appearance was vaguely familiar to Campion, and he had the impression that he had seen her somewhere recently. She was not a usual type and he was struck by something indefinable about her which he could only describe to himself as passive rather than active grief. She was middle-aged and, although smartly dressed, had none of Gina's essential style. It occurred to him that she belonged to the category known to his father's generation as "handsome women." She came forward timidly.

"I don't know if you're Mr. Campion," she said, "but if you are, could I speak to you for a minute?"

Her voice came as a surprise. Without being actually vulgar or uneducated, its refinement was not quite genuine.

Mr. Campion took out his key.

"Why, yes, of course. In just one moment," he said, and unlocked the door.

Miss Curley took Gina inside and as the light from the inner hall fell upon the girl's face Campion heard a smothered exclamation from his unknown visitor. He turned round to find her looking after Gina, an embarrassed and defeated expression in her eyes.

"That's Mrs. Brande, isn't it?" she said. "I didn't recognize her at first, in this light. I'm sorry I bothered you, Mr. Campion. Good evening."

She was halfway across the passage to the stairs before she had finished speaking, and Mr. Campion was puzzled.

"Won't you leave your name?" he said rather idiotically.

"No, no, it doesn't matter. I made a mistake. It doesn't matter in the least."

Her voice came back to him as she clattered down the staircase in her high-heeled black patent shoes. Looking over the banisters he saw her fox fur flopping up and down on her plumpish shoulders as she hurried.

Slightly bewildered, he went into the flat and put a question.

Gina looked up from the depths of his big armchair.

"Yes, I saw her," she said wearily, "but I didn't know her. I've never seen her before in my life. What did she want?"

"Goodness knows," said Mr. Campion.

9
The Daring Young Man

On any other occasion and in any other circumstances the spectacle of Mr. Lugg in his latest rôle, serving afternoon tea to one of the principals in a *cause célèbre*, might easily have delighted Mr. Campion; but as it happened, such is the perversity of fortune, he found it irritating.

The change which had occurred to Gina in the anteroom of the court still persisted. The agitation and ill-suppressed terror of the last few days had now given place to a weary, broken weakness a thousand times more pathetic.

Miss Curley, on the other hand, had reacted by becoming an intensified edition of her normal self. Campion suspected her of being extra busy and efficient so that she might not have time to think. All the same, it was a difficult gathering and John's arrival was a relief.

He came in, scowled at Lugg, sat down in the chair which Campion had vacated on rising to welcome him, and announced querulously that he would like a cup of tea.

Lugg served him ungraciously, the expression in his little black eyes intimating clearly that he did not like his manners and was quite prepared to subject him to a course of instruction if the opportunity arose.

Having averted this danger by banishing Lugg, Campion glanced enquiringly at his new visitor.

Mr. Widdowson was fast recovering from his hysteria of earlier in the afternoon. The pink pouches had disappeared from his gills and his eyes were cold and steady.

"I've been talking to Scruby," he began peremptorily, his thin, academic voice raised a little above its normal tone, "and he agrees with me, of course, that the police are making a fantastic mistake. Apparently the Coroner is strictly within his rights, although Scruby feels he may come in for considerable censure. However, that's not the point. What we have to think about now is the best way of clearing up the ghastly business satisfactorily."

Mr. Campion eyed the man and wondered if it could be possible that even now he had not realized the full gravity of the position.

John leant back in his chair.

"I think Scruby feels that the police used the inquest to avoid shouldering full responsibility for the arrest," he announced. "He didn't say so in as many words, of course, but that's what I understood."

Gina had shrunk back into her chair and he appeared to notice her for the first time.

"We shall need you, Gina," he observed, pointing a long bony finger at her. "Scruby wanted me to impress it upon you that you're likely to be a very important witness."

She did not speak, and he evidently did not expect her to, for he returned to Campion.

"Scruby feels with me that an independent investigation on behalf of the family is absolutely necessary," he said slowly. "Time, you see, is going to be short."

Mr. Campion, who had drawn up a small, hard chair, now sat upon it and blinked at his client, his pale eyes vague behind his horn-rimmed spectacles.

"I'm sure Mr. Campion will do all he can to help Mike," put in Miss Curley so hastily that he smiled at her.

"Of course he will. Of course." John brushed aside the interruption irritably. "Now. Campion, we all know Paul's death was an accident. What I ask you to do is to prove it to the satisfaction of the most unintelligent member of the police and Press."

Mr. Campion rose. Wandering across the room, he took up a position of vantage, his hands in his pockets and his body supported by the edge of the desk.

"I say, I do hope you won't mind my saying it," he began gently, "but you're making a most unfortunate mistake, you know."

John stared at him. The quiet authority in the casual voice was unexpected.

Mr. Campion continued diffidently.

"I don't want to alarm you all, but frankly, you know, I've a tremendous respect for the police. They're about as good at their jobs as people ever get. Their occasional mistakes are the exceptions which prove the rule. They aren't trying anything out, or shelving any responsibility, or anything like that. I'm afraid it's much more devastating. You see, they feel they've got an open-and-shut case and so they're dealing with it in the quickest and most efficient manner possible. It's rather revolting when you see it from our present angle, I know, but there you are. . . ."

Mr. Widdowson appeared to be temporarily silenced, and it was Gina who spoke, her voice husky.

"Albert, you don't think Mike killed Paul, do you?"

"No, old dear," said Mr. Campion, "but somebody did. Don't let's lose sight of that."

There was a long pause. Miss Curley moistened her lips with the tip of her tongue, a regular movement more nervous than feverish.

"Moreover, someone murdered him very neatly indeed." Campion sounded apologetic when he spoke again. "And in spite of that the method has been detected already. That's another point I don't think we should miss. Our astute friends Tanner and Pillow aren't so very inefficient.

They've dogged that much out all right, although they didn't get on the scene until the body had been moved and the most appalling mess made of the strong room. They're not fools and they're not dishonest. They don't want to arrest an innocent man, believe me. That's every policeman's nightmare. But on the other hand, they do want to do their job decently. Someone has murdered Paul and they're employed to catch him and stop him doing it to anybody else."

John sat up slowly and turned the full force of his famous disapproving eye upon Campion.

"You seem to be a very outspoken young man," he observed.

Mr. Campion appeared to be embarrassed.

"It's a very outspoken business," he said. "Do you still want me to have a look round?"

"Albert, you must." Gina had risen. The pallor of her face was accentuated, and her mouth quivered uncontrollably. "I do see the danger. I've seen it all the time. It's been haunting me ever since that dreadful Monday morning. You must find out that Mike couldn't have locked the strongroom door and put the key away. You must find out why he didn't say he'd seen Paul when he went down there on Sunday—because he must have been there—and you must find out what he was really doing before I phoned him on Thursday night."

Her voice ceased abruptly and she stood holding out her hand to him, an involuntary gesture oddly appealing. He looked at her gravely.

"I'll do all I can," he promised.

John rose. "I know it was an accident," he said, and there was conviction in his tone. "If you want to oblige me, Campion, you'll prove it. Get to the bottom of the mystery and you'll find I'm right. Now, Gina, you're to come back with me. I want you in the house when Cousin Alexander arrives."

The girl rose obediently. A lifetime of authority had endowed John with a gift for it.

"An accident," he repeated firmly as he shook hands with Campion in the hall, adding naïvely: "Terrible publicity. Good night."

Gina clutched Campion's hand; her lips were trembling.

"Let me know what's happening, won't you—please," she whispered.

John was halfway to the staircase and she glanced over her shoulder at him, dropping her voice to a whisper.

"Albert, will they open his letters there?"

Campion met her eyes.

"I shouldn't write if I were you," he said earnestly.

"I see." Her voice died away and the dullness returned to her eyes. "Good-bye, and thank you."

Campion watched her until she disappeared and then went slowly back into the sitting room. He had forgotten Miss Curley, and now the sight of her sitting quietly in an armchair, her hat slipping back until it looked like a three-cornered halo and her near-sighted eyes thoughtful behind her pince-nez, startled him. He smiled at her guiltily.

"I thought I had better stay to tell you that I'll give you all the help I can," she said. "Mr. Widdowson is really terribly grateful to you for taking up the case, but of course he's worried just now. The shock has been tremendous, for one thing. But I thought I'd like to tell you that if you care to examine any room in the office or get access to any papers I'll see that you can do it without interference."

"I shall hold you to that," he said gratefully, and added impulsively: "I'm not really the sensitive soul you seem to think."

She sighed. "Well, as long as you're not . . ." she said. "Mr. Widdowson does give offence quite unconsciously at times. It's being in the office so long, I suppose."

And then, to his consternation, her voice broke and she began to cry.

"I'm all right—I'm all right," she said, waving him away with one hand and dabbing at her eyes with the other. "I don't know what made me so stupid. It's the suddenness of it all, I suppose, although I've woken up in terror of something very like it every night this week. Mr. Campion, why didn't they arrest her as an accomplice?"

Before this mixture of muddled thought and penetration Mr. Campion found himself a trifle bewildered, but he answered the direct question.

"Gina came out very well on the stand," he said cautiously. "Besides, there's no direct evidence of an affair—no letters or anything. The charwoman was pretty damaging, but it was fairly obvious she'd go to pieces in cross-examination."

"But there's no direct evidence against Mike," Miss Curley protested. "It's all circumstantial."

He nodded gloomily. "I know. But there's a devil of a lot of it. I rather fancy that Salley has been stewing up for a row with his critics for some time and is spoiling for a showdown. You see," he went on gently, "the police evidently believe not only that they're right, but that they're obviously right."

Miss Curley's moist eyes darkened reflectively.

"I've known Mike ever since he was a child," she said, "and I don't think——"

She paused and he regarded her quizzically.

"Are you sure?"

The old woman looked up at him.

"Men in love are not quite normal," she said. "I've seen it over and over again. But I don't—I can't think Mike would *kill* Paul. And, anyway," she added triumphantly, "if he had he wouldn't have done it like that."

Campion brightened. "That's what I'm banking on," he said.

Lugg put his head round the door.

"Bloke outside," he remarked, and then, catching sight of Miss Curley, started visibly. "I thought you had gorn, madam," he remarked when he had recovered his composure, and straightening up announced with remarkable change of personality: "A gentleman is waiting in the hall, sir. Would you see 'im?"

"Of course," said Campion, slightly ashamed of his old friend. "Do drop that accent, it's getting on my nerves."

A spiteful expression appeared in Mr. Lugg's small black eyes and he surpassed himself.

"Very blinking good, sir," he said, and stalked out.

Ritchie came in, stooping unconsciously to avoid the lintel.

"Gina gone?" he enquired. "Oh, hello, Miss Curley. Thought I'd come and see you, Campion. Been down to the place with some of Mike's things—pyjamas, toothbrush, comb, and so on. Still got to live, wash, eat, poor chap. It's a mistake, Campion."

He dropped into a chair as he spoke and his pale blue eyes regarded the younger man with that questioning, inarticulate expression which Campion had seen there before.

"Got to find out who did it," said Ritchie. "Must."

Miss Curley rose and held out her hand.

"Don't forget," she repeated, "if there's anything you want to see in the office, come to me."

Campion showed her out and on the steps she looked up at him.

"You're a good boy to help us," she said suddenly, and patted his arm.

Campion went back to Ritchie, who had drawn up to the fire and was gloating over it like some huge but benevolent spider trying to get warm.

"Cousin Alexander," he remarked, without turning round. "Eloquent—dramatic."

Campion took his mind off the immediate problem for a moment to consider Alexander Barnabas, K.C. The grand old man had been comparatively quiet for a month or so, he reflected. He could not remember seeing his name about since the Shadows trials in the summer. In view of the circumstances, he regretted that he had never seen the barrister in the flesh, although photographs of that magnificent head were familiar enough and the very mention of his name brought recollections of dramatic cross-examinations and sensational speeches.

Sir Alexander's history was stormy. Although he was Jacoby Barnabas's only son, he had avoided publishing and taken to law, with his father's full consent and approval, and had made his name as a junior in the great days of Marshall Hall before the bar had followed stage into a quieter and less rhetorical style. After taking silk his practice had grown and he had been greatly sought after as a leader, until the unfortunate quarrel with the Judge in the Leahbourne case had done his reputation irreparable damage.

However, although it was still felt that his temper was not to be trusted, his triumphal return in the Dallas trial had restored him to popular, if not academic, favour, and he was now considered a fine showy counsel for the defence in sensational criminal trials and was often briefed by solicitors whose clients were backed by a newspaper.

Campion thought he understood Mr. Scruby's apprehension. A remark from Ritchie recalled his attention.

"Thought of something. Ought to mention it."

The man had turned in his chair and was looking up anxiously.

"Hose pipe—car exhaust—locked room—all that, not original," he blurted out at last. "Plagiarism. All in a book."

"In a book?" enquired Mr. Campion, a trifle mystified.

A vigorous nodding affirmed the question.

"Book called *Died on a Saturday*. Most of it in there. Read it myself. Recognized it in court."

"Who published it?"

Ritchie's face lengthened. "Us. Ten—twelve months ago. Not much of a sale."

Mr. Campion was looking at him anxiously.

"Who read this book besides you?—in the office, I mean?"

Ritchie's tremendous bony shoulders hunched in a shrug.

"Anyone. Handled by Mike's department."

"Are you saying that Mike brought out a book describing the method of murder which was used to kill Paul less than a year ago?" Campion demanded, aghast.

Ritchie's wretchedness increased.

"Fifteen months perhaps," he suggested.

Mr. Campion passed his hand over his sleek yellow hair and whistled.

Ritchie was silent for some moments, his awkward figure twisted over the arm of his chair.

"Somebody did it," he said at last. "Evidence showed that."

Campion looked down at him.

"What's your private opinion?" he enquired unexpectedly. "You were much closer to it all than I was. Who did it?"

Ritchie shook his ponderous head.

"Anyone," he murmured, and added with a sigh and a flail-like gesture: "No one."

Mr. Campion pursued his private thoughts.

"That Miss Netley, tell me about her."

Ritchie wrinkled his nose and achieved a masterpiece of pantomimic disapproval.

"Affected girl," he said. "Silly. Sly. Superior. Little snob. Stupid clothes."

"Anything else?"

The other man hesitated.

"Don't know much. Only seen her about. Fond of the ballet. Has a Post Office Savings Book. Arch," he added in triumph. "That's it—she's arch. Don't like her."

He rose to go shame-facedly, evidently feeling that he had not been very helpful in the cause, for he shook hands earnestly and, his blue eyes peering beseechingly into Campion's own, made a long and for him coherent speech.

"Do what you can, Campion, Mike's a good fellow— decent fellow. Never hurt a soul. Kind fellow—kind. Pleasant, friendly to me. Couldn't possibly get anything out of it. If we don't find out who killed affected ass Paul they'll hang Mike—kill him. Stop it, there's a dear chap."

After he had gone Mr. Campion sat at his desk and scribbled idly on the blotting-paper. He had no illusions concerning the task in front of him. Events had moved more swiftly than he had contemplated and the need for urgency was great.

Suddenly the thought which had been playing round the edges of his conscious mind so irritatingly for some time past came out into the open. He reached for the telephone directory and got on to Miss Curley just as she had entered her home in Hammersmith.

She heard his question with surprise.

"Mr. *Tom* Barnabas?" she echoed. "The one who—who disappeared?"

"That's the man." Campion's voice sounded eager. "What sort of person was he? What was he like?"

Miss Curley cast her mind back twenty years.

"A nice man," she said at last. "Good-looking, inclined to be reserved, but very odd. Why?"

"Odd?" Campion seized upon the word. "In what way?"

Miss Curley laughed, but when she spoke her words had a flavour of the macabre.

"He could walk upstairs on his hands," she said.

10
Twenty Years After

It was wet and bitterly cold, with sludge on the pavement and dark grey blankets in the sky, when Mr. Campion walked thoughtfully down Nemetia Crescent, Streatham, and tried to imagine it as it had been on a May morning twenty years before.

To his relief, there was no sign of any recent building operations, and, although the neighborhood had gone down a little, he suspected, there was no evidence of any structural alteration.

It was a melancholy little enclosure, a half hoop of flat-fronted houses looking out across a strip of wet tarmac at a bank of dilapidated shrubs.

He found the house out of which Tom Barnabas had walked on May the eighth, nineteen hundred and eleven, and stood in the rain looking at it. Dingy lace curtains covered the windows and a fly-blown black card in the transom over the unexpectedly nice door announced in silver letters that there were apartments within.

Mr. Campion passed on and turned the corner at the end of the Crescent. To his relief he saw that the deserted road in front of him tallied exactly with the description Miss Curley had given. A wall over six feet high and completely blank ran down the whole length of the road on the side nearest the Crescent, while on the other a row of little villas recessed from the road by overgrown gardens straggled down to the trams and the main street.

Campion paused and let his imagination dwell upon the facts of the story as he knew them.

It had been about nine o'clock in the morning. Mr. Barnabas had come striding from his house in the Crescent, had turned the corner, and was apparently marching on to the little tobacconist's at the end of the street, where it was his custom to stop and pick up a copy of the *Times* and the *Standard*, when unfortunately he stepped into the fourth dimension or was the victim of spontaneous combustion or some sort of accident to an atom.

The tobacconist's was still there. A row of newspaper boards decorated the far end of the wall, in spite of the rain. Mr. Campion wandered on, pausing now and again in spite of the weather and reflecting upon the few facts he had been able to glean that morning from the files of a newspaper.

For May 8th, 1911, the prophets had predicted fair to fine weather, warm temperature and slight mist. There had been an air smash in the Paris to Madrid race on the day before, when Monsieur Train had crashed at Issy, killing himself and seriously injuring Monsieur Monis, Premier of France, who had been present to see him start. The Court was just out of mourning for Edward VII, the Imperial Conference was opening the following day, and Freeman (J.) had been bowled by Hobbs for twenty-one in the presence of Their Royal Highnesses the Prince of Wales and Prince George.

The information was not very helpful. The world, in fact, seemed to have been going on in much the same way as ever. And since it is always easier to believe in a miracle which happened twenty years ago than in one of yesterday morning, Mr. Campion felt his suspicions aroused.

He looked at the wall. There was no way of telling what was on the other side. It might have hidden a pool, a back garden, or fairyland itself.

He walked on to the newspaper and tobacconist's shop. As he entered it his spirits rose. This stuffy little room with its doorway narrowed to the verge of the impassable by ancient paper-racks filled with brightly coloured periodicals, its acrid smell of newsprint, its two counters, one piled high with papers and the other decorated with every known brand of tobacco grouped round an immense pair of shining scales, could not have altered for forty or fifty, much less twenty, years.

He stood hesitating on the square foot or so of floor space for some moments before he realized that he was not alone in this sanctuary of smoke and light literature.

Over the paper department there was a species of canopy composed of yet more periodicals clipped into wire frames, and in the narrow opening between this and the counter he caught sight of two very bright eyes peering at him from out a pepper-and-salt wilderness of hair and whisker.

"Paper or a nice box of cigarettes, sir?" said a voice at once friendly and a trifle pert.

Mr. Campion bought both and had the satisfaction of seeing the remainder of the man as he came running out of his lurking place to attend to the tobacconist's side of his business.

He was very small, spry and compact, and his feet, which were tiny, were thrust into old sheep-skin slippers which flapped as he walked.

"Haven't seen you about here before, sir?" he enquired. "Moved into the district?"

"Not yet," said Mr. Campion cautiously.

"No offence meant and none taken, I hope," said the old man, running all the words together until they formed a single apologetic sound. "Only I saw you wandering up and down the road just now and it came into my head that you might be looking for lodgings. This part isn't what it used to be, but I could put you on to several nice respectable women who'd look after you very well. Perhaps you'd like a widow, now?" he finished, his little bright eyes watching Campion with the inquisitive yet impersonal interest of a sparrow.

"Not at present," said Mr. Campion, who had a literal mind. "As a matter of fact, I came down here on a sort of sentimental errand. A friend of mine disappeared, or is supposed to have disappeared, walking along this street."

Tremendous interest appeared at once on the small face.

"I believe you're referring to my phenomenon," he

118

said. "I always call it mine, although it wasn't really. I just happened to be there. Now that *was* a funny thing, if you like."

"Do you remember it?"

"Remember it? Wasn't I in this very shop?" The little man seemed hurt. "Wasn't it me who gave interviews to all the newspapers?—or would have done, only they didn't believe me. It was hushed up really. Did you know that? In my opinion, sir," he went on, eyeing Mr. Campion with portentous solemnity, "that was the most important thing that ever happened to me in all my life. And, luck being what it is—" he spread out his hands and hunched his shoulders in a gesture of resignation, "—I turned me back on it."

"Infuriating," murmured Mr. Campion sympathetically.

"It was," said his informant and, returning to his position behind the paper counter, leant across it and took a deep breath. "I didn't always talk about this," he began. "My name's Higgleton, by the way."

"How d'you do?" said Campion pleasantly.

"Pleased to meet *you*, sir," complied Mr. Higgleton, with grace, and plunged into his story. "It was on a Monday—no, a Tuesday morning, I think it was. Or it may have been a Thursday—I can't really remember—but I can see it as plain as daylight. I didn't talk about it much at the time because—well, you know what people are. Once you start seeing things that other people know can't have happened, you're apt to get the reputation of being a bit queer."

"Fanciful," suggested Mr. Campion.

"Exactly. But I remember that Wednesday morning as though it was yesterday. Only it was May then, not February like it is now. It was a beautiful clear morning, bright sunlight—we didn't have summertime then, so there was no hanky-panky—just a bright clear summer's day. This place is very pretty in the summer, though you might not think so. When there's leaves on those trees over there you can't see the houses. There were more trees in those days. It was when the children kept getting run over that they had one or two of 'em down. The children couldn't see the road from the gardens because of the trees and they used to run out and—there you are, as the saying is."

"I suppose that's why no one saw Mr. Barnabas from the houses?" said Mr. Campion.

"Barnabas!" said Mr. Higgleton, pouncing on the name. "That's it! That's it! Couldn't remember it for a moment, although it was on the tip of me tongue. That's why I was hedging about. Oh, I knew him as well as I know—you, I was going to say. Used to come in here every day for his papers. He was an ornament to the neighbourhood. I don't know what his business was; it was something in the City. But he used to turn out to it as though he was going to a——" Mr. Higgleton paused and searched in his mind for a simile.

"Ball?" suggested Mr. Campion idiotically.

His new friend glanced at him reproachfully.

"Well, not exactly a ball, but a wedding. City gentlemen used to dress more tastefully then than they do now. You probably wouldn't remember it very well, but they did. Silk hats and tail coats and fancy trousers were all the go, and a nice pair of yellow gloves to top everything off."

"And was Mr. Barnabas dressed like that when he disappeared?" said Mr. Campion.

"He was. A very well-dressed man indeed was Mr. Barnabas. I can see him now—in me mind's eye, of course—silk hat, nicely brushed, gold-topped cane and spats. A big handsome man he was, too, and very nicely spoken."

"How did it happen?" The question escaped Mr. Campion involuntarily.

"In the twinkling of a hand—like that!" said Mr. Higgleton, and snapped his fingers.

He had an odd trick of pausing after he had made an announcement and surveying his listener with a wide-eyed expression, as though inviting him to join in a wonder.

Mr. Campion, who had liked him from the start, began to feel a positive affection for him.

"I'll show you how it happened," said Mr. Higgleton, and, running out from behind the counter, he planted himself on the door-step. "Now here am I—see," he said over his shoulder, "standing on the corner of the street. It's nine o'clock in the morning, but I'm not so busy as all that, and I'm just standing here taking a deep breath of the ozone."

He gulped a lungful of rain-soaked, soot-laden air, and glanced at Campion for approval.

"Well, I see Mr. Barnabas turn the corner of the street down there."

He waved his hand in the direction of Nemetia Crescent.

"Now I *know* it is him—there's no doubt about that. (My eyes are better than what they are now, it being twenty years ago.) And I watch him coming up the street for a bit. There he is, striding along in the sunlight swinging his cane, looking as calm and happy as you please.

"Well, when he's about fifty yards away I say to myself, 'I'd better get his papers.' So I turn back into me shop like this," he trotted back to the counter and picked up a couple of newspapers which he thrust under Campion's nose. "There they are—see? Then I hurry back to the door and—" he stopped, and peered up and down the street, ventured out into the rain, and finally returned, bewilderment expressed in every line of his features, "—not a sign of him," he said. "Street empty all ways. You could knock me down with a wave of the hand, as the saying has it.

"'Well,' I said, 'he's vanished!' And he had, too."

Again the look of wonder.

"Of course you'll say," he continued after a silence which Mr. Campion had not liked to break, "that he must have snapped into a trot and run past the shop. But he couldn't have done. I wasn't in here above five seconds. Besides, the constable who was standing on the corner saw him go. One minute he was there and one minute he wasn't. In the middle of the pavement about fifteen yards from this shop, just along by the wall there, he disappeared and was never seen by mortal eye again."

"Top hat, gold-headed cane and all?" said Mr. Campion.

"Yellow gloves *and* spats," said Mr. Higgleton. "Clean as kiss yer hand."

"I'd like to have met the policeman." Mr. Campion sounded wistful.

"So you should have. I'd have taken you round myself if he hadn't retired and gone to live in the country. Somewhere Norfolk way he is. But he drops in here now and again when he comes to town. He was here as little as two years ago. Next time I see him I'll tell him you're interested and perhaps he'll let you have his side of the story. His name's on tip of me tongue, but I've forgotten it."

Mr. Higgleton thought for a while but to no purpose.

Mr. Campion expressed his thanks and made an attempt to leave, but he was not to get away so easily.

"I don't like to pretend I know what happened because I don't," said his new friend, skilfully edging between him and the exit. "But then funny things do happen. There was a man in that house over there—you can see it if you stand on the step—who ran off with every servant-girl his wife had in the course of twelve years. Every single one of them!"

This time the expression of wonder was a little overdone.

"She fetched him back one week and off he'd go with the new girl the next."

"What happened in the end?" said Mr. Campion, interested in spite of himself.

"Cut his throat on a golf-course in Scotland," said Mr. Higgleton. "And then there was the woman with the snakes."

"Really?" murmured Mr. Campion, moving adroitly to the right and gaining six inches in his progress to the door.

"She used to live in this house at the back of mine, on the other side," said Mr. Higgleton frantically. "Her garden used to run down behind mine and finish up alongside this wall. Of course, she left before the war, but at one time her place was *alive* with 'em. She used to breed 'em and train 'em. Some of them were very clever, I believe, but I never liked them."

He sighed. Mr. Campion was going to get away; he could see it.

"If ever that police sergeant should drop it, sir, perhaps you'd like me to give him your name?" he ventured, breathless with defeat.

"That's very kind of you." Campion drew a card from his wallet and Mr. Higgleton took it and placed it with great care behind a jar of tobacco on the shelf at the back of the shop. "Any time you want to know anything about this district," he said wistfully, "you'll come to me, won't you?"

Mr. Campion felt a cad.

"I certainly shall," he said. "Thank you very much."

"It's been a pleasure, sir," said Mr. Higgleton truthfully, and Campion went down to the High Street to find a cab, convinced in spite of his stern belief in the material that something very odd indeed had happened to Tom Barnabas twenty years before.

When he arrived back at Bottle Street he was still absorbed by the past and the urgent message from the present head of the firm of Barnabas and Company, Limited, demanding his immediate attendance at Twenty-three, Horsecollar Yard, brought him back to the problem of the moment with uncomfortable conviction that he had spent an unprofitable morning.

He arrived at the office at a little after two o'clock and was shown at once into John's big room on the ground floor, where a conference was in progress. Before he entered the room, while he was still in the hall, the sonorous voice from within warned him what to expect, and he did not come upon Cousin Alexander altogether unprepared.

The first thing he saw upon entering the room was the back of John's head and the arc of his forehead. He was leaning back in his chair, which had been turned away from the door, and appeared to be entranced or even stupefied by the spectacle confronting him.

On the hearth rug Sir Alexander Barnabas stood in one of his more famous attitudes, and Campion had the full benefit of his commanding presence. He was a big man, tall and heavy, with a magnificent physique and a great head surmounted by a mass of iron-grey curls parted sleekly down the middle and brushed up at the sides so that, whether by accident or design, one was almost deceived into thinking that his barrister's wig was a fixture.

His face was handsome in an orthodox way and its clean-shaven mobility had a trick of emphasizing the slightest inflection in its owner's voice with appropriate expression.

At the moment he was radiating authority. One long

graceful hand was upraised to drive home some point while the other rested behind his broad, dark-coated back.

"There is no question of that," he was saying. "Ab-so-lute-ly no question." And Mr. Campion was quite convinced that, whatever the subject of conversation might be, there could indeed be absolutely no question about it.

At Campion's entrance John pulled himself out of the stupor into which he had fallen and performed the introduction.

Mr. Campion was aware of a personage condescending to do a great honour. Two immense fingers rested in his hand for a second, and then he was dismissed to the realm of unimportant things and Cousin Alexander's melodious voice took up the thread of his discourse once again.

"We must have an acquittal," he said. "Complete and unconditional acquittal with no stain left upon the boy's character. I shall work for that and I shall achieve it."

Mr. Campion sat down on the edge of a chair in the far corner of the room and listened politely. Miracles seemed to be the order of the day.

"But you must understand, John," the Counsel continued firmly. "The case against Mike is very strong. Circumstantial evidence can be very deadly indeed. At the moment Michael is in a position of the gravest danger."

Mr. Campion pulled himself together with a jerk. The effect of so powerful a personality at close range was disconcerting. When Sir Alexander spoke of gravity one automatically thought of international crises and in his mouth the word "danger" had the shrill insistence of a fire alarm.

John attempted to speak, but was answered before a word had left his mouth.

"I have seen the boy," said Cousin Alexander, "and I am convinced of his innocence. Innocence," he repeated and stared at Campion, who found himself feeling like a rabbit caught in the glare of a headlight. "Innocent." Sir Alexander again dropped his voice to a whisper. "I heard his statement. Only an innocent man would have dared to make such a damaging confession. Why did he admit he had no alibi? Because he was telling the truth. Because he was innocent."

His glance swept round the room.

"Can't you see what happened?" he went on passionately. "Are you blind? Or does the very nakedness of truth offend your modesty? Imagine it . . ."

His voice had become persuasive, his excitement passing as rapidly as it had arisen.

"Think of the story he told the police. Think of the damaging history of that fatal night, related as simply as a child might have told it, a child not only innocent, but so guileless as to believe that not for a moment would its innocence be called into question."

Mr. Campion settled back in his chair and reflected how much more bearable drama was when it had a little art to help it along. On the witness-stand Mike had presented a depressing tale, but in Sir Alexander's hands his story became an exhilarating experience if not in particularly good taste. Meanwhile the great man was off again filling the room with melodious but overpowering sound.

"The Coroner demanded to know where Mike was between the hours of five and nine in the evening, hours which have since proved to be critical in the history of this terrible case. What did the boy do? Did he invent a history of little alibis to be broken down one by one by a pitiless police enquiry? Or did he tell the truth? 'I walked,' he said. 'I walked alone through the London streets, amid thousands of my fellow men, not one of whom will come forward to bear me witness. I was unknown to them—a stranger. I was alone.'"

"Yes, but what was he doing?" said John irritably, the paralyzing quality of Cousin Alexander's peroration having apparently passed over his head. "What purpose could he possibly have had in wandering about like that?"

Just for a moment the great man seemed to have been taken off his balance. He was evidently not used to interruptions, for his eye wavered and when he spoke again there was a reproving quality in the beautiful voice which had very little to do with art.

"If you will have patience," he said, "I will tell you. Mike is a young man and he committed a crime which, although reprehensible, is one of those misfortunes which overtake young men in spite of themselves. He fell in love with another man's wife. But he did not tell her so. He stood by and saw her neglected and tyrannized over by a man who did not realize her worth. From beginning to end their association was innocent. It does not follow that because of this restraint his passion was any the less real. An evening came when he knew the woman he loved was going to have a long interview with the man to whom she was bound by every legal and moral tie which our civilization has devised. Imagine him——"

The sonorous voice took on a hushed quality that Mr. Campion, who felt he was listening to the truth in dramatized form, found a little shocking.

"Imagine him sitting at his desk early in the evening of that cold January day. He was due to attend some literary function where a great deal of rubbish, some of it witty, some of it not, would be bandied from mouth to mouth, while in the very house in which he lived, in the very room two floors above that in which he slept, the woman whose being was the very core of his existence was talking to the man against whom she was completely defenceless, the man to whom the law gave every conceivable right in her, the man from whom she could not escape and from whom he dared not protect her.

"Do you see him there?" he went on, fixing Campion with a steely blue eye strangely reminiscent of the portrait in the waiting room. And then, in an even quieter voice: "I do. He cannot work, he does not want to go to the witty gathering whose chatter cannot save him from himself, nor can he go to his own home because he knows that in the room upstairs *she* is talking to his rival, her husband.

"What more natural for him, then—" the voice became musical as its rich tones played over the euphonious words, "—than to feel he must get away? Even his car is denied him: the fog is too thick. So he walks. He takes refuge in the time-honoured escape which men of every age and every generation have used to soothe their troubled spirits.

"He walks through London, through the crowds, thinking of her, trying to reason with himself, no doubt: trying to wrest himself from the cloying embraces of the pitiless emotion which consumes him."

John attempted to rise to his feet at this juncture, but was subdued by the famous eye.

"The little shop in Bayswater," said Cousin Alexander. "A secondhand jewellery store. A little place of curios, sentimental trifles scarcely of any value. He went there to buy her something, so engrossed in his thoughts that he forgot the day, forgot that it was a Thursday afternoon, upon which the keeper of the shop took his holiday and closed the shutters over the little trinkets, bidding lovers and their ladies wait until the morrow."

He paused, evidently feeling that he was navigating a dangerous stretch, and his keen eyes appraised their discomfort.

"He turned back. He walked on through the wet, cold streets. He did not notice they were wet, he did not notice they were cold; he was thinking of her, he was thinking of the woman. When he reached his home he had still come no nearer his goal, he had still not thrashed out his problem. It remained as large, as terrifying, as piteous, as wearying as ever before. He still felt the need of escape."

The great voice quivered and boomed, and at such close quarters was well-nigh pulverizing.

"What did he do? He saw the night was clearer. He thought of his car. He thought of the cool roads, the open fields, little remote villages—freedom, solitude. He went round to the garage and because it was his habit, because he wanted complete obedience from his car, he switched on the engine, intending to let it run for a while so that the cylinders should be warm, the oil moving smoothly and evenly.

"And at that time he was completely unaware that his car had been, or was going to be, used by some enemy to destroy the very man to whom the woman he loved was tied. Unfortunately for him he did not take the car straight out of the garage. Instead he remembered the key of the yard gate and went to his lonely little flat to fetch it.

"Imagine the thoughts which must have come into his mind as he entered that room and realized that she was above him, closeted, so he thought, remember, with the husband who neglected and had no respect for her.

"Then, just as he was about to take the key, what happened? The telephone bell rang and he heard her voice. He went down, turned off the car, and these two young people went out together. Is that the sort of man who would have gone to see a moving picture if he knew that down in the strong room beneath the office, in the very house next to the one in which he was going to sleep that night, a man lay suffocated to death? Of course not! It is not feasible."

He allowed the last word to die away and then quite surprisingly dropped his artificial manner and became a different sort of person altogether.

"That's the truth, you know," he said. "That's what happened."

John pulled a crisp white handkerchief out of his pocket and wiped his forehead.

"I think you're right about Mike," he said. "You convinced me."

A smile, pleased and schoolboyish, appeared upon Cousin Alexander's handsome face.

"It's effective, isn't it?" he said, including Campion in the question. "Awfully effective, and true. But we can't possibly use it."

Mr. Campion said nothing. A purely academic consideration concerning the importance of technique in all phases of modern life had sprung unbidden to his mind.

"Not use it?" said John in exasperation.

"Oh, no, we couldn't use it." Sir Alexander was quite definite. "Not in this case, not in London. It's not suitable. We simply must not admit any love at all. In law love is suspicious. Bendex—he's going to be one junior and is devilling for me at the moment—points out that that is absolutely without question, and I see that he's right. I was only telling you privately why I know Mike's innocent. We'll think of something else. But that's the truth of that point, I'm sure of it. Who is that?"

The final remark was made with a trace of his old manner and both John and Mr. Campion turned towards the door, through which faint sounds, as of a slight scuffle, reached them.

"Come in," said John peremptorily and, the handle turning abruptly, the door burst open and Mr. Rigget was precipitated into the room.

It was evident at once that something more than the business of the Accounts Department had occasioned his sudden appearance. He was neat, as usual, but considerably more pink and clearly a little above himself. He was also breathless.

At the sight of the K.C. he wavered and for a moment it seemed as though his determination would desert him, but a glimpse of John's stony face seemed to pull him together.

"I thought it my duty to come to you at once, sir," he said in a squeaky rush, his eyes snapping behind his pince-nez and his phraseology oddly stilted. "I reached the decision to tell something of which I had become cognizant to the police only this morning and now that I have done so I thought it would be only fair to tell you as well."

He stood for a moment wavering. John was looking at him as though he were some particularly unpleasant species of life, repellent but not dangerous.

Cousin Alexander, on the other hand, was staring over his head, no doubt considering Truth from yet another angle. Mr. Campion alone remained politely interested.

From pink Mr. Rigget became crimson and a dappling of sweat appeared upon his forehead.

"I've just told Sergeant Pillow about the quarrel I heard," he said sulkily. "It was on the Wednesday morning before the Thursday on which Mr. Paul was killed. The door between Mr. Paul's rooms and the File Copy Office was ajar and I didn't like to shut it."

Cousin Alexander bent his gaze upon the wretched man for the first time.

"Eavesdropping?" he enquired blandly.

"I happened to hear certain words," said Mr. Rigget indignantly. "And," he added, a suggestion of a snarl appearing for a fleeting instant across his mouth with the surprisingly white teeth, "I thought it was my duty to repeat them to the police."

"Get out!" said John, suddenly losing his temper. "Get out! Get straight out of the Office."

"Wait a minute." Cousin Alexander's voice had become pleasant again. "Let's hear what this gentleman has to say. You've come here to help us, haven't you? That's extremely kind of you. My cousin appreciates it. What did you hear when the door was ajar? First of all, who was speaking? You were sure of the voices, were you?"

"Yes, I was," said Mr. Rigget, considerably taken aback by this mercurial change in the magnificent-looking old gentleman in front of him. "Besides, I'd seen Mr. Paul and Mr. Mike when I went through the room first."

"Mr. Paul and Mr. Michael . . ." said Cousin Alexander soothingly. "And what were the words you heard?"

"Well, they'd stopped talking when I went in first," said Mr. Rigget truculently, "and then I suppose they thought the door was shut so they went on with their quarrel."

"Or conversation," murmured Sir Alexander pleasantly. "And then what?"

Mr. Rigget swung round on John. There was intense satisfaction upon his ignoble face.

"Mr. Paul said, 'You mind your own damned business, Mike. She's mine and I'll manage my own life in my own way.'"

There was complete silence in the room after he had spoken and he had the satisfaction of knowing that he had achieved a sensation.

"And did you hear anything else?" Cousin Alexander's voice was cloying.

"Yes," said Mr. Rigget, blushing to the roots of his black hair. "He said, 'Make love to her if you want—God knows I'm not stopping you.'"

"And then?"

"I didn't hear any more," said Mr. Rigget. "I came out then. But I could see what Mr. Mike was thinking."

"That's not evidence," said Cousin Alexander.

11
Fuse Cap

After a tedious magisterial hearing Michael Wedgwood was committed for trial and on the afternoon before the day on which he was to appear at the Old Bailey Mr. Campion, with Ritchie at his side, steered the Lagonda through the traffic in New Oxford Street. It was one of those warm blowy days when every street corner is a flower garden presided over by a stalwart London nymph still clad in the wools and tippets of winter and the air is redolent with an exciting mixture of tar, exhaust and face powder.

However, neither of the men in the big car was in the mood to appreciate the eternal hopefulness of spring. Ritchie was talking, curbing his gestures with considerable difficulty because of the confined space.

"Want you to see her," he said. "Don't like her like this. It's getting her down, Campion. She's fond of him, you know. Loves him and probably feels responsible. Women always take responsibility. It's a form of vanity. Can't help it. Natural with them."

His anxiety seemed to have loosened his tongue and the fact that he now considered Campion an old friend made him more coherent.

"Bound to get him off, don't you think?" he added, cocking a wistful eye at the young man beside him. "Terrible experience anyway. All terrible," he went on, waving a tremendous arm between Mr. Campion's eyes and the windscreen. "All this. All these people. They're all in prison. All miserable. All slaves. All got to work when they don't want to, eat when they don't want to, sleep when they don't want to. Can't drink until someone says they may. Can't hide their faces, got to hide their bodies. No freedom anywhere. I hate it. Frightens me. Knew a man once who chucked it. I couldn't."

"It's a feeling one does get sometimes," Mr. Campion conceded.

"I always feel like it," said Ritchie and hesitated on the brink of some further confidence but thought better of it and was silent.

They found Gina sitting by the open window in the big studio and Campion, who had not seen her for some weeks, was shocked by the change in her. She was harder, more sophisticated, older. Nervous exhaustion had been replaced by general deterioration. She looked less chic, less graceful, less charming.

Her greeting was artificial and it was not until he had been sitting on the big white sofa for some minutes that she suddenly turned to him with something of her old genuineness.

"It was good of you to come," she said. "I'm not going to cry or do anything silly and I shall be perfectly composed in the witness-box. It's not hearing from him," she added, her defences suddenly collapsing. "No mental contact at all. He's just gone. He might be dead."

The natural embarrassment which the confidence might have engendered was swept away by the relief which Campion felt at seeing that her artificiality went no deeper. This was only a warning then of the damage which might be done to her and had not the awful finality of the accomplished fact.

"You—you haven't found out what really happened? I know you haven't. You'd have told me, of course. But haven't you got just an inkling—haven't you got a clue? When I asked John he said something about a new witness. Can't you tell me about that? Or is it all a secret, like everything else?"

The mixture of bitterness and pleading in her deep voice was disturbing. Mr. Campion wished in his heart that he had better news for her.

"The new witness may be useful," he said. "His name's Widgeon. I had an awful job getting hold of him. He didn't want to talk but when he realized how much depended on it he shelved his private considerations like a sportsman and came out with all he knew. He's employed by the Tolleshunt Press people. They've got a small office on the second floor of Number Twenty-one. Apparently he got tight at lunch on the Thursday and it took him all the afternoon to sober up, so that he came to himself about five with a splitting headache and all the afternoon's work on his hands. So he stayed and did it and was still hard at it between six and nine, when Mrs. Tripper was making herself cups of tea and coming home from pictures and trotting along to the fried-fish shop."

He paused and smiled at her encouragingly.

"His story is that he heard the car start up soon after six—he can't say how soon—and that the engine was running continuously until eight or thereabouts, and that he didn't hear it again until ten to nine, when it ran for only a short time."

"But that lets Mike out! That bears out Mike's story!"

For the first time during the interview a faint tinge of colour appeared in her pale cheeks and she seemed to take new life.

Campion looked uncomfortable.

"It bears out his story," he said, "but it doesn't let him out. He can't establish his alibi between six and the time you phoned him, remember."

"I see," she said. She sank back again, her slender body in the sleek, man-tailored gown lifeless and pathetic.

"It'll help," said Campion, anxious to be reassuring. "Apart from fixing in the jury's mind that the whole thing probably happened on the Thursday, it refutes the evidence of the Tripper woman, or muddles it at any rate."

"And you've discovered nothing else?"

"Nothing of value," he confessed. "There's been so little to go upon. Usually in these things you can get your teeth in somewhere and worry the whole thing out, but in this business there hasn't been a gripping place. I had great hopes of Miss Netley, but either she can't talk and simply tried to look as though she could out of vanity, or else there's no earthly reason why she should and she doesn't want to."

"Netley," said Ritchie and, getting to his feet, walked out of the room.

His exit was so abrupt that they both looked after him. Gina's eyes were wet when she returned to Campion.

"He's been so kind," he said. "I used to think he was inhuman, a sort of creature; not a lunatic, you know, but, well, just not quite a right thing; but since—since Paul died he's been the only person who's behaved normally, to me at any rate. He's genuinely sorry for me and terrified for Mike. The others, John and even dear old Curley and Mrs. Austin and the doctor and all the other normal people who I always thought were ordinary and real, and who I expected to have ordinary human reactions, have their own points of view so strongly that they have no room for mine or Mike's. D'you know, John's *only* thinking about the publicity and the firm, and Curley follows him. Mrs. Austin's thinking about her personal appearance. It's as though she was going on the stage . . ."

Mr. Campion looked sympathetic.

"They're in it, you see, old dear," he said. "It's touched their lives."

She nodded gloomily. "It's the first time I've ever seen anything terrible close to," she said. "I haven't shown up very well to myself."

There was a silence which Mr. Campion did not like to break and presently she spoke again.

"John brought that man he calls Cousin Alexander up here. I got hysterical and they sent a doctor to me. I didn't mean to but he just wasn't human as far as I was concerned. He was like an author planning a book or a play. They talked about hostile witnesses and witness for the defence not as though they were people but as though they were stray ideas, little pieces of construction."

"Sir Alexander is convinced that he'll get an acquittal," said Campion.

"I know." Her voice became strident. "Insufficient evidence! And what good'll that be? I talked all this out with Ritchie and he was as appalled as I was when he realized it. Don't you see an acquittal will only save Mike's life? The great damage is done."

She leant forward, her intelligent face turned to him and her eyes very steady.

"Don't you see," she said, speaking carefully, as though he were a child, "if they acquit him without finding the man who did the murder everyone will always believe Mike did it, and if ever he is seen speaking to me that'll prove it from their point of view."

"I suppose what other people think matters?" said Mr. Campion weakly.

"Of course it matters," she said angrily. "It becomes the truth. What everybody thinks *is* the truth."

Mr. Campion was silent, knowing from experience that a discourse on ethics is rarely comforting to anyone in genuine distress.

"Somebody must have done it," she said. "Who was it? I've gone over it again and again so often that I sometimes think I shall go mad and imagine I did it myself. It was someone clever enough to think of arranging an accident, someone who had no idea how clever the police are. Albert, it wasn't Mike, was it?"

"No," said Mr. Campion quietly but with complete conviction. "It wasn't Mike."

She laughed unsteadily.

"When you're alone thinking, you believe anything."

Her voice died on the last word and she turned round. The door clattered open and Ritchie returned. Because of his excitement he was clumsier than ever and he lurched across the room dangerously.

"Any good?" he enquired, dropping something into Mr. Campion's lap.

Mr. Campion turned over the battered cardboard-backed book in some astonishment.

"Post Office Savings Bank?" he said. "Whose is it?"

"Girl Netley's." Ritchie seemed tremendously pleased with himself. "Might be interesting. Never know. Often thought it funny she brought it to the office. Keep bank books at home, not lying about."

"Where did you get it from?" Mr. Campion turned over the pages carefully.

"Out of her bag," said Ritchie without hesitation or attempt at mitigation. "Can't be conventional at a time like this."

Mr. Campion made no comment. Something in the book had attracted his attention and he sat for some considerable time turning over the pages and comparing entries.

"Thrifty kid," he said at last. "She saves ten bob a week regularly, every Saturday. There it is. It goes back nearly a year. Handed in at the same office just down the road here in Holborn. There were several sums paid in at Christmas—that's presents, I suppose—and she took out three pounds then too. I'm afraid it doesn't tell us much about her, unless—Hello! What's this?"

Gina rose to look over his shoulder while Ritchie leant back in his chair, his long hands dropping over the arms and his eyes mild and inquisitive, like a dog who has brought a parcel and is content to see his master open it.

Mr. Campion ran a finger down a paying-in column and traced certain entries across the page to the circular stamp which showed at which office the deposits had been made.

"These can't all be birthdays," he said. "They're funny amounts, too; so irregular. A pound on October the twenty-second last year, paid in at St. James's of all places. Ten shillings in the middle of the first week in November at the same place. Then there's just the ordinary ten shillings until December the first, when she paid two pounds in at the St. Martin's Lane office. Then nothing odd until January, and then there's quite a lot. Three pounds on the tenth, another three pounds on the thirteenth, two pounds on the seventeenth, then three again on the twentieth and—I say—five pounds on the twenty-ninth. That was the day after Paul disappeared. I wonder . . ."

He turned over the pages and his frown deepened.

"And there's nothing since. That's odd in a way."

"Source of blackmail dead," suggested Ritchie crudely.

Mr. Campion did not scout the suggestion openly.

"It's not very much for blackmail," he murmured. "Eighteen pounds odd all told. It's the paying-in places that strike me as being odd. They're all over the shop. Only the first two alike. Of course, we're catching at straws now, you know. This doesn't prove anything. It may mean absolutely nothing. Still, it's worth looking up."

He closed the book and slipped it into his pocket.

"I think I'll go across and have a word with her."

"Say I took it if you have to," said Ritchie recklessly.

"God forbid." Mr. Campion spoke piously and left them.

In spite of the fact that he had become a familiar figure at Twenty-three during the last few months, custom insisted that he should be shown into the waiting room and there left to kick his heels until the person whom he sought should be discovered and delivered to him.

He was standing with his back to the door, surveying the portrait of Jacoby Barnabas afresh, when Miss Netley came in. She went to meet him, a smile upon her lips and the same smug secretiveness in her eyes which he had noticed at their first meeting.

"Here again, Mr. Campion?" she said pleasantly but with the faintest suggestion of amusement in her tone. "I thought perhaps you'd brought us a manuscript!"

Mr. Campion's smile was wholly charming.

"That's what I call intuition," he said. "Look at this."

He had the satisfaction of seeing her complaisance vanish as she caught sight of the little brown book in his hand. Her round eyes lost their ingenuous expression and her colour vanished.

"It's mine," she said. "Where did you get it? Thank you for returning it."

"Ah, but I'm not returning it," murmured Mr. Campion and she gaped at him.

"I've never heard such impudence in all my life," she burst out finally. "How dare you! Where *did* you get it anyway?"

"Took it," said Mr. Campion and put the book back in his pocket.

Miss Netley trembled. "It's outrageous!" she said unsteadily. "It's illegal, it's—it's stealing!"

"Of course it is," he agreed. "Let's go and tell Inspector Tanner all about it, shall we? He's a policemen."

She drew back from him, her lips sulky, her eyes narrowed and frightened.

"What do you want to know? I can't tell you anything."

Mr. Campion sighed with relief. They taught them to be quick-witted in offices, he reflected.

"I thought we might have a chat," he said.

"I've told the police everything—absolutely everything."

"About the murder? Yes, of course you have," he said,

wondering how long they were going to be left alone in peace in the waiting room. "Let's talk about yourself."

Her suspicion increased.

"I don't understand."

Mr. Campion leant on the large table which filled the centre of the room. His expression was vague to the point of idiocy and his eyes looked guileless behind his spectacles.

"I hate to sound inquisitive and my question may sound a little in bad taste," he began, "but however much one's upset by a death one has to face facts, hasn't one? I do hope you won't think it impertinent of me to ask if your finanical position has been very much upset by Mr. Paul Brande's death? It is frightfully inquisitive, I know, but I would be really obliged if you'd tell me."

She looked relieved and he saw at once that he was on a wrong tack.

"Well, I haven't lost my job, if that's what you mean," she said. "What other difference could it make?"

"None, of course. If you're staying on that's all right." Mr. Campion covered his tracks but her interest had been aroused.

"Just exactly what are you getting at?" she demanded.

He took the bank book out of his pocket, looked at it thoughtfully, and replaced it again.

"You told the police exactly what happened when Mr. Paul Brande got a letter by the afternoon post on the Thursday that he disappeared. You haven't remembered anything else since, have you?"

"I've told it all, every single word, over and over again."

There was an edge to her voice which warned him to be careful. He smiled at her brightly.

"You've got awfully strong nerves, haven't you?" he said. "Let's go into his old office and—just go through it. Please don't think I'm being a nuisance, but I would like to know just exactly what happened. It'll fix the picture in my mind, you see."

Miss Netley looked at him witheringly but the retort which rose to her lips did not come and without a word she led him up to the first floor and into the big comfortable room, a little too preciously furnished for an office, in which Paul had worked.

Mr. Campion sat down at the desk after placing his hat and stick carefully on a side table.

"Now," he said, "where were you when the letter came?"

Still sullen, and looking her contempt, Miss Netley seated herself at the typewriter in the corner.

"Now," said Mr. Campion, "I suppose the boy brought the letter in, gave it to you and you handed it to Mr. Brande?"

She bowed her head. It was evident that she did not trust herself to speak. Mr. Campion tore open an imaginary envelope, exhibiting much pantomimic skill.

"Now," he demanded briskly, "what do I do now?"

"Mr. Paul got up," said Miss Netley, indicating that she was not going to play, "scrunched up the paper and envelope and threw them into the fireplace."

"Like that?" said Mr. Campion, hurling an imaginary ball from him violently.

"No," she said unwillingly. "Just casually."

"And it burned?" he enquired, his eyes resting on her quizzically.

"It did."

"All of it? Every scrap of it?"

"Every tiny bit."

"You looked to see?"

She met his eyes defiantly. "After he had gone, yes, I did."

"We're getting on," said Mr. Campion cheerfully. "Now I get up, don't I? And I seem excited? What happens? Do I get red and seem a little flustered? Do I take up my hat and stick and make for the door without a word or a glance in your direction? Or do I say something?"

The girl hesitated. She seemed to be considering her course of action.

"No," she said at last, grudgingly. "Mr. Paul asked me if a parcel had come."

"Oh, did he? What did he say? Can you remember his actual words?"

"He said"—she still spoke unwillingly—"'Has that parcel come from Fortnum and Mason's yet?'"

"Fortnum and Mason's? And what did you say?"

139

"I said, 'No, Mr. Brande, I don't think it has.' And he said, 'Oh, well, it doesn't matter,' and went out without it. And now I hope you're satisfied."

"Well, it's a crumb," said Mr. Campion. "It's a crumb. Ten bob here, a pound there. Two pounds and five pounds—it all tells up, doesn't it?"

He stopped abruptly. If he had meant to terrify her he could not have been more successful. She was staring at him, her eyes wide and her lips open.

"What do you know?" she asked huskily.

"Much more than you'd think." Mr. Campion spoke cryptically and he hoped convincingly. "Let's get back to Mr. Paul. You said the parcel hadn't come and then what happened?"

"I told you. He said it didn't matter. 'It does not matter,' he said. 'I will go without it.' Then he went out and shut the door and I never saw him again."

"Splendid!" said Mr. Campion. "You're not a good witness, you know, but it makes a lot of difference when you try. Now what happened to the parcel? Did it ever come?"

"Yes. It came about an hour after he left. I put it in that cupboard over there."

"Is it still there?"

"I don't know. I haven't looked."

"Then shall we look now?" he suggested.

She got up, sauntered across the room and jerked open the cupboard.

"Yes," she said. "There it is."

"Bring it here," said Mr. Campion. "I wouldn't have you for a secretary as a gift."

Miss Netley reddened and opened her mouth to speak. A single unprintable epithet left her lips and then, as he looked completely shocked, she strode over to her typewriter and burst into tears.

Campion examined the parcel. There seemed to be nothing in any way extraordinary about it and he loosened the string. Inside was a square box, tastefully ornamented and containing two pounds of crystallized Cape gooseberries.

He sat looking at them in their green and pink sugar jackets, his head slightly on one side and his eyes puzzled.

"Who was the lady?" he enquired at last.

Miss Netley wiped her eyes.

"I don't know."

"Of course you do. Ten bob—two pounds—"

She laughed. "You're wrong. I knew you were wrong."

Her watery-eyed triumph was vindictive.

"Well, I know now," said Mr. Campion mercilessly.
"Come on, I want the address."

"I don't know it."

He had the uncomfortable impression that she was
telling the truth.

"Look here, young woman," he said severely, "an
accident of nature has given you a certain amount of
intelligence. Believe me when I tell you that now is the
time to use it. Think! Pull your scattered little wits
together. Get it into your head that now is the time to talk."

This sudden ferocity from the hitherto mild young man
had the desired effect.

"There was a telephone number he used to ring up
sometimes," she admitted. "He used to send me out of the
room and then just as I was going I would hear him give the
number."

"Well, then, out with it, for the love of Mike," said Mr.
Campion, using the expression unconsciously.

"Maida Vale 58423. Now I can't tell you any more. I
can't—can't! I don't know any more!"

"Maida Vale 58423," said Mr. Campion, scribbling the
number on the blotter in front of him. "All right. You clear
off now and get your face washed."

"What about my book? You can't keep my book."

"I should trust me with it for a day or two," said Mr.
Campion. "I might put something in it. You never know."

A stifled scream escaped the girl. He had a vision of
her, white and trembling, and then the door banged behind
her. Enlightenment dawned in Mr. Campion's pale eyes.

"So that's how he did it," he said and pulled the
telephone towards him.

He heard the bell ringing in the far-off room for some
time before a voice answered him.

"Yes? Maida Vale 58423. Who is it, please?"

Mr. Campion was puzzled. It was a woman's voice and

it was familiar, but he could not place it. Completely in the dark, he proceeded cautiously.

"I say, I'm afraid you'll think it frightfully odd of me ringing up like this," he began. "I wonder if it would be too much to ask you if I could come along and see you? It really is important and I wouldn't take up more than ten minutes of your time."

"Do you know the address?" whispered the voice. "It's Thirty-two, Dorothy Studios, Denbigh Road, Kilburn. You open the garden gate and come down the steps."

"Splendid. I'll be right along," he said, completely startled. "My name's Campion, by the way."

"Yes, I know. I've been expecting you. My name's Teddie Dell."

Mr. Campion hung up the receiver slowly.

He was very conscious of the fact that he had never heard either the name or the address in his life before.

12

Somebody Died

Mr. Campion saw the studio as soon as he pushed open the gate in the blank wall behind the huge margarine-coloured block of flats and came out on to the iron staircase high above the untidy strip of sunken garden.

It sat opposite him in the grass, trying to look like a country cottage and succeeding in suggesting a garden suburb. Its four tall windows faced south and the back of the flats and had diamond panes. The skylight had been leaded over.

There was a trimness about the whole building and a preponderance of bright colours which conveyed a personality childish or at least uneducated. The paint was green, the curtains blue, the window sills and step red-ochred, while a ridiculous little green dog kennel stood beside the door. It looked extraordinarily clean and new in the dinginess of Kilburn and no more in bad taste than a painted Noah's Ark, which it resembled.

It was six o'clock and not yet dusk, although the sun had gone in. The flats and the studio appeared to be deserted and there was a quiet evening melancholy upon the scene.

Mr. Campion went slowly down the iron staircase and, picking his way over the grass, tapped with the brass knocker which bore a relief of Worcester cathedral and had come from Birmingham via Bruges.

An excited yapping from within answered him, followed by a woman's voice admonishing the dog. Then the door opened.

"Come in," said Teddie Dell.

Enlightenment came to Mr. Campion as he recognized the woman who had been waiting for him outside the Bottle Street flat when he had come home from the inquest with Gina and Curley. She looked bigger and older in her indoor clothes. Her fairish hair was dressed close to her head and was cut in a thin unfashionably curled fringe, while her smooth capable body was sturdy and unsuitably dressed in a very smooth blue skirt and a very frilly blouse.

There was a suggestion of strength about her face also, with its square jawbone and thick cream skin, its good teeth and wide-set blue-grey eyes.

"I'm glad you came," she said. "I've been wondering if I ought to ring you. Come in and sit down and have a cigarette."

The over-carefulness of her pronunciation struck him again, but her self-possession was unconscious and superb.

The dog was frantic with delight at his arrival and danced round him noisily in spite of his mistress's rebuke. He was a small smooth-haired yellow mongrel, spry and wiry on thin legs. Campion put out a hand and he offered a paw instantly. Campion took it and laughed.

"George, don't be a fool. Lie down! He's absurd, isn't he?"

The woman was laughing as she spoke and Campion glanced up to see that her eyes were swimming. She turned away to the mantelshelf and brought back cigarettes and matches, waiting on her visitor with the complete lack of self-consciousness of a nurse or a teashop waitress.

He found himself fumbling for a case to offer her at the moment when she held a lighted match to his cigarette.

The room in which they stood reflected the outside of the building. The floor was covered with imitation red and grey tiles and shone like a ship's deck. The dark oak furniture was ordinary and unpretentious. There was a divan under the windows and a comfortable chesterfield, flanked by two chintz-covered easy chairs by the fire.

Teddie Dell drew up the largest and most comfortable chair.

"Sit down," she said, indicating it, and he obeyed her.

Mr. Campion, the most unassuming of men, did not imagine for a moment that her solicitude for his comfort, her tacit acceptance of the fact that his ease was all-important, was due in any way to his personal charm. Teddie Dell, he realized, was behaving as she always had and always would behave, since she belonged to that most ill-used sisterhood, some of them wives, some of them mothers, and all of them lovers, who really believe that there is in the mere quality of manhood something magnificent and worthy to be served.

"You were pointed out to me at the inquest and I heard you were interested in the case," she said, seating herself opposite him and holding one hand up to the fire to shield her face from the blaze. "I didn't want to go to the police for obvious reasons. He wouldn't have liked it and she's only a kid, isn't she, and mixed up with nice people who don't understand this sort of thing. So I went round to your place. When I saw her come up with you I thought I'd better slip off. She's never heard of me, you see."

Mr. Campion nodded. He was wondering irrelevantly what Teddie Dell thought she meant by "nice people."

"It's been on my mind," she continued. "He came here when he left the office on the Thursday and the police don't know that. I wanted to ask someone about it and find out if it was any good telling. He kept me a secret from his family for fourteen years and I didn't see any point in it all coming out now if it wouldn't help."

"Fourteen years?" said Mr. Campion involuntarily.

Her eyes rested upon him for a moment.

"We met in the war, in France," she said. "I've had this place since '23."

Her glance left his face and travelled round the yellow walls and there was an indefinable expression in her eyes.

"I never thought he'd marry," she went on abruptly. "But he was right: it didn't make any difference. That's why I was sorry for the kid. That's no marriage for a girl. I suppose she got hold of the young cousin and egged him on and teased him till he went out of his mind—although I don't know why they think he did it. My dear old boy had a lot of other enemies—ooh, he had a temper——!"

She broke off. Her eyes were a blank and her mouth very hard.

Mr. Campion looked at the dog, who lay upon the hearth rug, his nose between his paws and his ears cocked. Gradually he became aware of other things: a small silver golf trophy on the dresser and a pair of slippers, grey with age and long discarded, stuffed behind the coal-box, which was also a fireside seat.

"Was Mr. Brande here very long on the Thursday?"

He put the question diffidently but the woman gave him her whole attention at once.

"No, he couldn't stay. That often happened. He was such a busy man. I suppose they'll miss him at the office. He held the business together, didn't he?"

She spoke wistfully and for a moment Mr. Campion was able to take the impulsive, excitable, slightly ridiculous Paul at the dead man's own valuation. The woman was still speaking.

"We were going to have a bit of dinner and then he was going to read. We didn't go out much together since he got so well known. I didn't ask him to take me; I'm not a fool. But he came in just about four and said he couldn't stay, so I made him a cup of tea and he went. I wondered why he didn't ring up on the Sunday, but on the Monday I saw the papers."

Her voice wavered on the last word but she controlled it magnificently, out of deference, Mr. Campion felt, to the presence of a stranger.

"Do you know where he went when he left here?" he enquired.

"I know where he said he was going and there was no point in him lying. Besides, he never did to me. We knew each other too well. He said, 'I'm so sorry I can't stay, Ted. I've got to go down to fetch a key from Camden Town of all places, and then I've got to dash back and slip into the British Museum.' I asked him if there was any chance of him dropping in later but he said, 'No luck, I'm going to be busy tonight. I'll ring you Sunday.'"

Her voice ceased and she moved her position slightly so that her face was in the shadow. Mr. Campion felt he dared intrude no more.

"It's been very kind of you," he began awkwardly. "I'll let you know, of course, if I think you ought to come forward, but it's quite possible that it won't be at all necessary—if you don't want to."

She got up, raising herself wearily as if her bones were unusually heavy.

"Why should I?" she said. "It's not as if he were ill. He's dead."

The dog rose and yawned and stretched himself, only to lie down again, his nose between his forepaws. The room was growing dark and the firelight flickered over the bright floor and was reflected in some little bits of brass on the dresser. There was comfort in the place and an utterly unbearable sense of waiting. Mr. Campion hurried.

Teddie Dell escorted him to the door.

"I'll keep in touch with you," he promised and paused. Paul had not died penniless and Campion had a strong sense of justice. "Forgive me if I am saying the wrong thing," he ventured, "but are you all right for cash?"

She smiled and there were so many varying emotions in her expression that he only understood that she appreciated his thoughtfulness.

"Better let her have it," she said. "There isn't much. He spent like a lunatic. It would be charity too. I haven't any rights."

She was silent for a moment and he had a very vivid impression of her, square and sturdy in her little painted home, the dog peering round her skirts.

"We loved each other," she said and her voice was as proud and forlorn as high tragedy itself.

Mr. Campion came away.

13

A Craftsman of Camden Town

"Would it be possible, Lugg," enquired Mr. Campion delicately, "for you to forget for a moment this respectability to which you are not accustomed and delve into the past?"

Mr. Lugg, who was taking off his collar because it was only his employer whom he had admitted, kept his back turned to the speaker and his attention fixed upon the drawer into which he was tucking this badge of refinement. The white roll of fat at the back of his neck looked smug and obstinate. Mr. Lugg had not heard.

"I suppose if I asked you to come off it," Mr. Campion began sarcastically.

Mr. Lugg swung round, his small black eyes unconvincingly innocent.

"I shouldn't understand what you meant," he said placidly, and returned to the drawer. "Some of the fellows down at the Mews wear butterfly collars and some wear straight," he observed over his shoulder. "I 'aven't made up me mind for good yet. Butterflies let yer neck through, but they're apt to look untidy."

Mr. Campion made no response to this implied question. Instead he put another.

"Lugg," he said, "if a man who had something to hide went to Camden Town to get a key, who would he go to?"

Surprise took Mr. Lugg unawares.

"Lumme," he said, "old Wardie Samson! He's not still at it, is 'e? Must be well over a 'undred. I remember 'im in my dad's day."

This family reminiscence was cut short by what was no

doubt a recollection of the rigid society of the hostelry in the "Mews."

"A very low person," said the new Mr. Lugg. "Dishonest, reely."

"Do you know him?"

Lugg wriggled uncomfortably.

"I visited 'im as a lad with my father," he said at last, "but I shouldn't think 'e was the party to which you was referrin'."

"Well, take off that awful coat and get in the car, which is downstairs," said Mr. Campion. "We're going to see him."

"Not me." Mr. Lugg was defiant. "I'll give you 'is address if you like, but I'm not coming with you. It's more than me reputation's worth. You never know 'ow a thing like this might tell two or three years hence when your relation 'as gorn the way all good relations should go and you and me are established in our rightful place. What sort of a position should I be in if one of the 'ousemaids, or per'aps another gentleman who'd come up in the world, should say, 'Surely I saw you in Camden Town, Mr. Lugg?' What sort of position should I be in then?"

"Even if I become a Duke," said Mr. Campion brutally, "the chances of you becoming a respectable person are remote—or at any rate, I shouldn't count on it. Come on. Hurry."

Before the authority in the tone Mr. Lugg's defiance turned to pathos.

"What's the good of me tryin' to better meself if you keep draggin' me down?" he said. "I've put the old life be'ind me. I've forgot it, see?"

"Well, this is where you do a spot of remembering," insisted Mr. Campion heartlessly. "And don't spoil everything by trying to impress your old pal with your new vulgarity, you fat oaf."

Mr. Lugg bridled. "That's a bit too thick, that is," he said. "You're destroying my ambition, that's about what you're doing. Mucking up me perishin' soul, see? All right, I'll come with you."

They drove for some time in silence, but as the wealthier parts of the city were left behind and they slid into the noisy poverty of the Hampstead Road some of Mr. Lugg's gloom deserted him.

"It's like old times, isn't it?" he observed.

Campion accepted the olive branch.

"We've got a delicate job ahead," he said. "I suppose your friend Wardie would give away a client if he was dead?"

"Wardie doesn't *give* anything." Lugg spoke reminiscently. "Doesn't know the meanin' of the word 'tick' either. Still, we can but try 'im. I 'aven't seen 'im for ten years, remember."

"When you were a lad," said Mr. Campion unkindly.

"When I was one of the lads," said Mr. Lugg, whose spirits were soaring. "'E was a clever old bloke, Wardie," he continued. "Give 'im an impression one day and in a little while 'e'd drop you a line and down you'd go to find a better key than the original. 'E did name plates, too—not for the same people. Only one thing aginst 'im, 'e was slow. Lumme, 'ow slow that man was! So busy making snide 'e never 'ad time for honest work. Used to make lovely 'alf-crowns. Made 'em out of the tops of soda-water siphons. That metal's just the right weight, y'know."

Mr. Campion showed polite interest. "Was he pinched?"

"Wardie? No. He was too careful. 'E never passed 'em. Wouldn't let any of 'is relations 'andle 'em either. Used to sell 'em—so much a gross—to one of these lads in the Ditch. 'E's a handy man, if you take me. I'm surprised at 'im still working, especially for outsiders. It's round 'ere, guv'nor. Better leave the car at a garridge. It's no good parkin' it. We don't want to turn up to Wardie's lookin' like bloomin' millionaires. Might give 'im ideas."

They left the car and continued on foot. For one who professed to have left this particular world behind him Mr. Lugg found his way among the maze of small streets with remarkable precision.

"'Ere we are," he said at last. "Now, look casual but not 'alf-witted. I don't want 'im to think I've turned up with a Killarney."

Mr. Campion, who in the course of a long association had come to realize that living up to Mr. Lugg was an impossibility, remained much as usual and they paused in the narrow, dusty little road littered with paper bags and kitchen refuse while Lugg went through an elaborate pantomime of noticing a small shop some few doors down on the opposite side.

"Why, there's Mr. Samson's joint!" he said, with theatrical astonishment. "I wonder if 'e's still alive? I'd better go and look 'im up. Just the same! The ole place 'asn't changed since I was a boy."

At first sight the Samson emporium was not impressive. It consisted of a very narrow door and a small window. Both were incredibly dirty and, while one revealed an even dingier interior, the other displayed a collection of old-iron ranging from nails to the back of bedsteads, a notice which announced that shoe leather could be purchased within, and a quantity of cheap new razor blades. There was also, Mr. Campion noticed, a hank of bass, two large bales of twine and a skein of very thick elastic labelled "For Catapults." This last was crossed out very lightly and "Model Aëroplanes" substituted in wavering pencil.

With the nonchalance of a loiterer observing a policeman, Mr. Lugg lounged into the shop, beckoning Mr. Campion to follow him with a jerk of his shoulder.

It took them some moments to accustom their eyes to the darkness. The atmosphere, which was composed of a nice blend of rust, leather and Irish stew, took a bit of assimilating also, and Campion felt his feet sink into a sand of dust and iron filings.

There was a movement in the shop, followed by a snuffling, and presently a bright young man with a white face, dusty yellow hair and an enquiring manner sauntered towards them. Mr. Lugg showed surprise.

"Business changed 'ands?" he asked suspiciously. "I come reely to enquire after an old friend, Mr. Samson."

The young man eyed Mr. Lugg from the toes of his boots to the top of his hat.

"One of the old brigade, aren't yer?" he said cheekily, his narrow blue eyes astute and appraising.

Mr. Lugg was momentarily taken off his balance.

"'Ere, what're you gettin' at?" he said, taking a

menacing step forward. "When I want any lip from two penn'orth of string-bag I'll ask for it."

In spite of a certain flabbiness induced by high life, Mr. Lugg was still a formidable opponent, and he was not alone. The young man retreated.

"Gran'dad's in the back," he said. "If you'll tell me your name I'll go and see if he remembers you."

"Gran'dad?" said Mr. Lugg, a repulsively sentimental smile appearing on his great white face. "Don't tell me you're little Alfie? Not little Alfie what I danced up an' down on my knee?"

"Charlie," said the young man, without enthusiasm.

"Charlie! That was it. Rosie's boy—little Rosie. 'Ow's your mother, son?"

"'Aven't seen 'er since she went off with a rozzer," said the young man, with that complete carelessness which is more chilling than any rebuke. "I'll go and tell Gran'dad. What's yer name?"

"Just tell 'im Maggers is 'ere," said Lugg, who was beginning to enjoy himself for the first time, Mr. Campion felt, for years.

"Shall I come with you?"

"No. You stay 'ere," said Charlie, with the first show of animation he had yet exhibited and disappeared into the darkness.

Mr. Lugg chuckled in a fatherly fashion.

"I remember 'im being born," he said, with inexplicable pride. "'Ear what 'e called me?—'Old Brigade!' That's 'cos 'e knows I'm after a key. 'Is pals use oxy-acetylene. Nasty dangerous stuff. When that come on the market I knew my time was over."

"'E'll see yer. Come on."

Charlie did not emerge from the shadows to make this announcement and they groped forward in the direction of his voice. After passing through a living room, into which the iron filings had percolated in the course of years, and which was apparently the fountainhead of the Irish stew, they came quite unexpectedly into the bright light of day. Their way led across a minute yard, dirty to a degree unknown by most users of the word, and into a small shed festooned with old bicycle tyres.

Seated at a bench was a large blank-faced old man, bald as an egg and clad in a very loose shirt and surprisingly tight trousers whose original colour could only be surmised. The round face was at once mild and cunning and possessed the serenity of a Buddha.

"Wardie!" said Mr. Lugg, enraptured, adding a little inopportunely: "I thought you was dead."

The old man smiled enigmatically as he held out a hand, and it occurred to Mr. Campion that he was deaf.

"Afternoon, gentlemen," he said, and his voice had a husky, secretive quality.

Lugg deserted Campion. He went round the back of the bench and seated himself beside the old man.

"I'm Maggers, Wardie," he said, thrusting a mighty arm round the other man's shoulders. "You remember me. I'm the fellow what was sweet on yer second daughter—the one what died. I'm coming back to yer, aren't I?"

"Lugg," said the old man suddenly. "Young Lugg."

They shook hands again solemnly and with great sentiment.

"Can you 'ear me?" said Mr. Lugg, rumbling into one of the great ears.

"Course," said the old man. "'Eard you all the time. Didn't know oo you were. Oo's yer friend?"

"Young fellow I go round with," said Mr. Lugg shamelessly. "You know me, Wardie: I wouldn't tell you wrong. Me and my pal we want a bit of 'elp from you."

He cocked an eye at his employer.

"You tell 'im, Bert."

Mr. Campion explained his business as well as he could.

"It's about a key," he said. "Lugg and I wondered if you could tell us anything about a key which a man picked up down here in Camden Town on Thursday, the twenty-eighth of January last. It's a long time ago, I know, but I thought you might remember. He was a well-dressed fellow, forty-fiveish, dark, and spoke well."

Wardie Samson shook his large round head.

"I don't know anything about keys," he said. "We don't sell 'em."

Lugg burst into a roar of unnatural laughter.

"You're takin' Bert for a 'tec!" he said. "That's a good one, that is! Old Bert a split! That'll be one to tell the boys!"

Wardie's inflamed and rheumy eyes shifted nervously.

"Can't tell yer about a key," he said. "Don't know."

Mr. Campion took a chance.

"It's private information I want," he said. "I'm willing to pay for it and I'll give you any assurance you like that you will never be questioned about it again. I am a detective, if you like, but I'm not a police detective. I'm not interested in your business, and all I want is a description, or, better still, a mould, of a key which the man I am interested in had made in this district. That's all I want. After I walk out of this shop you can swear blindly you've never seen me before. Lugg won't act as a witness."

The old man, who had been watching Campion carefully throughout this recital, seemed impressed.

"What date did you say, guv'nor? The twenty-eighth of January? Seems to me I read an interestin' bit in the paper about a gentleman who got his on that day. It wouldn't be him you was interested in, would it?"

"That's the ticket," said Mr. Lugg heartily. "Now you're bein' sensible. We're just blokes oo've come to an old pal for a bit of 'elp. As for that chap, 'e can't buy anything off you again, can 'e? 'E's in 'is box."

Mr. Samson seemed to have decided that his visitors were on the level, but he retained his caution of voice and expression, which seemed to be habitual.

"I sent 'im a letter telling 'im it was ready and 'e come down right away. Said 'e'd destroyed the letter for 'is own sake."

He cocked an eye at Campion, who nodded reassuringly.

"He had. We come to you by chance. Have you destroyed the impression?"

The old man nodded and seemed to debate within himself for a moment or so. Then, with a glance at Lugg that was almost affectionate, he opened a small drawer in the bench in front of him and, after rummaging in it for some time, produced a large, old-fashioned key. He threw it down in front of Campion.

"Always make two for luck," he said, and the faintest

suggestion of a smile flickered for an instant round his mouth.

Another search in the drawer produced a dirty envelope. "Paul R. Brande," he spelt out awkwardly. "Twenty-three, Horsecollar Yard, Holborn, W.C.1."

Mr. Campion took the key and Lugg waved him out of the shed.

"Me and Wardie will fix this little matter up between us," he said magnificently.

Mr. Campion waited in the filth of the yard for some considerable time, and Lugg finally appeared.

"Three pound ten," he said. "I know it's a lot, but you 'ave to pay for these things."

Mr. Campion parted with the money and presently, with the key safely stowed in his pocket, he once more approached the garage where the car was parked. As they settled down and Campion turned the Lagonda out into Hampstead Road Lugg nudged him.

"'Ere's thirty-five shillings that belongs to you," he said. "I did a split with Wardie. It's the worst of these dishonest people. They always expect you to live down to 'em."

14

The Damned

Even if Mr. Lugg was as hurt as he looked when his employer dropped him at the corner of Regent Street, at least he refrained from referring to himself as a "worn-out glove," an unsuitable simile of which he was very fond, having, so he said, read it somewhere and thought it "the ticket."

Campion went on alone to Horsecollar Yard. He had no desire to discuss his afternoon's work with Gina, and was wondering how he could get into Number Twenty-three without disturbing her, John, or an inquisitive policeman when he observed a familiar figure striding out of the cul-de-sac.

Ritchie Barnabas possessed a striking appearance at all times, but, seen at a reasonable distance in the lamp-lit dusk of a spring evening, he presented a spectacle of fantasy. He lolloped along at a great pace, each knee giving a little as it took his weight, and his great arms flapping about him like the wings of an intoxicated crow.

He pulled up with a jerk which almost overbalanced him as the Lagonda slid to a standstill at his side and thrust an anxious face into Campion's own.

"The key of the office?" he repeated after the younger man had made the request. "Certainly. Let you in myself. All the cousins and Miss Curley have keys. John's out, anyway. Gone to see Alexander."

All the time he was speaking he watched Campion's face with the eager but diffident curiosity of a child. The other man found himself apologizing.

"If I had anything definite I'd tell you," he said, "but at the moment I've only got an idea, supported by two or three dubious facts."

Ritchie nodded humbly and his blue eyes blinked trustingly at his friend. He opened the front door of Twenty-three and hesitated.

"Wait for you?" he enquired hopefully.

"I shouldn't." Unconsciously Mr. Campion spoke in that firm but regretful tone with which one tries to persuade a strange and friendly dog not to accompany one home.

"All right," Ritchie agreed sadly. "Lock up behind you. Good night."

He strode off, to return at once.

"Only live in Red Lion Square, you know address," he murmured. "There if wanted. Any hour."

He went off again, successfully this time, and Mr. Campion set about his investigations, blessing the idiosyncrasy of the firm of Barnabas which made them elect to have their offices cleaned out in the early morning instead of at night.

It was practically dark indoors, and the big untidy

rooms looked unfamiliar in the gloom; nor were they particularly silent. The ticking of clocks, the stir of papers in a draught and the vibrations of the nearby Underground railway combined to make the place sound alive.

Anxious not to advertise himself, Campion did not turn on the lights, but relied upon his torch. He went up to Miss Curley's room, a neatly kept glass-and-panelling cubicle built round one window in the typists' office. The strong-room key hung upon its hook on the inside of the old-fashioned desk. As soon as he handled it one of Mr. Campion's minor theories collapsed gently, to be replaced by a sense of misgiving and a wholly unwarrantable suspicion of the innate honesty of Wardie Samson.

He compared the two keys as they lay side by side on the desk in the gleam of his torch. Apart from the fact that they were both of the ordinary or old-fashioned type and were both over four inches long, it would have been difficult to find two such instruments more dissimilar. The key of the strong-room door was long and slender with three wards, but the key which Wardie Samson had made for luck was squat and heavy and had that curious unsatis-factory appearance which is peculiar to old-fashioned patent devices which have never been really successful.

Mr. Campion turned it over thoughtfully and an idea occurred to him. Placing both keys in his pocket, he went slowly downstairs. It was growing darker and the well of the front hall, which had no windows to admit the gleam from the street lamps, was completely black.

Because it is natural to keep quiet in the dark, Mr. Campion trod gently. At the top of the stone staircase leading down into the basement he paused to listen. His quick ears had detected something that was not one of the ordinary night noises and his interest quickened. It did not come again, however, and he went on.

On the landing, where the stair turned to face the basement wall, he paused abruptly, extinguishing his torch. Below him, at the end of the passage, a thin angle of light gleamed in the darkness. The strong-room door was ajar and there was a light within, a fact which might not have been so very astonishing even out of office hours had he not carried the only official key in his pocket.

Campion advanced cautiously, feeling his way down the shallow worn stone steps. His foot had just touched the concrete floor of the passage when the angle vanished as the light in the room went out.

He stood motionless, listening. The silence was uncanny and he hesitated to use the torch until he knew more of the situation. An unarmed man with a torch is an admirable target.

He was some half-dozen yards from the door and the basement was less disturbed by vibrations and draught-disturbed papers than the rest of the building, yet he could hear nothing. There was not a breath, not a rustle, not even the almost undetectable whisper of a well-oiled hinge. It was a paralyzed silence, not altogether natural.

Mr. Campion did not consider himself a nervous man, but neither was he sufficiently thick-skinned to let the piquancy of the situation pass by him. Someone, presumably with a guilty conscience and possibly with a gun, was aware of his presence and was waiting for him.

Campion stood quite still, holding his breath lest any sound should reveal his exact position.

The silence continued.

It came to an end at last, and in so unnerving a fashion that all his preparation was wasted. At the moment when he had decided that he must breathe deeply or burst, a yell so loud that its nature or even its origin was indeterminate sounded within a few feet of his ear and practically at the same time something apparently demoniacal struck him in the chest, knocking the torch out of his hand and most of the breath from his body.

There is to most of us a secret savage satisfaction in receiving a blow that one knows that one can repay with interest. As Campion staggered back against the wall beside the staircase his left came in contact with something that was hard enough to be a man's head. He heard a grunt and deep breathing and, as the knee came up to catch him in the stomach, he threw his arms round it, hurling his weight forward so that he went down on top of his unknown adversary.

During the next few seconds he had little time for speculation, but he became aware that he was fighting something human, since it was clothed, and of an iron hardness and ferocity which suggested a hank of steel rope temporarily possessed by a fiend.

Campion had some experience of catch-as-catch-can fighting. During his adventurous life he had enjoyed scraps in most stratas of society, so that he was aware that the Queensberry rules have many variations, but that evening in the pitch-dark basement he received an education.

The unseen creature bit, clawed, sobbed and pummelled, interspersing this unconventionality with occasional scientific blows. Campion was temporarily outclassed and was only relieved that his enemy had no weapon.

He was lying upon his face with a teetering, kicking thing trying to force him through the concrete floor when his groping hand caught an iron banister and he dragged himself up and let out with his right, the full weight of his body behind the blow.

It dawned upon him then, as he felt the wet chin go back under his fist, that he was fighting with a man in terror. The sobbing ceased and something thudded satisfactorily at his feet. Campion shook himself and waited, but there was no further sound from the floor. He moved unsteadily down the passage and, after a considerable delay, discovered the switch.

The first thing he saw as his surroundings leapt into view was a reflection of his own face in the mirror which hung just inside the open door of the little washroom. It was not a reassuring spectacle.

He did not stop to examine the damage, but swung round just in time to see a tousled object creeping furtively towards the stairs.

Mr. Campion leapt upon it, caught it by the remnants of what had once been a collar, and jerked back its head.

Shivering, whimpering, his face covered with blood and tears, cowered a star witness for the Crown, Mr. Peter Rigget.

Campion gaped at him and let him go. He dropped to the floor, crawled into a sitting position on the bottom step of the staircase, and wept. Never an irritable man, Mr. Campion felt himself excused in the exhibition of a little impatience. He pulled out his handkerchief and wiped some of the blood off his face.

"What in the name of all that's holy do you think you've been doing?" he enquired.

Mr. Rigget continued to blubber. Presently he stopped and his head fell forward on his chest. Campion bent over him, his eyebrows raised. But Mr. Rigget had not fainted. He was asleep.

Campion was not surprised. He had seen the same thing happen before when great physical exertion had been allied to the emotional upheaval. Since it is a natural phenomenon, only occurring to young people in exceptional health, Mr. Campion felt unreasonably angry with Mr. Rigget.

He left him where he was and retired to the washroom, where, with the door open, he could keep an eye upon the heavily breathing figure at the foot of the stairs.

A wrenched shoulder, a cut over the left eye, and four weals left by four fingernails travelling from his right temple to the top of his collar seemed to be his principal injuries. His clothes were in ribbons. There was a piece missing from the sleeve of his jacket which could only have been bitten away, and there was blood all over him.

He cleaned himself up as best he could and felt better after his head had been under the cold tap for a minute or two.

He let Mr. Rigget sleep for half an hour, and woke him by pouring a jug of cold water over his head. The puffed eyes opened sleepily and closed again.

Campion raised the stocky little body which was in such surprisingly good condition, and dragged it into the washroom, where he repeated his treatment until Mr. Rigget showed signs of returning life and intelligence.

"All right?" Campion enquired when once again the blue eyes looked out clearly from beneath their battered lids.

Mr. Rigget said nothing. He turned his back on Mr. Campion and began to wash his hands.

"I think we'd better have a chat, don't you, having been properly introduced?"

159

Still Mr. Rigget was silent. His hands seemed to require a lot of attention.

"What were you doing down here? You'll have to explain to somebody, you know. You'd better tell me."

Mr. Rigget was trembling violently, but no sound left his lips and he went on washing his hands.

Campion leant forward, turned off the tap and threw him a towel.

"Come on," he said, taking the other man by the arm. "We'll go into the strong room."

Mr. Rigget remained perfectly still. He was staring straight in front of him, his face pink where it was not discoloured and his eyes narrowed to pin-points.

Mr. Campion choked down his growing irritation.

"Since that face of yours is going to create a scandal in the witness-box, anyway, we may as well have the whole truth," he said. "And by the way, next time you go leaping on people in the dark don't lose your head, or you'll find yourself landed with a corpse which has been the victim of a murderous attack. Keeping yourself fit is all very well, but you don't want to turn yourself into a dangerous machine every time you get the wind up."

Mr. Rigget's trembling increased and suddenly, with an effect which was completely unnerving, he began to pray aloud. Mr. Campion took him by the shoulders and shook him.

"Pull yourself together!" he said firmly. "Don't try to mesmerize yourself. You need your brain at the moment. Use it."

Mr. Rigget relaxed cautiously.

"Where are you going to take me?" he demanded.

"Nowhere," said Campion. "We're going to stay here."

Mr. Rigget shuddered and glanced at the strong room.

"Not in there. I'll tell you. I'll tell you everything. I'm not really as bad as I look—at least I am, only I can't help it. Oh, God, I'm so tired!"

Mr. Campion sighed.

"My car's outside," he said. "I'll take you back to the flat."

Peter Rigget seemed agreeable to this suggestion, and they had started down the passage when he remembered

160

the strong-room door and went back to it. To Mr. Campion's intense interest he thrust his hand into his tattered pocket, drew out a slender three-ward key identical with the one which Campion himself had borrowed from Miss Curley's desk, locked the door and returned.

"I'm tired," he said again.

He dropped to sleep in the back of the car, and Campion had to wake him again when they arrived at Bottle Street. Lugg, curious and openly appalled at his employer's condition, went down obligingly to put the car away and Campion and his captive were alone.

In the bright light of Mr. Campion's comfortable room Peter Rigget made a pathetic and embarrassing spectacle. His pince-nez were gone, and his normally thin sensitive nose was no longer thin, and his puffy red wrists stuck out some three inches from his torn shirt-cuffs.

Mr. Campion, who knew a great deal about exhaustion, gave him some food, which he ate eagerly, swallowing great hunks of bread and lump sugar as though he realized instinctively how great was his need of them.

Gradually his unnatural lassitude disappeared, leaving him weary, but otherwise normal. Mr. Campion sat opposite him.

"Still feel like talking?" he enquired pleasantly.

Mr. Rigget looked at the ground. He was young, Campion decided, younger than he had thought; twenty-five or six at the most.

"I'm not a nice chap," he said. "I can't help it. I fight against it, but my instincts are all wrong. I keep letting myself down."

A dreadful sincerity in the statement robbed it of its humour and made it merely embarrassing. Mr. Rigget appeared to be speaking the simple truth from the depths of a resigned rather than a contrite heart.

"I've been educated," he went on, "but it hasn't altered me. I'm a cad. I'm dirty."

"Let's get back to the strong room, shall we?" suggested Mr. Campion gently. "You've got a key, I see."

Mr. Rigget shuddered. "I had it made. It was so easy. They ought not to put temptation in your way like that. I know I'm rotten, but I was tempted. Fancy leaving the key there where anybody could get it! I took it home with me for a week-end in the summer and had another one made. Nobody noticed. Nobody asked any questions. Even the man at the shop believed me when I said it was the key of my own front door. I live with my people. They're very respectable. This is going to break them. They've educated me and made me a better class than they are, and now I've disgraced them."

He spoke sullenly and with a sort of masochistic satisfaction.

"Been using the key pretty regularly?" Mr. Campion enquired.

The young man stirred. "Fairly often. Whenever I could stay behind. There wasn't much in there. I didn't do anything. I didn't take anything. I only turned things over. They didn't keep anything valuable there. It's a sort of junk room."

"What was the idea?" Mr. Campion sounded merely curious, even friendly.

"I'm nasty," said Mr. Rigget, raising very blue eyes bright with tears to his inquisitor's face. "I just wanted to see if there was anything interesting there—something that might be useful. You don't understand me. I'm not ordinary. I'm not decent. I haven't got any instincts against prying into other people's affairs. Most firms are dirty, and I wanted to find out anything I could."

Mr. Campion had an inspiration.

"Like little evasions of income tax?" he suggested.

A secretive, rather repulsive smile appeared on Mr. Rigget's swollen lips.

"Yes," he said. "That's the sort of thing. Only I couldn't find any books or anything. They didn't keep 'em there. I suppose they're in the safe. Or more probably the important ones'd be at the bank," he added gloomily. "You're shocked, aren't you?" He looked at Campion resentfully. "You ought to be if you've got the right instincts. But I'm not. I used to try to be, but I'm not. I'm dirty and mean and low and underhand, and all the things they educate you not to be."

It was all very distressing. Mr. Rigget's excellent accent and obvious misery made him well-nigh unbearable.

"Did you ever get the safe open?" Mr. Campion found himself trying to put the question so casually that it would not sound offensive.

"Oh, no, I didn't touch the safe! That's criminal. I haven't done anything criminal."

Mr. Rigget uttered the word as though it were blasphemous.

"I've had the key in my hand, I admit that, but I've never used it." He writhed in his chair. "I've got a key of the safe, I may as well admit that, but I've never used it. I swear I've never used it! I daren't do anything criminal. I want to, but I'm afraid to. That's the sort of chap I am. I ought never to be in the sort of job I'm in. I'm only educated. I haven't got any instincts."

Mr. Campion realized that he was confronted by a serious modern sociological problem, but he decided that it was far too large to tackle, especially at the moment. He concentrated on the keys. Producing the instrument which Wardie Samson had made "for luck," he handed it to the man whom he was trying not to think of as his victim.

"That's it! Where did you get it? It was in my collar drawer, locked up at home. Mother didn't know it was there, nor did Father, nor did anyone. Oh, God, you've been to them! They know about me. I'll never dare to go home now. I never want to see them again." Peter Rigget trembled on the verge of hysterics.

"This is my key," said Mr. Campion firmly. "It's nothing to do with your key. Pull yourself together."

Mr. Rigget wiped the tears angrily from his eyes and squared his powerful shoulders.

"I give way," he said unexpectedly. "That's weak. That shows I'm all wrong. I've been hiding myself up ever since I was a kid, but it's coming out now. You can't alter your instincts. You are what you are born to be, whatever you learn. If I'd been brave I'd have told what I knew on the Friday night, but I didn't want anybody to know I'd been down there. I was glad," he added, his voice rising. "I was *glad* it had happened, and I knew about it. I was *glad* there was going to be trouble. It made me feel excited and important."

It occurred to Mr. Campion that what Mr. Rigget really

needed was some sort of reverse process of psychoanalysis. To know the truth about oneself, if it were both unpleasant and incurable, must be a variety of hell, he decided. He became quite sorry for him, but there was obviously much to be learnt.

"When you say the Friday night, was that the evening after Mr. Brande disappeared?"

Mr. Rigget nodded. "I got a fright when I saw him. Afterwards I was pleased. I knew he was there, you see. I knew he was there all the week-end."

Mr. Campion sat up, but Mr. Rigget was too engrossed in his own unfortunate reactions to life to notice any added interest in his hearer.

"I stayed behind on Friday. It's easier on Fridays. People go home earlier and don't notice you're hanging about. I shut myself in the washroom with the light out until they'd all gone—I did that tonight, and then I let myself out and unlocked the strong-room door with my own key and went in. I didn't see the body at first. It wasn't by the door where they found it. It was lying crumpled up in a corner beside the safe, hidden from the door by a lot of boxes and things under the table."

He hesitated.

"That's where I got my key of the safe," he explained at last. "It was in the lock and the safe door was open. I thought the key might be useful, so I shut the door and turned it. I was frightened, of course, but I was excited, too. I never liked Mr. Paul."

Mr. Campion sat enthralled. He did not like to break the thread of the story, but at the same time the man's attitude towards his important discovery was incomprehensible.

"You were terrified, I suppose?" he ventured.

"No," said Mr. Rigget. "I wasn't frightened because he was dead—I made sure he *was* dead. I'd have been more frightened if he'd been alive."

He caught Mr. Campion's expression and attempted to excuse himself.

"It wasn't anything to do with me, I hadn't killed him. I didn't think he had been killed then. I thought he'd just fallen down in a fit. I was frightened they'd catch me by the

safe and think I'd opened it. I ought not to have taken the
key of the safe. That's criminal, really. But I didn't use it. I
never used it. I didn't bring it tonight because I thought I
might use it and I wanted to put the temptation behind me.
I took the other key, too," he went on, averting his eyes. "It
was in the lock when I pushed mine in and it fell out on the
floor on the inside. I picked it up and when I went out I put
it back in Miss Curley's desk after I'd locked the door."

"Why on earth did you do that?" Campion demanded
in astonishment.

Mr. Rigget was silent for some seconds and the
sulkiness on his face increased in intensity.

"Well, I thought I ought to leave the door locked in
case someone had tried it earlier in the day and had looked
for the key and found it wasn't there. Then I thought they'd
have to get him out some time, and I thought they'd
probably smash the lock. Then my own key that I'd had
made wouldn't fit any more. I'm mean!" he burst out
passionately. "I do things like that. I'm always thinking of
myself and how to save myself trouble—little petty things
like that."

Mr. Campion's face was very severe.

"Look here," he demanded, "do you realize that Mike
Wedgwood has been arrested and is going to be tried for his
life largely on the evidence that Brande was found dead in a
room locked on the outside? Now, according to your story,
the dead man was in a room locked on the inside. You must
see the difference."

Mr. Rigget shrugged his shoulders. "It wasn't anything
to do with me, as far as I saw. I've told you, I'm selfish, I'm
narrow, I'm mean."

Mr. Campion ignored the last part of his remark.

"You say when you found the body on the Friday night
it was lying in a corner so that no one entering the door
could see it immediately?"

"I didn't see it until I went over to the safe."

"But, good heavens!" exploded Mr. Campion. "Don't
you see, you're corroborating Wedgwood's story? Didn't
you follow the inquest?"

Mr. Rigget leant back in his chair. He looked ex-
hausted.

"It wasn't any affair of mine," he said stubbornly.

"Had you got a grudge against Wedgwood?"

"No." Mr. Rigget's sullenness increased. "I didn't have much to do with him. *I tell you*," he said, his voice breaking, "you think I'm a beastly filthy little twip, don't you? Well, *I am!* That's what I keep telling you. I am and I can't help it. I know I'm being an unspeakable cad not to own up to what I did, to get him off. I know I am: that makes it worse."

"Why did you go back there tonight?"

Mr. Rigget's wretchedness would have been distressing on any less momentous occasion.

"I shall get the sack when the trial's over," he muttered. "You were there that day when I went to Mr. Widdowson and Sir Alexander and told them about the quarrel I'd overheard. They daren't sack me now, but as soon as the trial's over they will—unless I can get something on them first. That's why I was hunting for something that I could use."

"Yes, well," said Mr. Campion, with disgust, "I don't think much of an education which taught you that tampering with a safe was criminal but didn't mention blackmail."

"Oh, it wouldn't be blackmail," murmured Mr. Rigget. "It would only be something I could just mention. All this is going to come out now, isn't it?"

"Some of it'll have to."

"How d'you know I shan't kill myself?" Mr. Rigget spoke cunningly.

Mr. Campion looked at him. "You poor little beast, you might," he murmured. "That's why I'm going to take you over to Scruby immediately."

Mr. Rigget shrank back in his chair.

"I'm a witness for the Crown. You can't tamper with me. You can't persuade me to say anything I don't want to. I've been talking to you as I've never talked to anybody else, but I'm not going to do it in court."

Mr. Campion got up heavily.

"I shouldn't worry so much about coming clean," he said. "Ever heard of Nemesis? Come on."

15
Night Shift

Those who live in that ghostly part of London which is the most crowded square mile by day and the most deserted by night insist that at three o'clock in the morning it is as peaceful as a country churchyard, and that there the black rats dance a leisurely saraband down the centres of the glossy streets.

Mr. Campion's hurrying footsteps made sharp echoes on the pavements as he strode through the unsavoury alley which is Red Lion Passage and came out into the shabby comfort of the square.

Most of the flat houses had been converted into offices long ago. Standing back from the road, they turned blank eyes to the street lamps and only a single brightly lit third-floor window twinkled at him mellowly through the budding plane trees in the dusty centre garden.

He made for it and was rewarded. Ritchie was evidently a man of his word and was sitting up. Having no desire to wake the whole house, Mr. Campion paused on the edge of the pavement and pitched a halfpenny expertly into the centre of the lighted pane.

Immediately a somewhat fantastic silhouette appeared at the sash, waved reassuringly and vanished.

Campion wandered up to the door, and it opened before him with so little delay that he experienced a slight shock of astonishment.

"Slide down the banisters?" he enquired facetiously.

Ritchie did not answer, and Campion, who could not see his face, received the disquieting impression that he was disconcerted. It was a ridiculous incident and passed at once. Ritchie's great hand caught his arm and forced him up

167

the dark staircase of the house which had seen much better days.

"People asleep," his host confided in a whisper which was like a roar of the wind in a turret. "Only kind to be quiet."

It was a long way up, but the older man moved at a great rate and Mr. Campion came thankfully and a trifle breathlessly into the bed-sitting-room which was Ritchie's home.

It was a huge apartment with a very high ceiling, some two feet below which a shelf had been constructed round all four sides of the room. This ledge was the most striking feature of the place, and first caught a visitor's attention, since it evidently contained practically all Mr. Richard Barnabas's worldly possessions. Books, clothes and manuscripts were there stacked together neatly, albeit a trifle dustily, and were, of course, extraordinarily inaccessible.

What furniture the room contained was huddled together along the darkest wall, as though space were restricted. The wash-stand stood at the end of the iron bedstead, rubbing elbows uncomfortably with a minute dressing-table.

The rest of the room was virtually bare, the floor covered with several layers of dusty under-felting. A small gas fire burned in the grate and a single folding armchair was drawn up before it.

"Sit down. Rather stand—sit all day."

A sweeping but completely meaningless gesture of one arm accompanied the hospitality, and Mr. Campion, who was beginning to understand his friend, obeyed meekly.

He was about to drop into the chair when he caught sight of something among the corduroy cushions and retrieved it in some astonishment. It was a spangled black tulle frill which immediately suggested to Mr. Campion a sentimental relic of a lady in tights dancing upon a *fin de siècle* stage.

If he showed surprise it was nothing to the effect the discovery had upon Ritchie. For a moment he stood gaping, utter consternation on his face, and then, whipping the furbelow out of Campion's hand, he thrust it for want of a better hiding place under the pillow on the iron bedstead.

"Never ask," he commanded, bright spots of colour appearing in his thin cheeks and his blue eyes unexpectedly belligerent. "Never ask."

Mr. Campion, who was tired and had by no means recovered from his encounter with the athletic Mr. Rigget, began to wonder if he himself were not a trifle light-headed. However, Ritchie was still regarding him truculently and he hastened to reassure him.

"Of course not," he said, with dignity.

There was a pause, during which Ritchie seated himself upon the floor, tucking his long awkward legs beneath him with extraordinary dexterity. His excitement evaporated and his eyes became mild and friendly, albeit a trifle worried.

Mr. Campion blinked. The vision of a youthful Ritchie and a lady in spangled tights provided a bizarre note in the sober business of the evening and he reflected what an odd, attractive, simple soul his host was. Ritchie glanced at Campion.

"Been fighting?" he observed.

Campion gave him a rough outline of his evening's adventure.

"I roused poor old Scruby and left Rigget with him," he finished at last. "It means a flutter among the legal gents tomorrow, I'm afraid, but that can't very well be helped. The important thing is that the little rat's story contains two pieces of new evidence: one that Paul was murdered, the key being on the inside of the strong-room door, and the other that the body was moved after rigor mortis had passed and probably Mike went down to the strong room on Sunday night."

He paused and Ritchie regarded him owlishly from the ground. Campion continued.

"I rather thought that something like that last had happened when I first heard about the hat. A man doesn't set his hat upon the floor and then lie down carefully beside it to die. But there was no proof, you see. Everything had been so mucked about by the time the police arrived that they were hampered on all sides."

Ritchie nodded his comprehension.

"New evidence important?" he enquired. "Vital? Mean release?"

"Oh, no, I'm afraid not." Mr. Campion succumbed to the impulse to explain things gently to Ritchie. "It'll weaken the case, of course, but Mike must stand his trial. You see, to do everybody justice, Mike is the obvious person to have killed Paul. He had opportunity, he admits going to the garage and starting the car, the shower tube had belonged to him, he had bought and read a book describing the method of murder in detail, and in the police opinion he had a motive."

"Gina?"

Mr. Campion bowed his battered head.

"The degrees of familiarity between the sexes in ordinary social life differ from clique to clique and class to class more than anything else," he pointed out. "It's practically the only subject on which the authorities are consistently muddled. I'm afraid police circles are inclined to be prurient-minded and lawyers worse."

"Understandable," said Ritchie unexpectedly. "Always having unfortunate experiences."

Mr. Campion continued his dissertation.

"That's the positive legal case, roughly. But then there's all the negative evidence, which only counts in the back of people's minds. Someone killed Paul, someone killed him intentionally and ingeniously. That someone apparently killed him between six in the evening, when the office went home, and nine in the same evening, when Mike turned off his engine and both Mrs. Tripper and my new friend Widgeon noticed the noise had ceased. That someone had access to either Twenty-three or Twenty-one, because it was only through either of these houses that the car could be reached. That someone either knew that Paul would be in the strong room at that particular time or inveigled him into the place. That someone knew of the hose pipe and therefore also knew the back entrance at Twenty-one. The only people who could have known and done all these things are Mike, you, Gina, John, Curley and the janitor— or possibly Paul himself, although it seems an idiotic way to commit suicide. And, anyway, in that case who moved the body?"

"Might be others," said Ritchie dubiously. "If Rigget stayed behind why not others? Girl Netley. Rigget himself. Anyone in the office?"

"Well, let's hope so," said Mr. Campion cheerfully. "Otherwise Mike and Gina are very unfortunately placed. Everyone else has an alibi."

He leant back in his chair and removed his spectacles as Ritchie's eyes watched his face.

"Miss Curley left the office on the Thursday evening at half past five and went to Peter Robinson's to have her hair shampooed. She left there at six and hurried on to the cocktail party which Mike should have attended in Manchester Square. At seven-thirty she left and went on to dinner at Rule's with Miss Betcherley of Blenheim's literary agency, and at eight-fifty she caught a Tube train to Hammersmith."

He paused and smiled.

"Then there's you. You left the office early and came back here, where you collected your landlord——"

"Landlady's husband," corrected Ritchie in the interests of strict accuracy.

"—And went to the circus at Olympia," continued Mr. Campion imperturbably, "where you stayed until ten-thirty. John left his office at five and went to his club, where he was recognized and where he had a business interview. He returned to his flat and dressed for the evening with his usual deliberation and attention to detail. His housekeeper waited upon him the whole time. At seven-forty he went off in a taxi to the Dorchester for the Quill Club dinner, at which he spent the evening. The janitor left the office at six sharp and went off with some pals to the Holborn Empire. In fact, everyone behaved normally except Mike, who went walking, an exercise he hardly ever takes."

His voice died away and he regarded Ritchie steadily.

"Do you realize," he demanded suddenly, "that whoever killed Paul must have stood by and let that car pump gas into the strong room for at least an hour, probably an hour and a half? It wouldn't take long to put Paul under, of course, but the murderer must have gone on with the treatment for some considerable time to make sure of death. That's why these alibis are so very convincing."

Ritchie was silent. He sat upon his feet, rocking gently before the fire, his eyes hidden.

171

"No motives," he murmured almost, it seemed to Mr. Campion, regretfully. "No motives either."

"All the same," Campion put in hastily, "it's not a strong case against Mike, and all that row the Coroner came in for will prejudice both Judge and Jury in his favour. He's almost certain to get off."

Ritchie shook his head gloomily.

"Not good enough. Stigma all his life. In love—can't marry. Poor fellow!"

He was quiet for a full minute, his huge bony hands twitching in little indeterminate gestures. Suddenly he sat up and Campion was surprised by the purpose and vigour in his tone.

"Got to prove who did it. Only way. Where now?"

Mr. Campion glanced at his watch. It was a quarter past four.

"I came to get your key to Twenty-three again," he said. "I'm going to burgle the safe. Like to come?"

"Yes," he said simply, and Campion grinned at him, despite his weariness.

They accomplished their short eerie walk without mishap and let themselves in through the big Queen Anne door at Twenty-three during that darkest moment of the night when the street lamps suddenly go out half an hour before the dawn.

"Can see in the dark," Ritchie remarked unexpectedly as he piloted Campion across the pitch-black hall to the top of the basement stairs. "Not like day, of course, but fairly well. Ten steps down to the landing and then twelve."

They reached the strong-room door and Campion unlocked it with Mr. Rigget's cherished key. There was something ghostly about the chaotic little apartment, and Mr. Campion found his mind, which was not used to such fancies, dwelling upon the crumpled body which had lain for so many hours among the dusty boxes by the safe and on the murderer who must have returned and dragged the helpless thing out to the clear space by the door at a time when the ravages of death were beginning to show.

There was no sign of Mr. Rigget's activities. His little inquisitions had been performed with the greatest discretion. Campion turned his attention to the safe and was glad that Lugg was not with him to express an opinion on a firm which entrusted anything of value to such an antiquated contraption. Ritchie divined his thoughts.

"Cupboard really," he observed apologetically. "Safe cupboard. Valuables at the bank."

Mr. Campion inserted the squat key which Mr. Samson had made for luck and mastered within a minute or two the simple arrangement of turns and half turns which shot back extremely heavy bolts. The door, which must have weighed a quarter of a ton at the lowest estimation, swung back, and Mr. Campion and Ritchie peered into the steel recess within.

At first sight the contents were not enlightening. Two or three half-calf ledgers, two small notebooks containing addresses, and a file of letters were neatly arranged upon the lower shelf. And that was all, save for a package neatly wrapped in green baize and tied with pink tape.

Mr. Campion took it out carefully and unpacked it on the table which Mike had cleared to receive Paul's body. Inside the baize wrapping was a well-made blue leather case designed to look like a book and very beautifully gilded. Examination proved that it had no lock, but pulled out in two pieces like a card-case and contained a slender manuscript.

"*Gallivant*," Ritchie remarked, looking over Campion's shoulder. "Never examined it. Uncle Jacoby Barnabas very strict. Thought it indecent. Would have destroyed it but for the value. John carries on tradition. Probably dull."

Campion turned back the thin octavo sheets, which were unbound save for the faded ribbon tied about the centre of the bundle. The brown ink made a spidery but decipherable pattern on the soft rag paper. He read a line or two.

> "*Gagewell:* '*O Sir, since Lady Frippet hath a bee*
> *in her bonnet, you must allow if the*
> *bee's not a queen the bonnet is at least*
> *à la mode.*'"

"Clean bit," said Ritchie, with that complete simplicity which was the mainspring of his personality. "Nothing to help us there. Valuable, of course. Wrote it himself, in his own hand. Insured. Stands at twenty thousand pounds in the balance-sheet."

Mr. Campion raised his eyebrow.

"Along with the office freehold and the printing plant at Gravesend?" he suggested.

"That's right," the older man agreed. "Best place for it. Never liked the classics. Put it away."

Campion was some little time repacking the treasure, and Ritchie wandered over to the safe.

"Nothing else," he observed, without turning round. "What are we looking for?"

"Whatever it was that made Paul go to the trouble of getting a key to the safe made for him," Campion explained as he tied the pink tape round the green baize once more and stowed it away in the safe. "There's only one official key to this elegant invention, I suppose. Who keeps it?"

"Head of the firm," said Ritchie. "Another tradition. Explains why there's nothing much kept in it."

"I see. That means that John had the original key?" Ritchie considered.

"Probably Curley," he said at last. "One or the other. Only a fetish."

Mr. Campion took off his spectacles and perched himself on the edge of the table.

"It seems very careless to keep *The Gallivant* there," he began. "I should have thought the insurance johnnies might have objected to a thing like that."

Ritchie's eyes clouded.

"Ought to go back to the bank," he agreed. "Fact is, this dreadful business—death, murder, trial, and so on— has probably put the whole thing out of their minds. Very likely they haven't been down here since. Can't blame them."

"Oh, it's usually kept at the bank, is it?" said Campion, pricking up his ears. "When was it put in here? Do you know?"

Ritchie's discomfort increased.

"Before Christmas. Silly business. Curley annoyed. Couldn't really blame her."

Mr. Campion was patient. Ritchie's cryptogrammic

replies were tantalizing, and he was thankful for everybody's sake that the well-meaning, inarticulate soul had not been subpœnaed for the morrow's trial.

After a certain amount of persuasion Ritchie amplified his story.

"Nothing in it," he said wretchedly. "Paul made an ass of himself over *The Gallivant*. Wanted to lend it to raremanuscript exhibition. Up against tradition at once. Grand old firm's vulgar classic. Wouldn't do. Old-fashioned. Stupid. But John and Curley had last word. Paul not content—silly fellow. Tried to get it from bank manager. Being partner, succeeded. Curley saw messenger who brought it. Went to John. John furious, backed her up. *Gallivant* put in safe."

Mr. Campion was bewildered. It seemed incredible that such a little domestic quarrel in the firm could have any connection with the grave issues at stake. He was silent for some moments, considering. John, he knew, had a fanatical pride in the honour of the firm; Miss Curley might easily have hidden depths of prudery; and Paul certainly seemed to have made a nuisance of himself all round. But compared with the scandal which had burst about their ears the public burning of *The Gallivant* by the police—an eventuality, after all, unlikely, since authors dead over a hundred years are permitted great license on the principle, no doubt, that their work has had time to air—would have been negligible, unless——? An idea occurred to him and he looked up, a startled expression in his pale eyes.

"Look here, I'll have to wander off now, Ritchie," he said. "I've been rather late for the bus all along, but I believe I'm catching up with it now. I shan't be down at the Old Bailey at the beginning this morning, but I'll come along later. Keep an eye on Gina, but don't tell her anything."

"No," said Ritchie, with the obedience of a child, and Campion, looking at him affectionately, wondered how much of the mystery about him he saw and what, if anything, he thought of it.

It was half past six on a cold spring morning, with drizzle in the air, when they parted, and Mr. Campion went home to bathe and shave, since it was too early to begin his day's business. He also took the opportunity to submit himself to a patching process, of which Mr. Lugg was a past master. The spectacle of that mournful figure, clad solely in a pair of trousers, standing upon a bath mat at seven-thirty in the morning, a minute pair of surgical scissors in one enormous hand and an even smaller strip of sticking-plaster in the other, was one of those experiences that Mr. Campion frankly enjoyed.

He was sorry that they were not on conversational terms. Mr. Lugg was the victim of a two-way complex. His newer self revolted at the unpleasant publicity with which he saw his employer's name surrounded as the trial progressed, while his elder spirit was deeply hurt that Campion should have enjoyed a scrap in which he had not been permitted to take part.

"There you are," he said at last, stepping back from his handiwork. "Now I've wasted my time on you making you look like a gent again, go and smear yourself with society filth. Roll in it like a dawg—but don't ask me to clean yer. Mud sticks closer than them patches I've put on your dial."

"Mud of the soul?" enquired Mr. Campion affably.

"You know what I mean," said Lugg warningly. "And if we 'ad that charwoman I've ben thinking of I'd drive 'ome me contemp' in the way I was brought up to, even if I 'ave learnt spittin's not quite the thing."

Mr. Campion dressed in silence. At nine o'clock he was waiting outside the door of a little office on the third floor of a building in St. Martin's Lane.

Ex-Detective-Inspector Beth found him there when he came heavily up the stairs to open the little private enquiry office he had established on his retirement.

"Can't get my assistant to turn up before half past, Mr. Campion," he explained as he unlocked the door. "My word, if I had him in the Force for half an hour!"

He paused, enquiry on his round good-natured face.

"Surely *we* can't do anything for you, can we? Well, well, I thought they even took in your laundry work down at the Yard these days."

"Working a little light humour into the act, I see," said his visitor approvingly. "'Divorce with a laugh' and 'Blackmail made fun'? It's not a bad idea. However, unfortunately, there's nothing very amusing about the small commission I am about to entrust to you at the moment. It is merely odd."

He took a limp brown bank book from his pocket and, opening it, entered into some careful instructions. The ex-inspector was puzzled.

"If it was a case of impersonation—someone taking it out—I could understand it," he said. "But who cares who pays money in?"

"I do," said Mr. Campion, who was very tired. "I'm a very proud young fellow, and I like to know where my money's coming from."

Beth turned the book over.

"Since when have you been called Dora Phyllis Netley?" he enquired suspiciously.

Campion leant forward confidentially.

"You must let a man have his secrets," he murmured. "Get on to it and let me have a report tonight."

"Tonight? What do you think we are?" protested his host.

"Private and enterprising. I read it on the door," said Mr. Campion, and hurried away.

It was just after ten when he reached the British Museum, and he paused for a moment at the foot of the great soot-stained granite flight of steps to feel in his breast pocket. His weariness was making him absent-minded, and just for a moment he could not remember if on changing his clothes he had slipped into his pocket a wallet containing a page of *The Gallivant* which he had stolen so shamelessly from beneath Ritchie's very nose. It was here, however, and he went on thankfully.

Time at the Museum is given the treatment it deserves from the custodians of the treasure of historic man, and Mr. Campion's godfather, Professor Bunney, did not arrive until late, so that the morning was considerably advanced when the tall pale young man in the horn-rimmed spectacles at last came out between the granite columns.

Mr. Campion walked slowly, accustoming himself to an idea. His godfather had been most helpful and he now knew without a possibility of doubt that the manuscript of *The Gallivant* in the blue leather box, which was insured for twenty thousand pounds and appeared in the balance-sheet of the famous firm of Barnabas, Limited as representing that sum, was certainly not, however genuine its contents might be, penned by the hand of Wm. Congreve, Dec. 1729, nor was the paper on which it was written manufactured one year earlier than 1863.

16

The Fourth Chair

One of the unexpected things about the Central Criminal Court at the Old Bailey is that it is perfectly new. The carving above the Judge's chair, where the great sword hangs, is not an old carving, and the light oak of the contraption so like a Punch and Judy show, which is the witness-box, is not worn by the nervous hands of a thousand testators but retains some of the varnished brightness of the cabinet-maker's shop.

This newness might perhaps destroy some of the court's undeniable impressiveness were it not for one significant difference between this particular new room and others of the time.

Here ancient things have been replaced not by copies vulgarly disguised to appear old, nor yet by new things different in design and purpose from the old out of deference to the changing manners and customs which have altered the surface of life during the past five hundred years, but by new things replacing those worn out in a room where customs and manners do not change and where the business conducted is not concerned with the surface but with that deeply set, unchangeable streak embedded in the rock of civilization which is crime.

Miss Curley sat beside Gina in the block of seats at the back of the court which is reserved for witnesses and, looking about her, wondered if Mike had been properly fed in Pentonville.

The two women were wedged in a corner some three rows from the front. Gina, at Cousin Alexander's hinted instigation, had succeeded in making herself look almost dowdy. Certainly she appeared very young and very tragic, the high collar of her black coat shadowing her pale, distinctive face.

Immediately before them in the well of the court was the enormous dock, looking as large as and not at all unlike a very superior sheep pen in a country market.

Three chairs, the one in the middle a little in front of the others and directly facing the judicial desk, stood lonely and inadequate in the midst of the expanse.

Beyond was Counsels' table, already littered with papers and glasses of water, with the jury and witness-boxes and the Press table on its left and the solicitors' table and the bank of expert witnesses on its right.

Farther away still were the clerks' desks, directly beneath the dais and facing into the well.

Last of all was the Bench itself.

The seven chairs on the dais were equidistant and all very much alike, since the Lord Mayor and Aldermen of London are entitled to sit. They each had high leather backs emblazoned with the city arms and managed to look impressive even when unoccupied.

The fourth chair fascinated Miss Curley. It stood between the carved columns, the state sword, hilt downward, immediately above it, while before it, at the wide desk, a little clerk was arranging sheaves of paper.

The court was full of people. The witness benches were crammed and the public gallery over the solicitors' table seemed in danger of bursting and jettisoning its load into the dock. Press and solicitors' tables were full and junior counsel and the clerks were clustering round their own headquarters. Everyone was talking. Men in gowns hurried to and fro with papers, their shoes squeaking noisily on the wood. Now and again a late arrival was thrust into a seat in the witness benches by a fatherly official clad in what appeared to be some sort of police uniform augmented by a beadle's gown.

The jury, ten men and two women, looked on at the preparations like an absurdly small audience at an amateur theatrical show which had got completely out of hand and swamped the auditorium. They looked apprehensive and painfully uncomfortable and the foreman, an elderly man with pince-nez and a bald head, mopped his face repeatedly although the morning was inclined to be cold.

John sat at the solicitors' table oddly in the picture, his round head held slightly on one side and his long thin neck sticking stiffly out of his elegant grey collar.

Ritchie was behind Gina and his expression of frightened disgust as he noticed each new evidence of human bondage was pathetic or comic according to the onlooker's fancy. He showed no signs of fatigue, but his gentle eyes were anxious and his enormous bony hands fidgeted on his knees.

Among the legal broiling circulating round the court with a familiarity which proclaimed it their own fishpond there was a certain amount of pleasurable anticipation. A *cause célèbre* at the Old Bailey is bound to have its moments. The Lord Chief Justice, Lord Lumley, affectionately called "Lor Lumme" by his admirers in the best legal, police and criminal circles, still preserved sufficient humanity in his omnipotence to lose his temper on occasions and there was a persistent rumour, utterly unfounded, that he cherished a personal antipathy towards Sir Alexander Barnabas.

Then, in accordance with the custom at poisoning trials at the Old Bailey, the Attorney-General himself, Sir Montague Brooch, was appearing for the Crown and was leading Sir Andrew Phelps, with Jerome Fyshe and Eric Battersby as juniors.

There were rumors of last-minute trouble with important witnesses and altogether the prospects looked good.

Gina sat trembling.

"I'm going to see him—I'm going to see him—I'm going to see him—I'm going to see him——"

The words made a singsong pattern completely without meaning in her brain, neither conveying nor expressing any thought at all, but providing a deadening chatter which prevented her from thinking.

Miss Curley sat forward, straining her eyes to see Counsels' table. Something was happening and she could see flickers of amusement appearing on dark faces beneath blue-white periwigs.

A clerk entered, laden with an assortment of paraphernalia which he proceeded to arrange. First a dark cushion was placed carefully on a chair, then a portfolio laid reverently on the table and round it a little ring of oddments carefully set out. Miss Curley discerned a pile of exquisite cambric handkerchiefs, a bottle of smelling salts, another of sal volatile, a box of throat pastilles and a glass of water.

There was a long pause. The clerk stepped back and gazed expectantly at the doorway behind him. His interest was not unnaturally echoed by those about him and finally, when everyone in the court was aware that somebody of importance was about to enter, a little door swung open, there was a rustle of an old silk gown, a glimpse of a grey-blue wig, and then, looking like a middle-aged Apollo in fancy dress, Cousin Alexander swept up to the table and sat down.

Miss Curley waited for the Attorney-General and, disappointed, had allowed her eyes to wander back to Cousin Alexander and away again before she suddenly caught sight of him at the same table and wondered if he had been there all the time.

The big hand of the court clock reached the half hour and there was a sudden silence, followed by a mighty rustle as everybody rose. The door on the right of the dais opened and an old gentleman in red appeared.

The squad of wigs bowed, looking slightly comic as black, brown and even pink heads appeared for an instant beneath the queues as necks were bent.

The Judge returned the bow as he settled himself, not in the fourth chair beneath the sword but in the one beside it, and the untidy little clerk rearranged his papers. The position brought him nearer the jury and the witness-box and farther from Counsel, and the change was probably pure pernicketiness and the desire to break the symmetry of the design.

The Lord Chief Justice, Lord Lumley, was a large old

man with the drooping jowls and bald bony eyesockets of a bloodhound. His upper lip was shaven but he affected a square of close-clipped white hair about as big as a piece of confetti in the centre of his lower one, which gave him a slightly sporting appearance. He was over seventy and forced from time to time to use eyeglasses, which he wore on a wide black ribbon.

As he sat in his high leather chair his scarlet robe fell sleekly with deep wine-coloured shadows over his heavy form, and his square wig, which was brown and inclined to look as though it were made of the bristles usually fashioned into carpet brooms, overshadowed his face.

In his hand he held a formal bouquet, the nosegay dating from the time when the air of the courtroom was not so hygienic as modern cleanliness has made it and a handful of flowers and herbs was at least some barrier between a fastidious gentleman and the plague.

After a pause, he seemed to remember it suddenly, for he leant forward and placed it carefully in the tumbler of water on his desk, where it stood for the remainder of the day looking like a motif from a Tudor tapestry or a chapter end for *Alice in Wonderland*.

Meanwhile there was a whispering hush over the room, and presently, from somewhere below the court, the sound of a door banging heralded the arrival of the prisoner.

Gina was unfamiliar with the geography of the place and Mike's sudden appearance from the well staircase in the bottom right-hand corner of the dock almost unnerved her. He came up slowly between two warders, whose care of him was that of hospital attendants. They were both square, short-legged men, considerably his senior, and they patted him and murmured what must have been encouraging words as he towered above them in the vast and shining sheep pen below the dome.

Miss Curley caught her breath. She had not seen him since his arrest and was unprepared for the change in him. He did not look particularly ill. His features were finer and his pallor made his eyes look darker, but his crisp shorn head was grey and, as he stood facing the Judge with his back directly to her, she saw the wide bones of his shoulders hunched under his coat.

She stole a glance at Gina. The girl was crying, angry, indignant tears hovering on the fringe of her lashes, and Miss Curley, who was liable to unexpected flashes of feminine intuition, realized that, whatever her other thoughts and emotions might be, Gina wept because his hair was grey.

She looked away abruptly. An entirely new personality had taken charge of the proceedings. The Clerk, who until now had been just another dark-faced, grey-wigged person sitting at a desk directly beneath the Judge's dais, had risen to his feet and revealed himself to be an unexpectedly distinguished man with a deep, cultured voice and a casual manner which robbed his words of their formality without over-emphasizing their meaning.

"Michael Wedgwood, you are charged for that you, on the twenty-eighth day of January, nineteen thirty-one, at London, murdered Paul Redfern Brande. You are also charged on a Coroner's inquisition with murder. How say you, Michael Wedgwood? Are you guilty or not guilty?"

As the last word left his lips he sat down again with a great rustle of papers and there was a pause until one of the wardens nudged his prisoner gently.

"Not guilty."

Mike's voice was unexpectedly loud and infused a note of tension into the friendly, businesslike atmosphere of the court. He remained upon his feet while the Clerk turned his attention to the business of swearing in the jury, and Lord Justice Lumley raised that part of his face where his left eyebrow should have been and remarked affably:

"You may sit down. The only time you have to stand in this court is when you are receiving sentence or when I address you."

He had a pleasant rumbling voice with a slight squeak in it at commas, which did nothing to detract from the magnificent oddity of his appearance or his unshakable dignity which clothed him as surely as his robe.

The jury being sworn, a proceeding conducted with the neatness and efficiency of a first-class acrobatic turn, the Clerk addressed them as they sat wriggling before him, twelve busy citizens with troubles enough of their own.

He sat down at last and bent over his desk and, while

Miss Curley trembled, the Attorney-General rose to open the case for the prosecution.

Montague Brooch was a little crow of a man. His silk gown enveloped him and his wig gave his face an even sharper, beakier appearance than it possessed without it. In repose he was inclined to look insignificant, and few would remark him, if even for his ugliness, but the moment he opened his mouth he became a personality that was as unforgettable as it was utterly charming.

"May it please Your Lordship, Members of the Jury——"

The voice was virile yet confiding, attractive, deferential and pleasing in the extreme.

"—the charge against the prisoner, as you have heard, is murder. I must, I am afraid, open to you with a story of considerable detail, and, while it is not without its difficulties, it must, I think, show a very serious case indeed against the prisoner."

For the first time since the arrival of Cousin Alexander upon the scene Miss Curley felt genuinely afraid. Until now she had accepted John's valuation of the famous man without question and had allayed all her qualms for Mike's eventual safety by a recollection of that handsome, sanguine figure with the face of a hero and the confidence of a Harley Street specialist. But here was a real adversary. Cousin Alexander's charm was definable and all the more vulnerable because of it, but the personality of Montague Brooch was not capable of analysis and had a disconcerting habit of confusing itself with clear and reasoned argument, so that it was his thought and not the man one most remembered.

Miss Curley glanced at John now and saw him sitting forward in his chair, his head held on one side and his cold eyes fixed unwaveringly upon the little crow with the sweet voice who spoke so convincingly, and at the same time somehow so regretfully, of the crime. There was no way of telling his thought but Miss Curley fancied that he was disconcerted.

Behind her Ritchie was breathing heavily and down in the other witness benches she caught a glimpse of Mrs. Austin's broad back and untidy hair.

"... *Now what happens on the Sunday night? On January the thirty-first you will hear that quite fortuitously, and when in the company of friends, the accused is asked to go down to the room where, it is the Crown's case, he knew the body lay*. ..."

To Gina the Attorney-General was just a voice repeating facts she already knew and had heard proved over and over again until their significance was lost upon her.

To her the one reality was Mike himself, sitting directly in front of her. She could see his grey head and the short hairs at the nape of his neck and her throat contracted until the pain of it alone seemed sufficient to suffocate her.

There was not complete silence in the court while the speech went on. To Miss Curley's surprise there seemed to be no rule against whispering, and clerks, with great armfuls of papers and noisy shoes, tiptoed about.

Cousin Alexander, looking tremendously important and more handsome than any man over fifty has any right to be in his immaculate wig and bands, was rustling his papers, conferring with his juniors and polishing his glasses with a great flourish of the topmost handkerchief.

"... *Let me take the next stage. Doctor Ferdie arrives. He agrees with Doctor Roe as to the cause of death and together these two men make a very careful autopsy*. ..."

The delightful voice played over the unpleasant words, giving them just sufficient emphasis. Miss Curley found herself listening with detached interest. At the inquest the central figure had been the dead man but here Mike had taken his place and the story was told afresh from a new angle.

It occurred to Miss Curley, who had known Paul and had been amused by him, that he was easily the least important person in the whole story and that his personality alone did not emerge in the dreadful résumé of the manner of his dying. She could not see the public gallery and even if she had been able she would not have recognized Teddie Dell.

"... *Inspector Tanner visited the strong room, where you have heard the body lay, and, after making a careful survey of the room and its environs, discovered a most ingenious device, of which he will tell you. . . ."*

Miss Curley, having located Doctors Ferdie and Roe in the benches behind the solicitors' table, was looking about for Inspector Tanner in the seats behind her when a large elderly man at her side turned round and, seeing her placid friendly face, whispered huskily:

"Makes you think, don't he? I remember him in a stuff gown."

Miss Curley gave the remark the conventional smile it needed and wondered who he was. There were a great many people in the benches whom she had never seen before and next time the stranger confided his admiration of Counsel to her with a muttered, "What a way with him!" she ventured to whisper back.

"Are you a witness?"

"No. Come in to watch."

He did not volunteer any information concerning the method by which he had obtained a seat and Miss Curley eyed his pleasant face, whose only striking feature was enormous eyebrows, covertly and reflected that it was difficult to generalize and that he was not at all the type she would have suspected of morbid curiosity.

Meanwhile, Sir Montague had spoken for the best part of an hour and his gentle voice was apologizing to Judge and Jury.

". . . I have little more to say now. You will hear in detail every part of the tragic and abominable story I have outlined to you. But there are a few points which I should like to put into your minds at this stage. It is usual to look for a motive in any crime and, although in this case you will not find a motive which you, or I, I hope, would think adequate, I think you will see that it is more than possible that the accused had a motive sufficient for him. I must admit to you that the Crown has no direct evidence of immoral relations between the murdered man's wife and the accused. It may be that when you see Mrs. Brande you will decide that she is not the sort of woman whose principles are those which would permit her to stoop to that sort of irregularity, but you will hear on her own submission that she was a neglected wife, and the accused has admitted in

his statement, which I have read to you, that he was in the habit of spending much of his time with her and that in fact at the very moment when, as I shall prove to you, her husband was lying dead in a basement room in the house next door, he took her to a cinema, bringing her back afterwards to the flat which she shared with her husband and returning immediately, I have no doubt, to his own home in the same building.

"You will also hear from Mrs. Austin, the honest woman who attended to Mrs. Brande's household work, of the scene which she witnessed when the accused came to break the news of Paul Brande's death to Mrs. Brande.

"Mrs. Austin came into the room to find them on the hearth rug, 'clinging together,' as she so graphically puts it. You may feel that this is not evidence of immoral relations and I would reiterate that the Crown does not allege immoral relations, but it does insist that there was deep friendship between the accused and Mrs. Brande, dating over a period of some years and increasing in intensity as Mrs. Brande's husband increased in his neglect.

"At what point, if any, a deep affection cherished by a young and virile man for a beautiful and virtuous woman some years his junior may grow into an overwhelming passion, in the grip of which his moral fibre is broken down utterly, it is for you to consider. The Crown is not dealing with conjecture. The Crown merely contends that a deep affection was entertained by the accused for Mrs. Brande.

"Mrs. Brande will tell you that she had visited a solicitor some days before her husband's death and had learned from him that there was no way open to her to obtain a divorce save through her husband's cruelty or through his co-operation. She will also tell you that the accused knew nothing of this, and indeed that he had no idea that any such project had entered her head. You must believe what you see to be the truth. If you believe that a deep friendship existed between these two you may think that it is improbable, even impossible, that any woman should keep such an important matter from such an intimate friend who saw her every day. If there was nothing but friendship between them, why should she hide it? If

there was more, might it not have been even at the accused's suggestion that she approached the solicitor?

"However, you will hear that Mr. Brande would not consider a divorce and that it was to discuss this very matter, and to make his strong views known to his wife, that he had arranged to meet her on the very evening that he met his death, an appointment which he never kept. . . ."

Miss Curley stirred in her seat. Gina was rigid, her cheeks pallid and her lips compressed. A woman in the gallery craned her neck to catch a glimpse of her.

Gradually the speech came to an end. The Attorney-General's voice had never lost its gentle and impartial reasonableness and now it became even more soothing, even more deferential, than before.

"It has been necessary to address you at this length because you must know exactly what the facts are in this story, the burden of which the Crown will attempt to prove. If you feel, as I feel you must, that the evidence leads you to the conclusion beyond all reasonable doubt that this man, in order to marry his cousin's wife, did kill his cousin on the night of January the twenty-eighth in this year, you will have no hesitation in doing your duty.

"If, however, you find there is insufficient direct evidence to make you so sure, and that you have a reasonable doubt, then again you will have no hesitation in doing your duty.

"The case is a difficult one. All the Crown will do is to set out the facts on which you must rely. This is not a case in which you will be concerned with any possible verdicts such as manslaughter. A murder has been done and it is for you to decide if it was committed by the accused. If it was, if the Crown proves to you, as I believe it will, that this man did what he is charged with doing, then it is a crime utterly foul and unpardonable. His cousin had done him no wrong. At worst he had neglected his own wife. And yet, if you so find it, he sent him slowly and insidiously to his death with a callousness which no rigour of the law can equal.

"If you think it is fairly proved against this man that he so murdered his cousin, then it will be your duty to send him to his account."

He paused, bowed to the Judge, and sat down.

And then, while the court was still tingling, a police

photographer bobbed up in the Punch and Judy witness-box, and began to testify as to photographs taken in connection with the crime.

A surveyor had taken his place and was painfully describing the survey of the ground floors and garden of Twenty-three and Twenty-one which he had made, and had produced plans and had sworn to them, when Miss Curley's neighbour turned to her.

"Shan't come back. Nothing more of interest today. Fireworks tomorrow," he confided in a warm whisper. "They'll adjourn in a minute."

"Adjourn?" murmured Miss Curley, who already saw Mike on the scaffold. "What for?"

Her neighbour gaped at her as at a lunatic.

"Lunch, of course," he said.

17

Mr. Campion's Case for the Defence

Ritchie was standing in the huge multi-coloured marble hall at the Old Bailey, which had the smell of a public library and was full of people who talked together with that peculiar excited anxiety almost always reserved for other people's troubles, when Mr. Campion found him and led him to one side.

He was obviously shaken by the experience of the morning and it was some time before Campion, who was tired, could be sure that he was getting his full attention.

"There won't be anything more of interest today," Campion repeated slowly and with emphasis. "I want you to come away with me now and give me a hand. It's important."

"Leave the court?" said Ritchie, his gentle eyes blinking at his friend.

"Yes, if you would." Mr. Campion was very patient. "I've seen Sir Alexander and Miss Curley will look after Gina. Are you coming?"

The sweet air, or it may have been the sweet freedom, of Newgate Street, revived Ritchie's powers of speech. He strode along to the car park talking with what was for him lucidity and volubility.

"Awful, Campion!" he shouted. "Ghastly! Jolly things like fancy dress, boxes for seats, coloured robes and policemen all made horrible and frightening. Like a serious harlequinade. Mike's grey. Hair's grey. Two men in delightful clothes arguing for his life. Like a game . . . rules . . . places to stand. Felt ill. Sick. Wanted to spew. Frightened, Campion."

The young man in the horn-rimmed spectacles was silent. The project he had in hand was a delicate one and he required co-operation. It seemed to him best in the circumstances to allow Ritchie's startled wits to reassort themselves without assistance.

As they climbed into the car and waited to slip out into the slothful stream of traffic Ritchie sighed and shook himself.

"Like a dream," he said. "Absurd, like a dream. They'll hang him, Campion. That fellow with the voice is cleverer than Cousin Alexander. That's what counts."

By the time they reached Ludgate Hill he was better and his companion, recognizing in him a worried edition of his normal self, thought it safe to broach the subject in hand.

"You get on very well with Mrs. Peel, don't you?" he enquired.

"John's housekeeper? Known her for years. Nice old body. Why?"

"She doesn't like me," explained Campion regretfully. "She didn't like to trust me in the flat. Afraid I was going to pinch the ormolu clock with the china figures. That's why I had to come and get hold of you."

He paused and concentrated on his driving, wondering how far Ritchie's perception would lead him and with what results.

The elder man did not seem to perceive at all. He

acquiesced quietly as they drove on in silence. It was warm and sunny when they arrived at the cul-de-sac and Twenty-one seemed to be deserted. Twenty-three was not closed but there was little sign of activity and the Morris sign of the Golden Quiver swung disconsolately in the light breeze.

"Mrs. Peel," remarked Mr. Campion as he sprang out of the car and came round to help Ritchie with the door, whose simple mechanism had defeated him, "thinks I am (A) a thief and (B) the police. You are coming with me to dispel both these delusions. Do you think you can do it?"

"Dear good intelligent woman." Ritchie observed, apparently in answer to the question. "Kind. Always liked her."

She stood in the dark entrance hall of John's flat when they presented themselves at the door a few minutes later and surveyed them with belligerent beady eyes, like some large elderly beetle surprised in its tree-trunk home.

She had a harsh unpleasing voice and when she said, "Back again?" Mr. Campion could not help feeling some of the shame which she intended to stir in him.

Ritchie stood looking at her helplessly for a moment and then, either by accident or design, achieved a master-stroke.

"No lunch. Peely . . . cocoa . . . bread and butter . . . anything," he murmured. "Campion and me, tired, hungry, want to sit down."

Mrs. Peel led the way into the dining room, grumbling as she went. Her brown serge dress hitched at the back, revealing untidy ankles, but her sparse hair was groomed and dressed to a neatness which suggested that each separate strand knew its duty in emergency and was determined to make up for its scarcity of companions.

As they sat waiting for food at the heavy mahogany table in the dark book-lined room with the thick curtains and half-drawn venetian blinds, Mr. Barnabas made a very curious remark.

"Pity about the food, Campion. Know how you feel. Old shibboleth, though. Couldn't be helped."

Mr. Campion's eyebrows rose and he shot his friend a single penetrating glance which completely destroyed for an instant the habitual vacuity of his expression, but Ritchie said no more and presently rose from his chair and opened a window, which Mrs. Peel promptly closed as soon as she returned with bread, butter, Gorgonzola and two cups of weak unpalatable cocoa.

"That two grown men with money in their pockets can't look after their creature comforts in a town of this size is extraordinary," she remarked angrily but as she looked only at Ritchie as she spoke Mr. Campion realized with relief that he was accepted, if ignored.

He even ate the horrible meal, Mrs. Peel waiting upon him as if he had been a six-year-old, buttering his bread and cutting him small chunks of odoriferous cheese.

"Been to the trial," Ritchie mumbled into his cocoa cup.

Mrs. Peel made an indignant sound like a French railway engine.

"That murder! I never heard such utter nonsense in all my born days. It was an accident. Mr. John told me so himself."

"Were you here on the night it happened?" Mr. Campion ventured.

The woman turned round and looked at him.

"Well, of all the questions!" she exclaimed. "Of course I was. What are you trying to insinuate? That I was turning on the gas in the office? No. I was in this flat the whole time. At four o'clock I began to lay out Mr. John's clothes and when he came in at five-thirty I went to my room and sat with the door open, so that I could hear when he called me."

"And did he call you?"

Mr. Campion's face expressed polite interest.

"Of course he did," she said impatiently. "If Mr. John could dress by himself I should think he was ill. He called me to turn on the bath and when it was ready I told him so and went back to my room."

Campion was silent for some time and his eyes were thoughtful. He was forming the next question carefully when she answered it unbidden.

"The murder wasn't the only accident that happened that night," she observed in the tone of one mentioning a genuine trouble in the midst of a discussion on imaginary ills. "When I knocked on Mr. John's bedroom door to tell him the bath was ready he didn't hear me and all the time I thought he was having his bath he was in here. He sat down for a moment and must have dozed off. Anyway, he didn't hear me and at a quarter to seven I hear him come out of the bathroom in a fine rage. He had been to see if the bath was ready and had found it lukewarm. I had to hot it up for him. In the end he didn't go into that bath until seven o'clock and of course he wouldn't hurry himself—never would, not if the house was afire. And finally he went off to his dinner at a quarter to eight, dressed nicely but not shaved. He hadn't, I know, because I looked at his brush and it was dry. That shows you how accidents happen."

"Yes," agreed Mr. Campion with a solemnity quite out of keeping with the circumstances. "Yes, that's exactly what it does do."

"Well, then," said Mrs. Peel and began to clear away with a great clatter.

Mr. Campion rose to his feet.

"Where is the bathroom?" he enquired.

The woman stared at him, her brows raised into acute angles on her wrinkled forehead and a flush spreading upward over her face.

"I never did!" she said at last. "Really! Oh, all right . . . the second door across the passage. There is a clean towel there."

A few minutes later when Ritchie entered the old-fashioned bathroom with the big copper geyser and the enormous antiquated bath he found Mr. Campion leaning out of the window. The younger man drew in his head and straightened his back. Ritchie took his place.

A fire escape sprawled its ungainly way up the back of the elegant old house and one green-painted iron landing stage abutted on to the wall less than two feet below the sill over which he leant. He looked at it for a moment and then stepped back and he and Mr. Campion eyed each other. Ritchie was first to speak.

"Talk," he said urgently. "Downstairs."

Mrs. Peel made it clear that she was glad to see the end of them, if indeed, as she very much doubted, it was the end. She also mentioned that something for nothing was a very common quarry in her experience, but that since Mr. Ritchie was a relation she did not see that she was entitled to begrudge the cocoa. She also wished them a very good afternoon.

Ritchie led Campion downstairs to the ground floor and let himself into Mike's domain.

"Mike gave it to me," he explained, observing Campion's eyes on the latchkey. "Had to fetch him some clothes when they took him to that place. He won't mind us here. Good fellow, Mike. Grey hair, poor chap."

He waved his friend toward a dusty armchair in the sitting room which they both knew well and perched himself opposite on the edge of the table, where he sat with his long arms swinging and his shaggy head held up alertly.

"Know now?" he asked anxiously and for the last time the younger man surprised the dog-like, enquiring expression in his face. "Clear?"

"Yes, I think so," said Mr. Campion and sighed.

"*Gallivant* only a copy?"

Although he put the words as a question Ritchie seemed to have very little doubt as to the answer and Campion wondered afresh at his extraordinary mixture of shrewdness and simplicity. Aloud he said:

"They think the stuff itself may be genuine, but it's not the original manuscript. It's probably a copy made sometime in the last half of the last century."

"Uncle Jacoby," observed Ritchie blandly. "All prudish Victorians secretly dirty. Probably had it made for private reading. Like him, rather. Funny old man. What happened to Paul?"

Mr. Campion leaned back in his chair. He looked very tired but his eyes were bright and intelligent.

"Paul was too energetic," he said slowly, and added apologetically, "You'll have to forgive me if I take my time, but I've learnt the story the wrong way round."

"Tell it that way. Begin at the end."

"I don't know the end," said Mr. Campion. "That's the trouble."

Ritchie sat silent and expectant and presently Campion went on.

"Paul made himself a nuisance in the firm for four years, ever since he returned from America," he said. "In that time he seems to have got on the nerves of most people in publishing generally. Then he was bitten by the idea of exhibiting *The Gallivant* and, of course, there were excellent reasons why the manuscript should not be shown in a place where interfering people might ask awkward questions about the age of the paper and the quality of the ink, not to mention the authenticity of the handwriting. So he was stopped, but, being an enquiring and obstinate beggar, it dawned upon him that there was probably something fishy about the precious manuscript and he decided to examine it. He got the bank to give it up, but again he was stopped from looking at it and the manuscript was put in the safe. Whether that was done with malice aforethought I don't know, but I rather think so, for the safe key was left in his way long enough for him to take an impression of it and from that time on a pretty close watch was kept on Paul's activities and the watcher was paid small sums for her trouble."

He paused and Ritchie nodded comprehendingly.

"The day came," continued Mr. Campion, "when the watcher reported that a letter had arrived which had made Paul dash off in excitement. It was a letter from Wardie Samson, for which he and his observers had waited. It was a signal for action.

"This is what happened to Paul. He came back to Twenty-three just after six o'clock, when he knew the place would be closed, let himself in and went up to Curley's desk, where he got the key of the strong room. He then went down to the basement. His new key fitted the safe, but the arrangement of turns and half turns got him bothered because he was nervous and in a high state of excitement. He had just got the safe door open when he was disturbed by footsteps in the yard outside. I imagine that a characteristic cough warned him, quite intentionally, that the newcomer was the one particular person he did not wish to find him there and I think he behaved quite normally and in the way the murderer foresaw he would behave, and not like that hysterical maniac Peter Rigget, who lost his head and went berserk."

Ritchie looked interested but so completely in the dark that Campion wondered if he could possibly be following this complicated reconstruction.

"Paul locked himself in and turned out the light," Campion continued. "He knew, or thought he knew, that he had the only key of the strong room, so that he was safe from the intruder, and as long as no chink of light showed anywhere there was no reason at all why anyone should suspect the place was occupied.

"In the dark he crept away from the door and waited for the other man to go. But the newcomer remained. He went into the garage and started the car and Paul, not sure if the back door was standing open, dared not slip out, even if he wanted to. Personally I think he decided to wait until the other man had gone. Probably he imagined that Mike was with him. Anyway, whatever he thought, it did not occur to him that carbon monoxide fumes were pouring into the unventilated room through the rubber pipe pushed through the grating in the opposite wall.

"He noticed the smell of exhaust gas, of course, but since he could hear the car and probably guessed there was an air brick leading into the garage somewhere he thought nothing of it.

"Within five minutes he was drowsy and sat down, I think by the safe. Five minutes later he was unconscious, and after the best part of an hour, when the murderer returned and switched off the engine, he was dead."

"Murderer returned?"

Mr. Campion looked up.

"Yes," he said. "In the interim he went back to his home by the way he had come, found his bath was cold, blew up his housekeeper, had the bath heated again and bathed. When he had finished he put on his underclothes and trousers, probably, under a dressing-gown, and went out once more through the bathroom window, down the fire escape, through the door in the garden wall, switched off the car, threw the rubber tubing in at the basement door as he returned, then finished his dressing and went out to dinner, unfortunately not having had time to shave.

"I'm open to bet that he wore gloves not because of

fingerprints, but so that he should not dirty or burn his hands."

There was a long silence. Ritchie was rocking himself slowly backwards and forwards.

"Not dozing in dining room, watching street for Paul to go into Twenty-three," he said at last. "Wouldn't have been seen on fire escape from street at other end of yard. Foggy all that week. Risky, Campion."

"Risky!" Mr. Campion caught his breath. "It was so risky that no one who did not imagine himself a species of god about the place would have thought of it, much less attempted it. Mike might have come home earlier, although, of course, he was supposed to be at the cocktail party. But anyone might have gone into the garage to see why the car was running. Hang it! Even a policeman might have enquired. . . . Besides, Paul might not have stayed there. He might have come out at the very beginning and asked him what the hell he thought he was up to."

"Wouldn't have mattered," Ritchie observed. "He'd have won. He'd have told Paul to mind his own business and go away. Paul would have gone. Strong personality . . . strict, you know . . . authoritative."

Mr. Campion remained thoughtful.

"On Sunday he must have been getting restive when he sent Mike down to the strong room," he said quietly. "He sent him to get a folder, expecting him to find the door locked and the key missing and so start the excitement which would lead to the finding of the body. It would have been a weak move if Mike had found Paul. As it turned out, of course, it complicated the issue tremendously. Mike didn't see the corpse and came back as though nothing had happened. That must have jolted our man considerably. So afterwards, probably late at night, he went down there himself, dragged the body into a prominent position, and, after placing the hat by its side, left it for Miss Marchant to find in the morning. He couldn't very well leave the door locked on the inside, so he put the key back in Miss Curley's desk.

"It's a mad sort of crime, so mad that it came off. It was the man's mental make-up which made it possible. All murderers are a little crazy. The people who get away with incredible things are those who never look round the subject, but just go straight ahead and make for their objective with blinkers on. It's like the drunk who walks across the parapet. He only knows he wants to get to a window next door, sees a straight path and takes it, oblivious to the ten-story drop on either side of him."

"John . . ." Ritchie. "Obvious really."

"Obvious?" enquired Mr. Campion, his professional pride stirring in its latent bed.

"From the beginning," said Ritchie placidly. "John said he knew it was an accident. John's not a fool. Got a logical mind. Reasonable, except where personal infallibility is concerned. If he knew it was an accident he must have arranged it himself: everyone else thought it was a murder. Queer chap . . . law of his own. Terrible for Mike."

"Not too good for Paul," murmured Mr. Campion dryly. "But that's not the question at the moment. The trouble is I can't prove this story. It depends too much on your friend Mrs. Peel, and even if she could be persuaded to tell the same yarn in the witness-box what should we have then? A case against John just about as strong as the one they've already got against Mike. The police wouldn't consider it. Why should they?"

Ritchie sat silent for a long time. Finally he looked at the younger man, his mild blue eyes dark and pained.

"Terrible for Mike," he repeated. "Caught, imprisoned, killed."

"No," said Campion hastily. "He'll be acquitted. I'm sure of it. If I wasn't I'd be at the Yard now doing anything I could, making a fool of myself probably. I'm banking on an acquittal. Anyway, there'll be the appeal. That's not the point. Unfortunately in an imperfect world acquittal does not mean that a man is proved innocent to the satisfaction of the people with whom he has got to live."

"What shall we do?"

Ritchie invited a command and Mr. Campion made up his mind. He rose and walked over to Mike's desk.

"I think we'll leave a note," he said.

Taking an envelope from a pigeon-hole, he addressed it to John, adding briefly: "With Mr. Campion's compliments."

Inside he placed the folded page from the copy of *The Gallivant* and the key of the safe which he had received from Mr. Rigget. Together he and Ritchie carried the missive up stairs and left it with Mrs. Peel.

18

In Reply to Your Letter

Their visit to John's flat and subsequent conversation had taken much longer than either Ritchie or Mr. Campion had dreamed, and when they met Gina and Miss Curley on the door-step of Twenty-one they were astounded to learn that the court had adjourned for the day.

Miss Curley was grimly capable, keeping her head with a conscious effort. Gina was silent and, had it not been for a glazed expression in her eyes, might have appeared sullen. Her chestnut hair warmed the whiteness of her skin and her mouth was resolute.

"She must eat," said Miss Curley in an undertone to Ritchie. "You come up with me and talk to her until I find something."

Gina looked at Campion.

"They're making a strong case," she whispered. "Even John's beginning to see it now. He stayed behind to speak to Cousin Alexander. It all fits in so horribly the way they put it."

"Wait till you hear the defence," said Campion, with forced cheerfulness. "The prosecution is always convincing till you hear the defence. Don't worry."

She looked at him as though he had said something absurd, smiled mechanically and passed on up the stairs, Miss Curley following her. Ritchie turned to Campion.

"Better go," he said. "Poor girl!"

There was a pause in which he seemed to be struggling for words. Campion thought he had never seen such intensity of feeling in a face before.

199

"To escape," said Ritchie suddenly. "Escape, Campion. Escape all . . . this."

A great wave of a flail-like arm included, as far as his hearer could judge, the civilized world and all that lay within it.

Mr. Campion made no direct reply. Apart from the fact that no one could ever be quite sure what Ritchie was talking about, there seemed to be no comment upon such passionate feeling which would not be an impertinence.

"Good-bye," he said. "See you to-morrow."

"To-morrow," said Ritchie, and in his mouth the word had the bitterness of eternity.

Mr. Campion went home. Age, he reflected, was beginning to tell on him, and, since he was a person not given to self-consideration, it came to him with all the force of a major discovery that nearly thirty-five and nearly twenty-five are two very different kettles of fish where nervous stamina and the ability to do without sleep are concerned.

He was so depressed by the thought that he decided to go to bed immediately upon arriving at Bottle Street, and would have done so had it not been for the visitor who awaited him.

Ex-Inspector Beth rose from his chair in the sitting room and grinned as his host came in.

"Didn't expect to see me here, did you?" he said. "And with the goods."

"No," said Campion truthfully. "I did not."

"He's bin 'ere for an hour talking about 'imself, until you'd think 'e was still a flattie," observed Mr. Lugg, who had wandered in from the next room, collarless and in his house coat.

"Oh, I have, have I? Well, no one would think you were still a cat burglar," countered the ex-inspector spitefully.

"No, I've bettered meself," said Lugg, with ineffable complacency. "I'm a house gentleman now."

"What's the report?" cut in Mr. Campion, who was not in the mood for cross-talk. "Anything definite?"

The visitor became businesslike immediately.

"Pretty good, Mr. Campion, pretty good. As far as I

can ascertain, nearly all the amounts paid into the bank book since December last, and not handed in at the Holborn post office, were paid in by an elderly gentleman. Is that what you expected?"

"Only 'nearly all'?" enquired Campion, with interest.

"All those I could ascertain," said the Inspector firmly and with reproach. "There are five instances in which the assistant remembered, because he or she thought it queer; two doubtfuls; and one plain rude and unhelpful."

"Any description of the man?"

"Fair." The ex-inspector consulted his notes. "Tall, thin, sixty-ish, well-dressed, yellow face—that's some person's word alone—quiet, stranger to each office. Any good?"

"Good enough," said Mr. Campion. "Good enough for my own information. No good as evidence."

"I don't see why not." The inspector was hurt. "Some of them remember him clearly. The idea of him doing it tickled 'em. You know what these youngsters are nowadays."

"Oh, it's not your end. That's fine." Campion spoke soothingly. "It's the information received. That's the part of the story I couldn't pin down."

Ex-Inspector Beth's large face assumed a puzzled expression. He had never been a man who liked to see good work wasted, and now mentioned the fact in passing.

"For information received, was it?" he continued. "That makes it darker still to me. I can't see at all what you're driving at, Mr. Campion. The amounts were so small. If there was any hanky-panky you'd imagine they'd have been paid in cash."

Campion sat down. He felt the ex-inspector was entitled to an explanation, but had never felt less like making one in his life.

"Beth," he demanded, "have you ever met a woman who conveyed interested information without actually saying it?"

"Hinting?" enquired the inspector dubiously.

"No, not exactly." Campion hesitated, looking for the word. "A woman who gossiped to the point," he said at last. "She knows, and you know, that she's telling you something, and yet for reasons of discipline or dignity or discretion neither of you ever admits to the other that you are interested or she is informing. See what I mean?"

"Exactly."

Beth nodded sagaciously and Mr. Campion, finding it easier than he had expected, went on.

"Now suppose you want to reward such a woman. You want to encourage her and yet you don't want to commit yourself by giving her money in her hand. You can't trust her not to come out into the open with a direct question if you leave a pound note on her typewriter."

"Yes?"

"Well, suppose she sees your difficulty and one day you find her Post Office Savings Bank Book lying in your room. It may have been a mistake; it may not. What is to prevent you paying a pound or two in at an unfamiliar post office? If she likes to query it you know nothing about it. If she accepts the cash and it encourages her, well, you're on the same footing as you were before. You've never come off your pedestal. You've never descended to a familiar word. You've done it and yet you haven't done it."

"And if an old ex-policeman goes round asking questions?" murmured the practical Inspector Beth.

"Ah," agreed Mr. Campion, "but I don't think you're the sort of man who would imagine that possible. You're a conceited beggar. You think your dignity gives you a special pass to ignore enquiring policemen and all their works. It's your own personal dignity in relation to the woman who is your employee which counts with you. That's the sort of man you are."

"Oh, am I?" said the ex-inspector. "Well, in that case, Mr. Campion, you can take it from me that I might do abso-bally-lutely anything. What a tale! If you'll pardon a professional question, how did you get on to it?"

"She's that sort of woman," said Mr. Campion, and Beth was satisfied.

It was half an hour later before Campion got rid of him. Lugg was in lordly mood and in the vein for a bout with an old sparring partner, while the ex-inspector evidently had time to waste. Eventually, however, he departed and Campion was thinking affectionately of his bed when the telephone summoned him to his feet again.

"Hello, is that you, Campion?" The dry precise voice sent a thrill through him. "John Widdowson here. I got your note."

"Oh, yes?" Campion heard his own voice studiously noncommittal.

"You made a most natural mistake." The tone was conciliatory, but by no means ingratiating. "You've discovered the manuscript in the safe is a copy, of course. I don't think anyone knew that except myself. I congratulate you. It was made for my uncle many years ago and for reasons of extra-special safety I put it in the place of the real play, so that if there should be any attempt at theft I should be doubly protected. You follow me?"

"Perfectly." Campion's inflection was unmistakable.

"Good. Well, what I want to say is this. I feel that since you have made the discovery and it has evidently led you to a mistaken conclusion, I naturally very much want you to see the real manuscript, so that any—ah—unfortunate surmises you may have made can be contradicted. That's quite reasonable, isn't it?"

Mr. Campion's tired brain considered the concrete evidence he had gathered against the man at the other end of the wire and found it nil. He had no doubt that John Widdowson could have murdered his cousin, and in his heart he believed he had done so, but he realized that if the real *Gallivant* was still in the firm's possession the motive he had so carefully reconstructed was gone, and if there was no motive the strongest part of the case fell to the ground.

John was still speaking.

"I want you to see that manuscript and I want you to see it at once, so that you can concentrate on finding the truth. Mike's life is in danger. We've got to move quickly before those imbeciles decide to hang him. I'm in conference with Sir Alexander now. He's hopeful, I may tell you, but he realizes that it's going to be a hard fight. We're grateful for Rigget, Campion, but it's not enough."

There were urgency and anxiety in the voice not unmixed with a hint of reproof, and Mr. Campion found himself shaken by that rarest of the emotions, honest astonishment.

John went on.

"I'm a little irritated, naturally. Although I do see exactly how the misapprehension arose. You are a friend of poor Mike's, but you don't know me. We will say no more about that. I admit that were I unable to produce the genuine manuscript my own position might very well be open to question. I see that now, although it certainly gave me a shock when you pointed it out. I want you to see the real manuscript, Campion."

"I should like to." Campion sounded annoyed, in spite of himself.

"You must. You must see it at once. I want all your energies concentrated on Mike's trouble. Will you give me your promise that you'll settle this point tonight?"

Mr. Campion's weariness had given place to bewildered resignation.

"Yes, of course. I want to see it."

"You'll be able to recognize it, you think?"

"I think so."

"Splendid. It's not in a very inaccessible spot, thank God, but one of the safest I know, one where I keep things when I want them protected from the inquisitiveness of my own family. Do you know our Paul Jones premises?"

"No," said Campion, who felt like a child waiting to see what would happen next.

"They're in the phone book, of course." John was clearly trying to keep civil in the face of crass idiocy, and finding it difficult. "Eighty-seven, Parrot Street, Pimlico. It's a large building. Take a cab. Any driver will know it. I can't come with you myself, unfortunately, because I shall be closeted with Sir Alexander into the small hours. But I want you to go at once. You can't do anything useful while you're still on a wild-goose chase. You see that?"

Mr. Campion found himself thinking, quite unpardonably, that he had never been treated as a blundering employee before and that the experience was refreshing, stimulating and probably good for the soul. Aloud he said:

"All right. I'll go."

"You'd be behaving like a young ass if you didn't," said the voice, with some asperity. "I'll telephone to the caretaker to admit you on your card. He won't know where the manuscript is, of course. You'll have to find that yourself from what I tell you now. It's very simple. The last room on the fourth floor, that is to say, at the top of the building, is the directors' office. The room number is forty-five. If you forget it the caretaker will show you. In the room is a carved desk—oak or ebony, I forget which—and in the left-hand top drawer you will find the key of the cupboard. Open it, and the manuscript is in a newspaper parcel on the second shelf with two or three others. My uncle always kept it like that. His contention was that no one would look for it there or recognize it if they found it, and when he gave over he passed the tip on to me. Lock up after you, of course."

"Yes," said Mr. Campion meekly.

"I shall expect you to phone me later in the evening to tell me you're satisfied, and, perhaps—" the cold authoritative voice betrayed a hint of condescending amusement, "—to apologize. I'll phone the caretaker immediately. Oh, wait a moment; Sir Alexander may want to speak to you."

There was a considerable pause while, presumably, Cousin Alexander was fetched from another room, and then the magnificent voice rumbled over the wire.

"That you, Campion? I'm sorry, but I must have John here some time yet. Terribly sorry, my dear fellow, but anxious times, you know—anxious times. Good night."

Before Mr. Campion could reply he had gone and John had taken his place again.

"Go along and satisfy your mind, my boy," he said. "You'll know where you are then. As soon as you clear the line I'll ring Jenkinson. He'll be waiting for you. Goodbye."

Mr. Campion hung up the receiver and walked slowly back across the room. Standing by the window, looking down into the lamplit street, he tried to sort out thought from instinct and wished he were not so incredibly tired. That afternoon he had been sure of John's guilt. Even now, when he considered his painfully forged chain of half-facts, he could not believe that it was composed entirely of unrelated coincidences; and yet, if John were innocent, could he possibly have made any more reasonable move than the present one? On the other hand, if he were guilty, what could he hope to gain by the production of yet another faked manuscript, or even no manuscript at all?

There was one other alternative, and Campion considered it in cold blood. In the course of an adventurous career he had received many invitations which had subsequently proved to be not at all as innocent as they at first appeared, and the common or garden trap was not by any means unknown to him. And yet, in cold blood, the absurdity of such a suggestion in the present case was inclined to overwhelm every other aspect.

While he was still wavering there returned to his mind a maxim often expounded by old Sergeant McBain, late of H Division: "If you think it's a frame, go and see. Frames is evidence."

Mr. Campion put on his coat and had reached the front door when another thought occurred to him, and rather shamefacedly he returned to his desk and, taking a little Webley from its drawer, slid it into his pocket.

Leaning back in a taxi cab nearly fifteen minute later he surveyed Parrot Street, Pimlico, with interest. It was a long dingy road lined with solid slabs of Georgian housing, intersected by occasional side streets or great yawning gaps where demolition and rebuilding were in progress. Office staffs had long ago displaced the comfortable families for whom the houses were built, and at eight o'clock in the evening Parrot Street was a gloomy and deserted thoroughfare.

Number Eighty-seven was a dishevelled building. Its windows were dirty and uncurtained and here and there patches of plaster had chipped away, showing the brick beneath. One of its immediate neighbours had been taken down and huge wooden joists supporting the structure along one side did not add to its distinction. Altogether it was not a likely sister for the elegant Twenty-three, Horsecollar Yard.

The explanation, of course, was the old one. Like hairdressing and hotel-keeping, publishing is forced to be class-conscious, and just as front-rank restaurateurs are sometimes known to have smaller, cheaper establishments tucked away in the back streets, where, under less dignified names, money is made and odds and ends used up without waste, so sometimes distinguished publishing houses have humbler sisters where less rare but equally filling mental dishes are prepared and distributed.

Messrs. Paul Jones, Ltd. published children's picture-books, light love stories of the cheaper sort, translations, and a vast quantity of reprints, and were kept alive by the possession of some twenty or thirty copyrights of the great Fairgreen Fields' earlier works, which they republished at three and six, half a crown, one and three, one shilling, ninepence, sixpence, and fourpence simultaneously and over a period of years, without ever, apparently, overlapping or saturating any of that fine "blood" writer's many markets.

The firm was owned by Messrs. Barnabas, without being in any way affiliated to them socially, and was run by a separate staff.

The taximan pulled up outside the dilapidated doorway and Mr. Campion got out. The dirty transom showed a faint light in the entrance hall, and as soon as he knocked the door was opened by a woman as untidy and disheartened as the house itself.

"Me husband's hurt his foot," she said before he had time to open his mouth, "and I said for him not to move himself now he was got comfortable. I knew you wouldn't mind."

She looked up at him with a confiding leer which showed gappy teeth in pale gums.

A wail from the lighted doorway at the far end of the passage indicated that she was not in attendance upon her husband alone.

"I'm coming!" she shouted in a voice surprisingly raucous after her husky conversation tone. "See to 'im, Dad, do!"

Mr. Campion gave her his card, and she took it under the bulb to read.

"That's right," she said, with idiotic but ingratiating surprise. "Campion. That was the name Mr. Widdowson said. Shall I keep this, sir? D'you know where to go? It's Room Forty-five, right at the top of the 'ouse."

She glanced abjectly at the dusty wooden staircase and back again.

"I can turn on the 'all lights from 'ere," she added, and rubbed her hands on the back of her skirt.

Mr. Campion looked down at her.

"How long ago did your husband hurt his foot?" he enquired unexpectedly.

"Week last Monday. One of the van boys let a box down on 'im—clumsy young monkey! Mr. Widdowson said surely it was well by now. I didn't 'alf tell 'im off over the phone. 'Well,' I said, ' 'he's not an idol, Mr. Widdowson.' "

She spoke without heat or humour, and her tired face turned towards the stairs again. In the back room the baby roared.

"I'll come up with you if you like," she said.

Suddenly Campion laughed.

"Don't bother. Is the door locked?"

"Oh, no, sir. We're always here, you see. There's only this entrance and the one at the back which we use. Nobody could get in. You'll go up, then?"

"I will. I'll see you when I come down."

"Thank you, sir." He saw her quick hopeful smile and she wiped her hands again. "I'll just turn on the lights."

The beautiful staircase, which had been a Georgian housewife's pride and responsibility and was now a danger trap to van boys and caretakers, was flooded with dusty light as Campion set foot upon it.

The premises at Eighty-seven were even less attractive inside than out. The two lower floors were used as a warehouse and stretched out behind over what once had been a garden in vast ramifications of the book-producer's trade. The very air was thick with dust and the sweet, acrid smell of ink.

Campion went up slowly, his hand on the Webley. In spite of his conviction that the idea of attack was absurd, he took no risks. His senses were alert and he walked with quiet springy steps.

He was not disturbed. The rows of greasy doors on each landing were silent and no creaking board, either behind or above him, answered the tread of his own feet.

It was a long way up. He climbed steadily on, pausing only once to look down the well to the hall, small and far away below.

The fourth floor was a little cleaner than the rest of the house. One or two of the doors had been freshly painted, throwing the shabbiness of the walls into painful prominence, and there was a strip of floor-covering of sorts down the centre of the passage.

Outside room number forty-five he paused and stood for a moment, listening. The silence was everywhere. Very gently he tried the handle. It turned easily and the door swung open, revealing an apartment only faintly lit by the light from the street lamps below.

With his left hand, his gun in his right, he shone his torch round the room. It was unoccupied and appeared to be in normal order.

A glance at the light fixtures assured him that there was nothing untoward in that direction, and he turned over the switch.

It was a big room, comfortably furnished with that particular brand of red Turkey carpet which is to the City office what the bowler hat is to the City clerk, a bookcase, a few chairs and the desk of which John had spoken. The walls were covered with show-cards, book jackets and galleys of advertisements.

Mr. Campion looked for the cupboard door and saw two, one beside the desk, the other behind it. They were both used as notice boards, the wooden panelling being particularly suitable for the reception of drawing-pins. The miscellany hanging there told him little more than the date, several publication fixtures for books of which he had never heard, and the details of the train service to Chelmsford.

He did not hurry. In the back of his mind something was warning him of impending danger. Looking about him, the instinct seemed ridiculous, and he remembered that he was tired and probably jumpy.

He went over to the desk unwillingly and pulled open the first drawer on the left-hand side. It contained at first sight nothing more remarkable than a tin of biscuits and a pair of gloves, but after removing these cautiously he saw a key with a piece of string through the ring lying half under the paper with which the drawer was lined.

He took it out and looked at it suspiciously, but it was quite ordinary and of no particular interest in itself.

Feeling foolish but still puzzled, he carried it over to the door behind the desk.

It fitted the lock, but he did not get the door open until he realized with a wave of self-dislike that it opened outwards and was not even locked. He thrust it open and stepped back, taking out his torch once more.

The cupboard proved to be a cloak-room containing an incredibly dirty wash-basin and a row of clothes-hooks, upon one of which a dilapidated umbrella hung dejectedly.

He came out and went over to the other door. Once again he fitted the key in the lock, the old sense of danger assailed him, and he swung round to face the landing, but all was silent and dirty and ordinary as before.

Then, from far below, he heard a little angry sound, thin, high and furious. Mrs. Jenkinson's baby was protesting violently at some parental indignity. It was too much. Mr Campion cursed himself for his hysteria, his cowardice and his approaching age. He turned the bolt over and pulled the handle.

The jamb did not move and he remembered it probably opened outwards. He tried it gently, but it was stuck and he drew himself back to throw his shoulder against it.

That miraculous sense which is either second sight or the lightning calculation of the subconscious mind, which nothing escapes, arrested him, and, changing his mind on the instant, he pulled his gun and kicked the door open, police fashion.

For a moment it still stuck and then shattered open sickeningly and he stood overbalancing, shuddering horror fighting with the realization of a certainty.

There was nothing there at all; only the wide sky threadbare with stars and fringed with a million chimney-pots, and, far, far below him in the cool darkness, the jagged stone foundations of the house that had been next door.

19
Under the Sword

Miss Curley cleared her throat, pushed her hat a little
further on to the back of her head, and wondered rather
helplessly if the truth could be any more apparent after five
days' talk, when it seemed to be so hopelessly hidden after
one and a half.

At her side Gina sat immobile. All through the day she
had preserved the same aloof expression. Her eyes were no
longer dazed, but had assumed instead a settled coldness.
Miss Curley was anxious about her.

In the luncheon recess she had taken the girl to a city
restaurant and had made her eat, but she had done so
without interest and had not talked.

Even John's absence, the non-appearance of Ritchie,
and the unaccountable desertion of Mr. Campion had
passed her by as unworthy of comment and only once,
when Mike had been brought back into the dock, had she
shown by a single quickening glance the least sign of
interest in the proceedings.

Miss Curley's other neighbour, on the contrary, was
evidently not only following, but enjoying, the case. He
had reappeared at the morning session as eager as a child at
a play, and Miss Curley, a patient, tolerant woman, had
gradually become used to his muttered commentary.

The afternoon was very warm for the time of the year,
and the sun shone on the dome, making the court
comfortable and bright. Lord Lumley leant back in his high
leather chair, his scarlet robe catching the sunlight and the
colour flickering on the lenses of his eyeglasses. Before him
the eternal bustle of the court continued.

Cousin Alexander sat in his place, his silk gown shining

and his eyes eloquent, ready at any moment to leap up and pounce upon a witness.

The first three sessions of the enquiry had established much of the Crown case and the Attorney-General had reason to be pleased with the way events were shaping. The jury now fully understood the mechanics of the crime. They had examined the hose pipe, seen the photographs of the strong room and garage, and had heard the medical evidence.

They had also heard Mrs. Austin do her well-meaning damnedest, and Mrs. Tripper had repeated her story of the running car engine.

At the moment the red-headed and vivacious Roberta Jeeves, author of *Died on a Saturday*, was giving her evidence, struggling between the desire to escape all responsibility and a certain shy pride in having invented a murder which would work.

She had, she said, no idea whether Mr. Michael Wedgwood had read her book or not. It did happen sometimes that a publisher did not read every book he sponsored.

Was that not usually only in the case of well-established authors? Fyshe put the question innocently.

Miss Jeeves reluctantly supposed it would be, and Counsel begged leave to enquire if Miss Jeeves considered that she had been a well-established author at the time of the publication of *Died on a Saturday*.

Miss Jeeves confessed with not unnatural irritation that she had no idea.

Fyshe asked humbly if it were true that in view of the complicated mechanics of the device described and the faithfulness with which they had been executed in real life Miss Jeeves had felt it her duty to call the attention of the police to her book.

Miss Jeeves, holding strong views on the subject of coincidence, was fairly embarked upon a dissertation upon them when she was gently and courteously stopped by the Judge.

Cousin Alexander did not cross-examine.

Miss Curley stirred and smiled nervously in reply to her unknown neighbour's wink and nod of appreciation. She looked round the court again. Until now she had believed that court proceedings were tedious beyond all bearing and that the greatest ordeal participators had to face was one by ennui, but so far the effect of cumulative drama had never faltered and always just in front of her there had been that strong wide back of the young man she knew, who might be going to die.

Others might find the technicalities of doctors and central-heating experts dull, but to Miss Curley every word was of vital importance, every point reached her, and every time the jury whispered together her heart contracted painfully.

Miss Jeeves having returned to her seat, there was a rustle at Counsels' table. Fyshe sat down and the Attorney-General rose to examine as Peter Rigget stepped into the box.

His slightly dilapidated appearance was not enhanced by the green reading light which, shining down upon his papers, was reflected up into his face. He looked puffy because of Mr. Campion, unhealthy because of the light, and thoroughly vindictive, which was his own affair.

Miss Curley, who knew nothing about his secret self-deploration, had no sympathy for him at all.

"Strong case," whispered the man at her side. "Now they're coming to it . . ."

Miss Curley wondered if it was her imagination or that a new excitement was, in fact, growing in the big bright room. The Lord Chief Justice looked as placid as before, but there was certainly a rustle among the clerks and the jury leant forward to see the witness better.

It was evident at once that Mr. Rigget was aware of his importance. He even permitted himself a sickly nervous smile, which was rendered frankly horrific by the green light reflected in his glasses.

Cousin Alexander noticed the little man's self-satisfaction with grim approval.

Miss Curley glanced at Gina. The girl was very still, her eyes fixed upon the silent figure in the dock. It occurred to the older woman that she was praying.

The Attorney-General began gently in his softest, most ingratiating tone, and Mr. Rigget made his opening statement happily.

213

"I am an accountant employed by Messrs. Barnabas. I have known the accused and the deceased for about two years, ever since I came to work in the office. On January the twenty-seventh I went into the deceased's room at the office and on into the book-file room, which leads off it. When I entered the room the two men were talking. They ceased when they saw me, but when I went into the little office they continued their conversation."

"Was the door open or shut?"

"Open."

"Could you hear what was said?"

"Clearly."

"Can you repeat what you overheard, word for word?"

"I can."

"Is it not extraordinary that you should remember a chance conversation so clearly?"

"No, because it was an extraordinary conversation."

"Will you repeat it?"

Mr. Rigget considered and began in a slightly affected voice.

"Mr. Paul, the deceased, said: 'You mind your own damned business, Mike. She's mine. I'll manage my own life in my own way.' And then after a pause he said: 'Make love to her if you want to. God knows I'm not stopping you.'"

"Did you hear any more?"

"No. I came out then and they stopped talking."

"Did you see both men?"

"Of course."

"How close to them were you?"

"I passed quite close to Mr.—to the accused, within two feet."

"Did you notice anything about him?"

"He was very white. His hands were clenched. He looked as if he could—he looked very angry."

"Had you ever seen him like that before?"

"I had never seen him like that before."

Miss Curley's neighbour nudged her.

"They'll get him," he whispered jubilantly, and then, as she turned to him, coughed apologetically into his handkerchief and reddened round the ears.

Cousin Alexander rose majestically and scattered a sheaf of papers to the floor with the sleeve of his gown. While Mr. Rigget's attention was still distracted by the incident he put his first question.

"Some time before you entered the employment of Messrs. Barnabas, Limited, you were employed by Messrs. Fitch and Sons, paper merchants, were you not?"

Mr. Rigget started violently.

"Yes."

"Is it true that after you left them you gave evidence for the prosecution in an action brought against that firm by the Inland Revenue Department and were rewarded by that Department for information received?"

The Attorney-General sprang up and protested violently, and for the first time real heat was infused into the chill argument which had taken place between the two Counsels. Lord Lumley blinked at Cousin Alexander.

"I confess I don't see the purpose of such a question, Sir Alexander," he rumbled mildly.

Cousin Alexander bowed.

"I will not press it, My Lord," he said virtuously, and Mr. Rigget was sufficiently ill-advised to smile.

"Are you an accountant?"

"I am."

"Have you very little to do with the book publishing side of Messrs. Barnabas' business?"

"I suppose I have." Mr. Rigget spoke grudgingly.

"Is it true you do not know even the titles of all the books they publish?"

"No, not all," said Mr. Rigget nervously.

"Is it true that you did not know, for instance, that in January Messrs. Barnabas acquired the rights of an auto-biography entitled *My Own Life*, by Lady Emily Trumpington?"

"No—o."

"Did you or did you not?"

Cousin Alexander's chill eyes suddenly reminded Mr. Rigget of the portrait in the waiting room.

"I may have heard of it."

"Did it occur to you then or does it occur to you now that what you really overheard the deceased say on the

occasion when you were 'overhearing' in the next office was:
'You mind your own damned business, Mike. She's mine.
I'll manage *My Own Life* in my own way,' meaning, of
course, the author, Lady Trumpington, is my client and I
will manage her book—that is to say, I will publish her
book—in my own way."

"No," said Mr. Rigget, turning a dull brown in the
green light. "No. I thought he was talking about his wife."

"You thought . . . !" began Cousin Alexander, apparently temporarily overwhelmed by the iniquity of fools, but
recovering himself with pretty dignity. "What made you
think that he was talking about his wife?"

"Well," said Mr. Rigget uncomfortably, "there had
been a bit of talk in the office about Mrs. Brande and the
accused carrying on, and I naturally thought—"

His voice trailed away.

"A bit of talk." Cousin Alexander's tone rose melodi-
ously. "A bit of talk in the office. Tittle-tattle among the
employees. A's wife has been seen with B, and so when A
and B talk heatedly it must be about Mrs. A. Is that how
you reasoned, Mr. Rigget?"

"I—I may have done."

Lord Lumley leant forward.

"When you heard the words 'my own life,' did they
sound like the title of a book? Were they said with equal
emphasis on each word, or on one or two words only?"

The quiet affable question brought the whole tricksy
business back to earth again, out of the realms of cleverness
into the quiet line of enquiry the results of which should
determine if Mike was to hang by the neck until he was
dead.

Mr. Rigget dithered while the court held its breath.

"I can't remember," he said at last, and the ready tears
which were such a constant source of embarrassment to him
crept into his eyes.

Cousin Alexander let the admission sink in before he
tackled the next stage of his enquiry.

"You have told us that you cannot remember the
inflection on the words 'my own life,'" he said quietly. "Are
you sure that you remember the words 'make love to her if
you want to, God knows I'm not stopping you'? You are sure
you heard them?".

"I am sure."

"Did the accused say anything at all while you were in the inner office?"

"Nothing."

"Are you saying that you heard him say nothing?"

"I heard nothing."

"Might he have whispered?"

"No. I should have heard him if he had."

"Were you listening carefully?"

"I was."

"Were you remembering everything you heard?"

"Everything."

"And yet you are not sure if the deceased was talking about his own life or the title of a book."

"That's your suggestion," sneered Mr. Rigget.

"Yes, it is," said Cousin Alexander, with lightning heat. "And it is also my suggestion that in order to convince yourself that you had heard Mr. Brande talking about his wife, you imagined the second part of the statement."

"No."

Cousin Alexander took a deep breath.

"Consider those two remarks, first side by side and then concurrently. Do you think they could have been made by the same man, the same man in the same mood and on the same point? Are they not directly contradictory? 'I'll manage my own married life in my own way; make love to my wife if you want to.' Taken together, do they not sound absurd?"

"I heard it," said Mr. Rigget obstinately.

"I suggest," said Cousin Alexander, "that you thought you heard it."

"No, I heard it."

"Is it possible, Mr. Rigget, that you may have been mistaken in what you heard?"

There was a blessed quality of moral absolution in the word "mistaken," and Mr. Rigget fell for it.

"Perhaps," he said, and Cousin Alexander sighed.

"Do you like the accused?—or rather, is it true that you bear no grudge against him?"

"I hardly know him."

"Yet you knew the intimate affairs of his life. You knew he had been 'carrying on' with Mrs. Brande."

"I had heard it."

"Do you think now that you may have been mistaken?"

"I had heard it."

"May it have been untrue?"

"It may."

Cousin Alexander began to enjoy himself. His elation, which had been slowly growing ever since Mr. Rigget had entered the box, was shared by all those whose personal feelings were not harrowed by the case. Throughout the last part of the cross-examination people had been coming into the room. Barristers from other courts slipped in unobtrusively and the undercurrent of whispers which broke out in every pause became a natural part of the proceedings.

Miss Curley was stirred by the excitement of it all, in spite of herself. She could not help reacting to the general animation which had arisen so suddenly. It frightened her. She felt that it was at moments like these when mistakes were made, but she could feel the exhilaration and her neighbour was quite frankly beside himself with delight.

There was so much movement going on all round the room that she did not notice that the Attorney-General had left the court. It was Gina who called her attention to the fact.

"Where's Sir Montague Brooch gone?" she whispered. "A note was brought in to him and he hurried out. Did you see? Where's Albert Campion? They'll need him, won't they? Something's happening."

Miss Curley realized with a shock of self-reproach that the different atmosphere in the court had not registered upon the girl. Gina was concerned only with the truth and the man in the dock. Cousin Alexander's dexterities had passed her by.

"I don't notice anything," she whispered back, and before she had time to consider the suggestion Cousin Alexander began again.

"We will leave for a moment the question of what you do and do not remember, Mr. Rigget," he said graciously, "what you are sure you heard and what you cannot remember if you heard, and go on to something which happened so short a while ago that I am sure you will have no difficulty in calling it to mind. I put it to you that you visited the strong room where the deceased was found after office hours on the ninth of this month on the eve of this trial. Did you or did you not?"

Mr. Rigget's glance turned nervously towards the prosecution and he saw for the first time that Sir Montague Brooch was not present. Sir Alexander was still waiting.

"Did you or did you not?"

"I may have done."

"Come, come, Mr. Rigget, that's no answer to a perfectly straightforward question. It is now Thursday. Did you on Tuesday night go down to the strong room of the office where you are employed after office hours?"

Again Mr. Rigget looked round helplessly, and this time even Miss Curley was aware that something untoward was afoot. Cousin Alexander's junior tugged his gown and slipped a note into his hand, and at the same time the Clerk, who had been in conference for some minutes with Fyshe, rose and whispered to the Judge.

Mr. Rigget, finding himself temporarily forgotten, said "Yes" sulkily, and the whole court waited.

" 'Ullo? 'Ullo?" murmured Miss Curley's unknown neighbour expressively, and at the same time Gina caught the older woman's hand.

"I told you something had happened. What is it? More evidence against Mike? I can't bear it, Curley, I can't bear it!"

"Hush, dear, hush," said Miss Curley, patting the hand she held and moistening her lips with the tip of her tongue.

Cousin Alexander bustled out of court and his junior rose to take his place. The Clerk still stood whispering and Lord Lumley, looking more like a very old and very wise bloodhound than ever, sat forward, his head on one side. Now and again he nodded gravely and sometimes put a muttered question, which was answered by more whispered volubility from the Clerk.

The junior for the defence repeated Cousin Alexander's last question and received the same sulky reply from Mr.

Rigget, but its importance was lost. The jury were whispering heatedly, and only the little group in the dock sat stolidly silent, waiting.

"While you were there, what did you do?"

"I looked for things."

"Were you on the firm's business?"

"Yes."

"Did anyone from the office know you were there?"

"They may have done."

Mr. Rigget's eyes were snapping. He saw his opportunity and was taking it. The junior had no terrors for him, and he saw his chance to deny the truth of the statement he had made in Mr. Scruby's office. He supposed he could get that respected firm of solicitors and the odious Mr. Campion into the devil of a row if he played his cards carefully.

Looking up, he saw Mike's eyes resting upon him, and he turned away hastily from that pale unhappy face.

"Will you tell the court what was the nature of the business on which you were engaged in the strong room at that unlikely hour?"

The fact that the court was certainly not listening to anything Mr. Rigget might have to tell unnerved the young barrister and the question lacked authority.

"I was looking up some royalty accounts for our department," said Mr. Rigget mendaciously, and remembered suddenly that perjury is a crime.

"Had you any authority to do that?"

"No, but I like to do my job thoroughly."

The whispered conversation at the bench had ceased, and now Sir Andrew Phelps was talking to the Clerk.

The cross-examination went on its desultory way.

"While you were there were you disturbed?"

"Yes, I was. I was set upon and nearly killed."

"Did you not attack the man who discovered you there?"

"No, he attacked me."

"You must be more explicit. Did your assailant come straight into the room and hit you?"

The quiet voice from the bench at his side startled Mr. Rigget out of his wits. Under cover of the mysterious upheaval which seemed to have distracted the entire court, he had been happily chirruping on. Now it was as though God had stretched out a great finger and pinned an impudent sparrow to the gate. He gasped.

"No. I went out to see who it was, and he hit me then." Counsel continued.

"Did you turn on the light?"

"No, I ran out into the passage in the dark."

Mr. Rigget's face grew rigid after he had spoken. His eyes blinked piteously and he trembled, waiting for the next question.

It was a very long time in coming, and at last he looked up in sheer desperation, only to see the Attorney-General and Cousin Alexander back at the table again. Both men seemed slightly excited. There was a flush on Sir Montague Brooch's thin dark cheekbones and Cousin Alexander was forcing a smile, which was clearly not genuine. There was a pause. The Attorney-General looked at the Judge, and when His Lordship nodded to him imperceptibly he rose.

"My Lord—" the beautiful voice was a little thin, "—in view of certain circumstances which have arisen, and of which I understand Your Lordship is already aware, it is the intention of the prosecution to call no further evidence."

Before the words were finally out of his mouth, Cousin Alexander was on his feet beside him. Even in that moment of bewilderment it flashed through Miss Curley's mind that his agility was extraordinary for his age and weight. An usher signalled Mr. Rigget out of the box, and was too startled to notice whether he obeyed.

"My Lord," said Cousin Alexander, "in view of my learned friend's decision, it is my duty to demand a verdict from the jury."

Mr. Rigget was still in the box, forgotten and too terrified to move.

The Lord Chief Justice cleared his throat and tapped gently with his eyeglasses upon the vivid sleeve of his robe.

"Yes, Sir Alexander," he said in a quiet unemotional voice which temporarily robbed, for Miss Curley at least, his words of their momentous meaning. "I think that is a very proper request."

He turned to the jury, where they sat gaping at him like a double row of somebody's stupid relations, and addressed them simply.

"Members of the Jury, as you have just heard, certain circumstances have arisen which have caused the prosecution to decide to call no further evidence in this case. That means the Crown does not press the charge against the accused. Therefore it is my duty to direct you to find the prisoner not guilty and to acquit him of the charges which have been brought against him. Do you understand?"

There was a mutter in the jury-box, too confused and hasty to be dignified by the word "consultation," and the foreman stumbled to his feet with a nervous nod.

"We have—I mean we do, My Lord, Not guilty, My Lord."

As the jury writhed and murmured, overcome with delight and relief, the Judge addressed the prisoner. Mike rose stiffly to his feet. He looked young, broken, and inexpressibly alone in the great bare dock. The Judge's voice was very kind.

"Michael Wedgwood, you have been found not guilty of the charges brought against you. You may go."

The young man stood quite still. The whispering around him turned into a roar, and Cousin Alexander hurried over to him.

"'S'truth," said the man next to Miss Curley, as they rose while the Judge made his stately exit, his flowers in his hand, "what's happened now?"

Gina clutched Curley's arm.

"I want to get out!" she said wildly. "I want to get out!"

Miss Curley put her arm round Gina's shoulders and they were swept by an excited throng to the doorway. Mike was surrounded, she saw, and it occurred to her that it would be better if the two young people did not leave the court together.

What's happened? Why? What's happened? The question overtopped all the other crowding thoughts racing through her bewildered mind. Mike free—no need for Gina to give evidence—what's happened?—where are they all?—what's happened?

Over her shoulder she had her last glimpse of the court, the empty bench, the sword, the coats-of-arms, the excited throng, wigs, bands and silk gowns shining in the sunlight under the dome, and the witness-box with Mr. Rigget still inside it, peeping out like a bewildered green parrot in a cage.

What's happened?

They came out into Newgate Street, running almost, with the weight of the crowd behind them. The sun shone in their eyes and the hubbub of the traffic surged about them.

What's happened? With the return from the slightly *Alice in Wonderland* atmosphere of the court to the sturdy matter-of-factness of a London afternoon the question became urgent.

"What's happened?" The words themselves were on her lips when Gina stopped abruptly on the pavement. "Look!" she said huskily.

An old man in a ragged raincoat, who wore three out-of-date hospital flags in his cap, was leaning against a brilliant pillar-box, an apron of newspaper bills round his waist.

WEDGWOOD TRIAL
MAN DEAD

Miss Curley's eyes let her down. She took the paper the old man proffered her and fumbled with it blindly.

"What's happened?"

Gina's voice sounded very harsh and far away.

Miss Curley was aware of a red, unshaven Cockney face and two very bright sparrow eyes looking at her with kindly curiosity.

"There it is, lady, right on the first page. It happened this morning, but trust the perlice to keep it dark until they knoo what was what. 'John Widdowson, cousin of the man on trial, found dead.' Look, Ma, *there.*"

Miss Curley did not speak. She was staring through the paper and her shoulders shook a little.

"Found dead in 'is bath, killed the same way as the

other bloke was, with carbon monoxide gas. 'Ousekeeper found 'im."

The paper-seller supplied the details out of pure kindness of heart.

"Suicide," said Gina, and drew a long breath.

"Very likely," agreed the old man, politely noncommittal. "But it looks to me as if the perlice thought it was murder. What price the case for the prosecution now? Get you a taxi, lady?"

20

The Fourth Dimension

It was nearly dark in the hallway at Twenty-one when Mike came home. He was alone. Because of John's death there was a man on the outside door and reporters, friends and sightseers were temporarily kept at bay.

He came slowly down the passage, feeling for his second key. His lean figure did not droop, but some of the dignity of his ordeal still clung to him, and he looked unapproachable, like a man in great grief.

As he paused to open the door a shadow detached itself from the darkness of the first half-landing and came slowly down to meet him. It was Gina.

She looked smaller and thinner then he remembered her, and her old quiet self-assurance had gone, leaving her pretty and young but not a commanding personality.

"Hallo, Mike," she said.

He paused and looked at her awkwardly, wishing she had not come.

"Hallo, Gina."

There was a painful silence and she stood on the bottom step, hesitating.

"I'm glad you're free."

"Thank you."

There was another gap, and he felt weary and very glad he could not see her face.

"It's terrible about John." Her voice had a quiver in it, and, because he could not bear any more emotion and because he felt sick and so flat that the Day of Judgment might have come and he been overlooked, he snubbed her.

"Quite terrible," he said over his shoulder, and he bent to unlock the door.

He did not step inside instantly, but turned back apologetically. She was in the passage and the light from the door caught her face.

"I'm tired, old girl," he said awkwardly. "Hopelessly tired." He went in and shut the door. The girl went quietly upstairs.

On the threshold of his sitting room Mike stopped abruptly. Mr. Campion was sitting there alone.

"Have a drink?" he suggested, raising a glass.

Without a word the newcomer helped himself from a decanter and siphon on the elbow-table and accepted a cigarette. He did not speak until he was seated and had half finished his glass. Then he looked at his friend and a hint of the old lazy humour returned to his eyes.

"What a mess," he said.

Mr. Campion stretched himself.

"The best possible thing in a way," he murmured depreciatingly.

"We couldn't have brought him to trial, poor chap, even if we'd felt like it."

"Alexander's been telling me." Mike shook his grey-black head. "I was in a bedroom at his club, hiding from newspapermen, while he was talking to you. Poor old chap! He seems quite cut up. I think he'd been looking forward to his speech in my defence. I was sorry I missed you, but I've heard all about *The Gallivant* and the fire escape and—"

"—the ever-open door," murmured Mr. Campion. "But I forgot, you don't know about that. John was a difficult chap. This was the best way."

"It was suicide, wasn't it?" Mike put the question anxiously. "Cousin Alexander struck me as being a trifle reticent on that point. What happened exactly? How did he die?"

Mr. Campion sipped his whiskey.

"At nine o'clock this morning," he said, "John turned on the bath in his flat, locking the door probably out of force of habit, although he was alone in the apartment. Mrs. Peel had been called out, so he had to light the geyser himself. The window wouldn't open—stuck or something—and he was shut in with that awful old brass death-trap, one of the first geysers ever produced, I should think. Water takes off the stink of carbon monoxide, you know, and very little of the beastly stuff can do you in. Anyway, when Mrs. Peel returned at about eleven o'clock she found the door still locked and, getting no reply to her knock, she got the janitor up and they forced the door open. John was in the bath, his head under the water. He had passed out with the gas and slipped under. Actually he was drowned."

Mike sat up and passed his hand wearily over his forehead.

"It sounds like an accident to me," he said. "How did I—I mean, how did it affect me?"

Mr. Campion blinked at him.

"Mrs. Peel had the presence of mind not to raise a general alarm. She phoned Tanner and he came hareing round to find that the vent-pipe on the geyser had been bunged up with a towel. You can reach it quite easily from the fire escape. From one or two other things Tanner began to suspect he'd made a mistake. Very soon he was quite sure he had. I had a little yarn to tell him which had a bearing on the case, and finally he did the necessary. The police don't want to convict the innocent, you know! That's the one thing they say their prayers about."

"What an extraordinary way to commit suicide," said Mike. "I suppose John thought it was self-explanatory, since he left no note."

Mr. Campion nodded absently. There were one or two points which he had no intention of mentioning at the moment. One of them was that the bathroom window had been wedged from the outside and another that the telegram which had summoned Mrs. Peel to her married daughter's untelephoneable house in East Putney had not been sent by the lady whose name appeared as its signature.

Mike leaned back and closed his eyes.

"It's true, Campion," he said. "The awful thing is that it's not a nightmare. It's happened."

"Let's clear off," said Campion unexpectedly. "Let's go abroad. Miss Curley is cut up now, but she'll get over it and running the office will—er—take her mind off things. Besides, you've got some good men. A personal telephone call to each author will keep the business sweeter than anything; that's one thing, authors do understand the desire for solitude."

A flicker of interest appeared in Mike's eyes.

"It wouldn't be bad."

"I'll hold you to it," said Campion. "Going to stay here alone now?"

"No. Jimmy Bengers was in court. He came up to me after the trial and suggested he should come round this evening. Know him?"

"The golfer?"

"That's him. He'll be here any minute now. Good chap, Jimmy. Understands how to shut up. I've know him all my life. Ritchie will roll in too, I expect. I suppose someone's told the poor old beggar about everything?"

"I suppose so," said Mr. Campion vaguely. "I say, I think I'll go now. I've got one or two things to look into. I'll phone you in the morning."

He left Mike in the armchair and had the satisfaction of passing Mr. James Bengers in the outside hall. That large young man had a straw-covered bottle in one hand, a hamper in the other and a hastily caught-up toothbrush peeping shyly from his breast pocket.

Mr. Campion nodded to the man on duty and pushed his way through the crowd on the pavement. Afterwards he went down to Scotland Yard and stayed there for some time, talking to Superintendent Stanislaus Oates, an old friend who had much that was interesting to tell him.

It was just after ten when he returned at last to Bottle Street, and was met by Lugg in the hall of the flat. Lugg was wearing his collar, a certain portent of strange company, and Campion's heart sank. Lugg was indignant.

"Bloomin' ex-rozzer," he murmured in an all-too-audible undertone. "Old Beth's bad enough for one week and all right in 'is way, but this chap's never bin more than a *sergeant*. Can't get rid of 'im. You 'ave a try."

Had Miss Curley been with Mr. Campion as he entered the sitting room she would have recognized the visitor immediately. Mr. Campion saw a large, oldish ex-policeman, with a round red face and very bushy eyebrows, who rose as he appeared and grinned at him in a fashion both shy and friendly.

"Mr. Campion, I presume?" he said. "I'm Mr. Livingstone, late of the Met-ro-politan Police. You'll have to excuse me calling on you so late in the evening, but I'm off on the six-forty back to Norwich to-morrow."

The mention of the Norfolk town brought a great light to Mr. Campion, and to Lugg's disgust he shook the newcomer's hand warmly.

"This is an Act of God," he said. "You're the man I want to see. Higgleton sent you, I suppose?"

"Yes." Mr. Livingstone sat down again and accepted the drink Campion offered him. "Old Charlie Higgleton and me are what you'd call friends, although we don't see much of each other now I've retired. On the quiet, I came up for the trial," he added confidentially. "I like to keep in touch with old times, as it were, and when I see a certain firm was implicated, in which I was interested because of a funny thing which happened in the past, I said to my wife, 'I'll have to go and see that.' And so I came."

"Did you get in?"

Mr. Livingtone drooped a heavy eyelid.

"There's ways and means," he said darkly, "naming no names, of course. But we—er—we—" He hesitated.

"Old blues?" suggested Mr. Campion affably.

Mr. Livingstone beamed.

"Exactly. We police, we stick together and remember old pals. The end come a a real shock to me this afternoon. I thought the youngster was for it."

He looked at Campion enquiringly, but his host did not

rise to the implied question, and after a pause he continued.

"Well, when I went back to Charlie's, where I'm staying, and was talking about it and about old times, he remembered you and found your card. I recollected seeing your name in connection with the case, so I hopped on a bus and here I am."

Mr. Campion purred over him.

"You're providential," he said. "Tell me, did Mr. Higgleton tell you about our conversation in the spring?"

Mr. Livingstone looked pointedly at Lugg, and when that excellent person had been persuaded to leave them he smiled self-consciously at Campion.

"It's not a tale to put about," he murmured apologetically, "but since you was interested I thought I'd like you to hear my side of it. We're referrin' to a certain party who disappeared about twenty years ago, aren't we?"

"That's right," said Campion. "Tom Barnabas was walking down the road from Nemetia Crescent, Streatham, when he vanished."

"And was never seen of more," added Ex-Sergeant Livingstone in a voice so sepulchral that Campion jumped. "Well, since you're interested I may tell you it's true. It was a sunny May morning with a touch of mist in the air and that shimmery look on the pavements and the trees. Mr. Barnabas was walking along the road on the side nearest the wall. Charlie Higgleton saw 'im and went in to get his paper for 'im, and I was standing on the corner on the opposite side of the road. I saw 'im coming and I recognized 'im. I didn't watch 'im closely, of course—why should I? I didn't know 'e was going to walk into the fourth dimension."

"Of course not," agreed Mr. Campion reasonably.

"It's a high wall," said his visitor. "You've seen it, so you know. As high as the top of 'is silk hat. I mention it because him being against it, as it were, he stood out very clear, if you take me."

Mr. Campion nodded comprehendingly and Livingstone went on earnestly.

"When he was about a hundred yards away from me on the opposite side of the road, and there wasn't another soul in sight, I looked away from him and glanced into Charlie's shop. But I could still see Mr. Barnabas, although it was only out of the tail of me eye and I wasn't really lookin' at him. You follow me?"

"Perfectly."

"Well, 'e vanished," said Mr. Livingstone, staring at Campion with boot-button eyes.

Mr. Campion was suitably impressed.

"Look here," he said, "let's get this right. When you looked once he was there, and when you looked a second time he wasn't."

"No, that was the funny thing," said Mr. Livingstone. "I saw 'im out of the corner of me eye the whole time. I saw 'im go."

"Did you, by Jove? Which way?"

"He went . . . up," said Mr. Livingstone.

There was a slightly uncanny silence and Mr. Campion rose.

"Higher than the wall?" he enquired at last.

"I think he did. I remember him melting into the foliage above the wall and then 'e was gone. It happened like *that*."

He struck one palm noiselessly against the other, an oddly expressive gesture.

"Of course I didn't report it quite like that at the station," Mr. Campion's visitor continued in a different tone. "We wasn't used to miracles twenty years ago, and if I'd gone to the Inspector and said I'd seen a big heavy bloke in a top hat, tail coat, white spats and gold-headed cane disappear into thin air in front of me very eyes I'd have been sent to the doctor and never heard the end of it all me born days. So I took the wise course, and you'll see in my reports that I saw 'im coming along and I looked away, and after that I didn't notice 'im any more. I thought he must have gone into the shop. It was Charlie Higgleton who stuck to the miracle story, although it was me who saw it. That was a funny road altogether. On the other side of the wall was a garden full of snakes. A woman used to breed 'em. London's a rum place. I miss it sometimes up there in Norwich. London's got the fascination of a girl you never quite get to know."

He made the final remark regretfully and without affectation.

Mr. Campion was silent for some time. Finally he looked up.

"Do you like miracles?" he enquired.

"Like 'em?"

"Do you mind them explained?"

"Oh, I see what you mean." Mr. Livingstone had the honesty to hesitate, and his host liked him for it. "Yes," he said at last. "Yes, I'd like to know what really happened. He wasn't never seen again, you know."

Mr. Campion went to the cupboard in the bureau and, after rummaging for some time in its depths with his back towards his visitor, he suddenly swung round, his left arm outstretched.

"Look," he commanded.

Mr. Livingstone's eyes bulged and he sprang to his feet with an exclamation. A particularly murderous-looking knife was sticking through Campion's forearm with about three inches of crimson blade projecting from the side opposite the hilt.

Mr. Campion was apologetic.

"Sorry to startle you," he said. "I thought you'd probably seen these things. They sell 'em at the toyshops. It's a sort of bracelet, see?"

He took the contraption off his arm and revealed its secret, which was no more mysterious than a half circle of steel wire connecting the hilt with a three-inch length of painted blade.

Ex-Sergeant Livingstone took a child-like delight in the trick.

"You startled me!" he said, chuckling. "I thought, 'Lumme! 'E's barmy,' before I see you laugh."

"Yes, well, there you are. There's the explanation of your miracle." Mr. Campion sounded a little regretful.

His visitor was still puzzled.

"Do you mean it was a trick wall, sir?" he ventured dubiously. "I dare say you know best, sir, but I knew that road pretty well and I'd have known at once if there was anything funny about the wall."

231

"Oh, no, not a trick wall," said Mr. Campion. "A trick man."

"A trick man, sir?"

"Yes, look here. Suppose if instead of a stolid city gentleman advancing on middle age you'd seen a great strong fellow in shorts and a singlet striding down the road towards you; and if you had read a poster which told you that Mr. Tom Barnabas, the vaulting champion of the world, was going to perform; and if, while you were looking at him, he suddenly swung up an enormous right arm, and caught the top of the wall, which was six foot ten high, and pulled himself over it as swiftly and neatly as a dog swallows a chunk of fish, would you still have thought it a miracle? No. You'd have thought what a first-class performance it was."

Mr. Livingstone took some moments to digest this revelation.

"Was Mr. Barnabas a champion vaulter, sir?" he said. "I never heard that."

"No," said Campion. "He wasn't. That's why it was such a good trick. I don't even know if there were such things; but he could walk upstairs on his hands and I imagine that he had one or two other accomplishments of a like nature. He also had a sense of theatre and I suspect a touch of humour."

"But the snakes . . ." protested Mr. Livingstone, impressed in spite of himself. "The garden on the other side of that wall was full of snakes."

Mr. Campion eyed the ex-sergeant.

"I think he was probably very fond of snakes," he said. "And I think he knew those particular creatures very well."

"Well!" said Mr. Livingstone, and was silent.

He sat quiet for some little time and finally glanced up wistfully.

"You've got it," he said. "I remember now after all these years I caught a glimpse of him turnin' in the air and I thought he was going up in a sort of spiral. But when I got me head round he was gone. Still," he added, taking leave of his miracle with reluctance, "what about his belongings, if he disappeared on purpose? He left everything, you know. Money in the bank as well."

"I think," said Mr. Campion, with deliberation, "that he only took one piece of luggage into the fourth dimension, and he sent that in advance."

It was clear that he did not mean to dilate further upon the subject, and Mr. Livingstone did not press him. The explanation of his miracle had saddened him and he was subdued.

Gradually, however, his thoughts drifted from the past to the present and he sat up.

"I'll be going," he said. "It's late. Thank you very much for your information, sir. It's explained a lot to me. I'm glad you told me, I am really. I wonder if you could tell me one other thing? In the present case the Crown stopped that trial because the police believed there'd been another murder done in exactly the same way as the first, and probably by the same man. Now are they going to hunt out the murderer, or are they going to let the papers think it was a case of suicide done in remorse and leave things alone?"

Campion looked at him, heavy-eyed.

"My dear chap, I don't know," he said, and his voice was sharp with anxiety. "I only wish I did."

After his visitor had gone he flung himself down in his chair and stared morosely at the carpet, a strange heaviness in his heart. For what he had not told Mike, and what the police were so far attempting to hide from the Press, was the indisputable fact that at eight o'clock that morning Mr. Ritchie Barnabas had paid his bill at his lodgings, divided his personal effects impartially between his landlady and his landlady's husband, and had gone out ostensibly to take his annual holiday and had vanished as utterly and unobtrusively as his brother had done twenty years before.

21
The Spangled Frill

It was September, and the hot airs of the long summer were beginning to be dispersed by the light breezes which precede the mistral, when Mr. Campion and Mike stood upon the long concrete platform of the railway station at Avignon and waited for the Paris train.

It was just dusk and inside the walls of the city the plane trees were making high tents against the sky, while down in the *place* the rival cafés jostled each other off the cobbles, the different colours of their painted chairs alone proclaiming their irregular boundaries.

Both men looked well and exceedingly pleased with themselves. Mike especially was frankly jubilant, as every now and again he glanced at his wrist-watch.

"I still think we ought to have gone on to Paris," he said. "I can't see why you're so insistent about staying here. Of course, I am very grateful to you. I shouldn't have sent that wire by myself. I hope it'll be all right though: this isn't exactly a pleasure city."

"It's a lovely town," said Mr. Campion, with dignity. "The French Colchester. When you compare the two you see the essential differences between the French and English temperaments. We've had a nice vulgar holiday all over the show, and this is journey's end, and very nice, too."

Mike grunted, and after a pause glanced at his friend sharply.

"I don't want to butt in," he said diffidently, "but have you had any idea in your mind while we've been gadding about?"

"Idea?" echoed Mr. Campion, a trifle hurt.

"Well, purpose. All this trip, ever since May, you've

been jittering around the Continent like an agitated tourist. We've avoided the cities, but I should think we've visited every second-size town in Italy, Dalmatia and France, stayed about ten minutes and rushed off again. Now at last you've settled down in Avignon of all places. Found anything?"

Mr. Campion was silent. He did not appear to have heard. Mike hesitated.

"Don't think I'm not grateful," he went on seriously. "I am. I've got everything in perspective now and my own troubles don't quite fill up the landscape any more. I had a line from Curley. Everything seems to have blown over. It seems extraordinary when you think back, but people soon forget. The latest rumpus in our world is the autobiography row. The author's hiding in a nursing home terrified of all the angry females who haven't been put in the book."

He laughed shortly, and Campion, eyeing him, decided that his cure was practically complete.

"Train's due," he said.

"Is it?" Mike swung round and gazed up the track and Mr. Campion felt himself forgotten.

The engine came roaring in, and instantly the dozens of recumbent blue figures who had hitherto lain moribund sprang to vociferous life and, amid all the excitement of the arrival of the winners in a motor rally, the daily mid-evening train drew in.

The door of the Pullman burst open and Campion heard Mike's "Gina" above the parrot-house hubbub all round him.

She stepped out, radiant and coolly excited, and Campion, who had a proper respect for any woman who could end a twelve-hour summer journey in a Paris-Sud train looking as though she had stepped out of a bandbox rather than an ash-pit, admired her elegance.

She did not see him at first. Mike absorbed her complete attention.

"I got your wire," she was saying as Campion drifted up to them.

Mike held her at arms' length, his eyes eloquent, although his words were hardly inspired.

"And you came?"

"I came," she said quietly, and he caught his breath as she linked her arm through his.

Mr. Campion shook hands hastily and said he was going to the circus. They watched him stride off, a long, thin, inoffensive figure, personable, but by no means arresting.

"We owe him a lot, that one," the girl remarked quietly.

"Too much," said Mike fervently. "I daren't think of it. Look here, sweetheart, you've got to hurry. The chef of the hotel is waiting for you. He tells me he is a man of perception. I'm afraid he may come and cry over us."

She laughed and they stepped out of the station together and climbed into the crazy old *voiture* which was to carry them into the walled city.

Mr. Campion crossed the bridge over the wide, lazy Rhone, reflecting idiotically that the new bridge was better than the old Pont d'Avignon of the nursery rhyme because there was enough of it to reach to the other side.

It was a magnificent dusky evening, the air soft and tainted by the wine-presses and jubilant with the excitement of autumn, which is so much more comfortable than the excitement of spring.

In the fields on the other bank of the river, on the road to Villeneuve, the *cirque* was already established. It was not a grand affair, designed to attract the *tourisme*, but a little noisy jollification for the natives now that the visitors had gone and left a few spare centimes behind them.

There was one big tent, five or six side-shows mainly of the freak variety, and a cluster of painted living wagons. Electric light bulbs strung on yards of dangerous cable sprawled everywhere and the Provençal *en toute famille* laughed and joked about the frankly comic sides of ordinary life which seem to be so very offensive if one is not amused.

The show in the big tent would not begin for half an hour, and Campion, having seen the spider lady and the tallest Ethiopian in the world, found himself outside the largest of the living wagons. This was a slightly baroque affair, decorated with the Queen of Sheba on one side and a view of Naples on the other, and glittered with brass rails and several varieties of scroll-work. A man sat upon the steps reading a newspaper by the light of a festoon of coloured bulbs draped over the wagon.

He was a large man, still tough at sixty and very fine to look at, in spite of a pink shirt, stiff collar, tight black trousers and Texan sombrero. There were two diamond rings on his fingers and his shoes were English hand-sewn.

He looked up at Campion, who saw his face and rejoiced.

"M'sieu'?" he enquired.

Campion presented him with his card. The stranger took it between an enormous finger and thumb and sat looking at it thoughtfully for some time. Campion bent forward.

"I came to tell you," he said quietly in French, "that John Widdowson killed his cousin Paul Brande, and afterwards, when he was discovered, was found dead in his bath. The general opinion in England now is that he committed suicide."

"And the police? What do they think?"

"The police," explained Mr. Campion, "preserve an open mind. There is one whom they would interview if they found him, but I do not think they are looking for him. As long as he does not reappear . . ." He shrugged his shoulders expressively.

The man rose to his feet and held out his hand.

"How d'you do?" he said in English. "Let me introduce you to Madame."

He went slowly up the steps and bent his head to enter the caravan. He was extremely tall, a giant of a man, with the long supple muscles of an acrobat. Campion caught a few of the murmured words within.

"Un ami vrai . . . absolument. C'est lui . . . le jeune gen lui-même. Ne vous enquietez pas."

There was a rustle and Madame appeared. She was large, dark and gracious, wearing a trifle too much jewellery for camping, perhaps, but she gave Mr. Campion her hand and flashed her black eyes at him and he liked her, snakes, diamonds and all.

They entertained him on the steps. It was a warm night, and it occurred to Campion that she might just possibly keep her more favourite pets in the caravan.

"How did you find us, my friend?"

It was Madame who enquired, and Mr. Campion, feeling he could do no less, explained.

"I went through the old mailing lists, and when I found that M. Robert, proprietor of Robert's *Cirque*, one time c/o the World's Fair, received copies of Spring and Autumn catalogues in company with several thousand householders, I thought he might be worth looking up. It has taken me three months."

The man who called himself Pierre Robert smiled, and reminded Campion of his brother.

"Rubbish!" he said. "It has taken you twenty years. Remember," he continued, speaking English carefully as though he were not used to the tongue, "you are a friend of his. We feel you are his friend."

"But of course," agreed Madame, "the young man is a friend. I knew it as soon as I saw him. "You see," she added, beaming upon Campion, "for so many years now he has spent his holidays with us. Now it is all holiday."

"He is free—that's the main thing," her husband remarked. "Been imprisoned, as I was, all his life. Now the fellow's free—free as air."

Mr. Campion hesitated. There was something he very much wanted to ask, and was wondering how to put it.

"It seems—er—unexpected," he ventured at last. "I mean, after *publishing* . . ."

His host turned to his wife.

"The portrait," he commanded, and while she scrambled into the wagon he launched into a brief and formal history.

"My father was an impulsive man, but very much under his brother Jacoby's influence. He fell in love with a beautiful woman, carried her off and married her. She gave up everything for him, but Jacoby still considered it a mésalliance, and after her two sons were born she died of a broken heart. They kept her mewed up in the country, where she was looked down upon and misunderstood."

His visitor had just time to nod his comprehension when Madame returned with a faded cabinet photograph, which she placed reverently in his hands.

Mr. Campion's startled eyes rested upon one of the most supremely comic figures of his life. A corseted lady in tights and a bustle had been caught in the act of gripping a broken column as though for support. He had a fleeting impression of gentle eyes, a coronet of flowers and a fine piece of gilt script announcing "*La Palone, the Queen of the Wires.*"

His host took the photograph away.

"My mother," he said, with a dignity which was as unassailable as Lord Lumley's own. "That's the explanation. My grandfather was a tumbler."

It was altogether a most delightful gathering. Madame brought glasses and a bottle of Royal Provence, that wine of Paradise which the tourist ices and derides because it does not taste like champagne. They drank it in the dusk and Mr. Campion no longer felt anxious.

As he rose to leave he turned to his new friends.

"Mr. Barnabas," he enquired unexpectedly, "what did you do with *The Gallivant?*"

"Sold it to a collector," said Tom Barnabas promptly. "Fellow was a crook. Believe he cheated me. Anyway, I got enough to buy the show, which was all that mattered."

A grin passed over his face and Campion saw him as he must have been in the days when Miss Curley had admired him.

"I didn't steal it, you know," he continued. "I wanted to sell out my share in the business when Uncle Jacoby died, but old John wouldn't hear of it. So to save trouble I took the firm's most mobile asset and went off, leaving John with my share in exchange. It was quite fair."

"Taking his fortune, he leapt into space?" murmured Mr. Campion under his breath.

Tom Barnabas sighed.

"What a leap that was!" he said. "I couldn't do it now." Madame laid a plump hand on his shoulder.

"Do you want to?" she demanded. "Of course not." Tom Barnabas looked at Campion and laughed.

" 'Voir, M'sieu. Au 'voir."

Mr. Campion wandered off into the fair. The big tent was crowded. An appreciative audience was applauding a lady who was hanging by her teeth from a trapeze, while her son and daughter swung lightheartedly from her ankles.

The turn finished with much bowing and kissing of hands and, while a resplendent attendant wound up their trapeze, a wild exuberant cry sounded from the artists' entrance and a flying figure came whooping into the ring.

He was attired as only French clowns are dressed, in a monstrous caricature of everyday clothes. An enormous black sleeping-suit, on which a white shirt and waistcoat front had been crudely painted, enveloped his gaunt form. Grease-paint half an inch thich obliterated his features and gave him a wide, pathetic smile.

A little white head covering, which Campion saw with a shock was a regulation barrister's wig, decorated his skull and round his neck was a tulle frill spangled with gold.

From the moment he appeared he was a success. His flail-like gestures were here understood. Here his mute appeal was answered, his wide smile echoed. The children shouted his name: "Moulin-Mou! Moulin-Mou! Moulin-Mou!"

He bowed to them gravely and lolloped to the side of the ring purposefully. There he took a basin from an unexpected cupboard in the skirting. He broke eggs in it and added sawdust from the track. His face, now miraculously anxious in spite of his painted smile, appealed to them to sympathize with him in his insuperable difficulties.

To his foredoomed concoction he added all sorts of unlikely ingredients, his dubiety growing and his eyes wild and apprehensive. He stirred, he looked, he smelled. He offered the basin to a little white dog, who lay down and covered its nose with its fore-feet. He wept. He went on stirring.

Then just at the moment when defeat and disgrace seemed inevitable he started. He smiled. He beamed at the breathless company and finally, amid howls of delight, produced triumphantly half a dozen very stale buns and threw five of them to the delirious audience. The sixth he held in his hand for an instant, looking about him with bright child-like eagerness.

Campion was aware of two very gentle blue eyes, infinitely appealing, infinitely friendly, and so far away that they peered at him from another world.

The sixth bun dropped into his lap.

He rose to his feet and waved and some of his neighbours rose with him. Moulin-Mou threw up his arms and bellowed. Campion saw him, rigid for an instant, his great flail-like arms outstretched, his face hidden forever behind the most impenetrable disguise in the world.

The next moment he had gone and a young lady on a horse had taken his place.

Mr. Campion went back over the Pont Neuf, the bun in his hand. He was still carrying it when Mike and Gina met him on the steps of the hotel.

"Horrible," said Mike, staring at the unattractive object with suspicion. "Who gave you that?"

Mr. Campion looked at them solemnly.

"The King's Executioner," he said so gravely that they did not question him.

ABOUT THE AUTHOR

MARGERY ALLINGHAM, who was born in London in 1904, came from a long line of writers. "I was brought up from babyhood in an atmosphere of ink and paper," she claimed. One ancestor wrote early nineteenth century melodramas, another wrote popular boys' school stories, and her grandfather was the proprietor of a religious newspaper. But it was her father, the author of serials for the popular weeklies, who gave her her earliest training as a writer. She began studying the craft at the age of seven and had published her first novel by the age of sixteen while still at boarding school. In 1927 she married Philip Youngman Carter, and the following year she produced the first of her Albert Campion detective stories, *The Crime at Black Dudley*. She and her husband lived a life "typical of the English countryside" she reported, with "horses, dogs, our garden and village activities" taking up leisure time. One wonders how much leisure time Margery Allingham, the author of more than thirty-three mystery novels in addition to short stories, serials and book reviews, managed to have.

Masters *of* Mystery

With these new mystery titles, Bantam takes you to the scene of the crime. These masters of mystery follow in the tradition of the Great British and American crime writers. You'll meet all these talented sleuths as they get to the bottom of even the most baffling crimes.

CATHERINE AIRD

For 15 years, Catherine Aird's mysteries have won praises for their brilliant plotting and style. Established alongside other successful English mystery ladies, she continues to thrill old and new mystery fans alike.

WHODUNIT?

Bantam did! By bringing you these masterful tales of murder, suspense and mystery!

SPECIAL
MONEY SAVING
OFFER

Now you can have an up-to-date listing of Bantam's hundreds of titles plus take advantage of our unique and exciting bonus book offer. A special offer which gives you the opportunity to purchase a Bantam book for only 50¢. Here's how!

By ordering any five books at the regular price per order, you can also choose any other single book listed (up to a $4.95 value) for just 50¢. Some restrictions do apply, but for further details why not send for Bantam's listing of titles today!

Just send us your name and address plus 50¢ to defray the postage and handling costs.